Also By Ashley Hawthorne

Deliver Me

Death Sentence

Death Sentence

ASHLEY HAWTHORNE

Author's Note

This book contains themes of death and violence. A more complete list of potentially upsetting or triggering content is available at ashleyhawthorne.net

Published in the United States by Creative James Media.

www.creativejamesmedia.com

978-1-956183-38-2 (trade paperback) First U.S. Edition 2024

To My Husband,
Because every unlikable female protagonist deserves a loving
partner in life, and I was lucky enough to find mine

One

Eloise's new neighbor was probably going to be the death of her. Admittedly, having a confrontation, even an unpleasant one, wasn't typically a death sentence but in less than twenty-four hours, he had already disrupted the carefully cultivated order and tranquility of her life. Even worse, he was rude, insulting, and showed no signs of remorse.

They had made a *scene*.

In front of the *whole neighborhood*.

While she was wearing her *pajamas*.

The indecency of such a confrontation might have been embarrassing if she hadn't been so livid about the fact that it was *entirely his fault*. The whole thing could have been avoided if he showed even the slightest sign of maturity or responsibility. This would never have happened with any of her other neighbors.

They knew how to behave. *They* had manners. She had chosen her house—a fully restored, one hundred-year-old Craftsman not far from the French Quarter in New Orleans—because it was in a quiet, well-tended neighborhood. Eloise knew she was careful, studious, and unflinchingly dependable and she expected her environment to reflect those things as well. It soothed her, made her feel like her life was finally her own to control.

She liked the older, well-kept homes and the wide sidewalks that were always swept. Like all her other neighbors, Eloise worked hard to make her home look nice. She kept the lawn neatly cut and the hedges trimmed. Her front yard beds had been professionally designed and all her flowers were fertilized at precise intervals to give her the biggest and brightest blooms on the block.

She did her part to adhere to the unspoken rules of neighborly behavior and, until this man had showed up, so had everyone else on her block. There had never been problems with anyone else before he moved in.

In fact, she had gotten along fabulously well with the neighbor who had previously lived in that particular house. Mr. Callaghan had been a lonely old man without family, and he'd appreciated her flowers, her baked goods, and her frequent visits. It had been an odd friendship. It wasn't often that a lonely old widower and his young, career driven neighbor found much to talk about, but it had worked very well for them. She'd been genuinely upset to learn about his death—once a week visits for a chat and cookies were more than she'd ever managed to pull from her own father, after all—but it had never occurred to her to be nervous about the new occupants.

It hadn't taken long at all for the house to lose its comfortable, lived-in appearance, whoever was handling his estate apparently coming in during the day while she was at work to deal with his belongings. She'd waited for the 'For Sale' sign to appear in the yard, but it never came, and the vacant windows looked out over the growing lawn for only a few short weeks before she'd seen the moving truck out front.

There had been no sign of whoever was moving in and a quick glance at the inside of the truck hadn't shown her anything of interest, most of what remained were sealed cardboard boxes of various sizes and shapes. The organized nature of the move had seemed like a good sign, an indication her new neighbors would be tolerable, if perhaps less charming than Mr. Callaghan. In her limited experience, delinquents didn't usually hire professional movers.

She'd smoothed the wrinkles out of her black pencil skirt, checked that none of the golden blonde hair she'd pulled up into a loose up-do had slipped free of its pins, and looked in her mirrors twice before backing out of the driveway and onto the street.

When she'd arrived home and found the moving truck gone, she'd been unpleasantly surprised to see a black motorcycle and a cherry red sports car in its place. The glaringly disruptive color of the car, and what she assumed would be an equally obnoxious amount of disruptive noise from the motorcycle, would have been bad enough, but the owner of the two vehicles had decided to park the bike in the driveway and the car on the *front lawn*.

More precisely, it was on the grass of the *shared* front lawn between her driveway on the left and his driveway on the right. His front tires were clearly *on her side*. It would leave ruts in the soil, flatten the grass, leave a large and unsightly dead spot in the center of her lawn if he did it with any regularity. Surely, he could not imagine that it would be acceptable to ruin the curb appeal of her home by parking that monstrosity of a vehicle on the lawn.

She would have to say something about it when she saw him, she'd decided, glaring at the car as she unlocked her front door. Her keys clattered as she dropped them with uncharacteristic force into the bowl by the door before kicking her shoes off and hitting the button on the remote that filled the downstairs with the soft sound of classical music. With any luck, it would help soothe her frazzled nerves.

It was easy to put the neighbor and his car aside, to settle into her usual routine of heating up a cup of fragrant tea while she prepared the vegetables for dinner on the cutting board that protected her pristine kitchen counter. She fell into the familiar routine of cooking as she sliced zucchini, artichoke hearts, and small heirloom tomatoes that she'd grown herself in the small garden in the backyard, layered it in the casserole dish over chicken breast, added the seasonings and the cheese, the crumbled bacon that was left over from breakfast, and slid it into the oven. There would be enough there for dinner and for leftovers. It wasn't easy to cook for one, even with her love for all things culinary, but she managed.

Cooking was a comfort to her, a leftover warmth from her time in college when her part time restaurant job had been all that kept her spirits up as she worked toward a degree in a field she was mostly indifferent about. She'd mentioned the idea of culinary school to her parents once and the meltdown that had followed had been enough to make sure she kept her passions to her own kitchen. Still, it was nice to see what she could do for herself, even if no one else ever tasted it.

Dinner would take a while to bake, and, in the meantime, she could ignore the series of texts she'd received from her mother—yes, she *did* know how long it had been since her last promotion, *thank you very much*—and instead settle down in her favorite chair and read the last few chapters of her most recent book.

She hadn't made it through the first page when the noise started.

It began with the rumble of motorcycle engines, the slamming of car doors, men shouting and laughing at decibels that seemed likely to rattle the windows. She resisted the urge to get up, to peek through the curtains like a stereotypically nosy neighbor. She already knew who was responsible, certainly no one else on this street would have guests that behaved like this, especially on a weeknight of all things, and she wouldn't stoop to his level by becoming a rude neighbor herself.

The music started soon after, drowning out the familiar melody created by talented fingers on the keys of a piano and subjecting her to the erratic beat of a drum and what she thought might possibly be an electric guitar. Whatever speakers they were pumping it from had to be nearing their capacity for noise making disruption, because this time the windows at the side of her house *were* rattling their frames. The lead singer, if indeed screaming profanities into the microphone could qualify him as a singer, was obviously oblivious to things like pitch and tone, rhythm, and tempo.

The skin on her knuckles turned white as she wrapped her fingers around her teacup too tightly, but she didn't make a scene.

It wasn't until well past ten, when she had already changed into her favorite set of soft pajamas, that she reached her limit.

She heard it first—the rev of a motorcycle engine that was much too loud and went on much too long to be necessary, then the squeal of tires and the hideous scrape of metal on concrete. By the time she made it to the window, the bike had been set upright again and the fool riding it was standing on the sidewalk looking sadly at the scratched paint and busted lights. In the dim glow of the streetlight, she could see that he had lost control pulling too quickly out of the driveway and slid straight into her hydrangeas.

That was quite enough for one day.

There were several men gathered around the bike and its rider when she stalked barefooted across her front yard. Tattooed, pierced, and dressed to the last man in unrelenting black, there was a dangerous look to them that she consciously ignored, the adrenaline in her system overriding her well-honed self-preservation instinct.

They all turned their heads to look at her—a series of marionettes being controlled by the same puppet master—and said nothing as she stared down at stripped blooms and broken stalks where the bike had crashed into her flowers. The plants were mangled and quite possibly beyond saving.

She sighed heavily and looked around until she spotted what she thought was the guilty party. "Are you responsible for this?"

The one that had done the damage was young and dark eyed, a kid with tousled brown curls and skin that was a few shades too pale as what little color had remained in his face drained away when he saw the look on hers. He swallowed hard, the act visible even in the dark and across the distance that separated them. "I'm sorry. It was an accident."

"Shut up, Myles. You're gonna apologize to a woman in her pajamas like you're scared? Grow a pair for fucks' sake."

She whirled, cheeks flaming, on the man that had spoken as Myles muttered a quiet, "Sorry, Dylan."

Dylan leaned against a different bike, arms crossed as he stared her down over the broken bits of flower between them. His hair and eyes were dark like the boy's but there was no touch of babyish youth or soft embarrassment on his bearded face. The family resemblance between them was clear, but the cold eyes told her the similarity went no deeper than the surface. A tingle of awareness, perhaps alarm, swept over her, and she crossed her arms defensively as she glared at him.

"You have damaged my property. You'll all be lucky if I don't call the police." She glanced around, noting with a sick feeling in her stomach that there was a face in at least one window of every house in the vicinity. They were making a spectacle out of this, and she did not appreciate it. "You're my new neighbor, I presume?"

"Nah, you got lucky. You won't be dealing with me. Ethan's still in the house." He smirked and jerked his chin toward the front door.

Eloise narrowed her eyes in that direction. "Ethan apparently needs a lesson in manners and disturbing the peace ordinances," she snapped, turning on her heel and marching back across the lawn, this time toward her neighbor's porch instead of her own. "And get that motorcycle away from my flowers!"

They all ignored her, choosing instead to follow a short distance behind her, clearly intent on watching as she confronted the man she blamed for all of this.

She pounded with the side of her fist, forgoing the usual polite knocking altogether because she knew it wouldn't be heard over the unholy racket still blaring from the speakers.

Her focus on summoning her new nemesis was so intense, and the music so loud, that she didn't notice the doorknob turning. He pulled the door open just as she swung arm forward to pound again and she found herself flying through the open air where the door had been and straight into the arms of a stranger.

It was like running into a wall, albeit one that was slightly softer and warmer than any she had encountered before. She felt hands come up to grasp her elbows, lifting her and steadying her back onto her feet. The men in the yard were all gathered at the bottom of the porch steps now, laughing at her again. She shot a disgruntled look over her shoulder as she righted herself, stepping back and slapping peevishly at the hands that had caught her. She had no patience left to be manhandled.

"*Excuse* me," she began loudly, infusing her voice with enough hostility to make certain anyone listening knew that she was not requesting to be excused at all, but whatever else she had been about to say was quickly forgotten.

She turned away from the miscreants in the yard and back to the man in the doorway. The barrier she had run into was his chest, which seemed to stretch impossibly from one side of the door frame to the other and to do so at about the same height level as her face. In order to see the rest of him, and there was rather a lot more of him to see, she had to retreat an extra step and tip her chin back so far that throat felt bare and exposed.

"*Hmng*," she said, swallowing hard against the sudden urge to run back to her own house and slam the door closed behind her. This man was nothing like his friends. He was neither small and timid, nor haughty and cruel, though she wasn't sure entirely what words she would use to describe him, besides enormous.

She wasn't particularly petite—she was slender but five foot seven without shoes—he simply overwhelmed her in height and breadth. Standing so close to him made her feel small and vulnerable even before she got a good look at him.

Looking down at her, his head nearly brushing the top of the door frame, was the most compelling looking man that she had ever laid eyes on. Like the man in the yard, he was bearded but his hair was shorter and lighter, bordering on blond, and his features held none of the cruelty of his companion. He had a long nose and though the shadows of the porch hid the color of his eyes she could see even in the dim light that his mouth was plush and pink.

He was amused, if the lazy curl of his lip was any kind of accurate indication, and entirely too smug for a man who had inconvenienced half the neighborhood with his antics. He leaned casually against the door frame, raising one arm above his head to curl his fingers around the top of the trim. The movement pulled the black T-shirt he was wearing tight across his chest, and with his arm this close she could see the tattoos that snaked from his wrist to somewhere beneath his sleeve. It was impossible to tell what they were, but they bled across his skin in a fascinating pattern of blacks and blues and reds.

"Can I help you, sweetheart?" His voice was deep, honey-over-butter smooth, and arrogant.

She scowled. Men tended to take that tone with her often. Lightly condescending. Annoyingly flirtatious. No one ever took her seriously. It was the gold shine in her hair. The powder blue of her eyes. The slight scattering of freckles across her nose, just enough to add interest to her features without overwhelming the soft pink of her cheeks. As a child, she had often been told she looked like a doll. People assumed that meant she would be bendable. Movable. An object that they could manipulate to their whims. That assumption was a mistake.

"You can begin by not calling me '*sweetheart*'. I'm Eloise Mason, your new neighbor. I live right there." She turned to point to her own house, and he leaned out the door to look, invading her personal space and letting his breath brush her ear as he did so. He was crowding her, but she refused to step back again. She turned to face him with her lips pressed in a discouraging line.

"All right, well, it's nice to meet you ..."

She ignored him, speaking over the end of his sentence until he trailed away into silence. "You've parked your car on my lawn, played your music far too loudly, and allowed your friends to damage my personal property."

Again, she pointed and, again, he leaned around her to look, this time at the sadly broken mess that was her hydrangeas.

He whistled. "The boys did that?"

"They did," she confirmed. "I don't know exactly what it is that you do for a living Mr. ...?"

"I'm Ethan."

"Fine. *Ethan*. I don't know what it is that you do, but

some of us, that is rather *all* of us, in this neighborhood have jobs and families and need to be awake at respectable hours, especially during the week. Are you aware it's a Tuesday night?"

"I am aware actually. Tell me, are you always going to be this cranky on a Tuesday night?"

She blinked up at him, mouth opening and closing silently before shutting on a snap. "If you're always going to be this disruptive.

He grinned. "I'll take that as a 'yes', then. You're welcome to come over in your PJ's any time you feel like yelling at me about not parking on your lawn." She flushed and glanced down at her cotton pajama pants, curling her bare toes into the painted wood of the porch while he continued. "Which is actually *my* lawn, by the way."

"Not that part of it," she insisted, chin lifting in challenge. "The dividing line between my portion of the yard and yours is quite clear. Please, park your car in the driveway, like the rest of us."

"I see," he murmured, and she didn't miss the pointed look he aimed at someone standing behind her.

"Well, I don't know what to tell you, Mrs. Mason. You aren't being very friendly. In fact, I'd say you're not doing a very good job at all of welcoming me to the neighborhood." He leaned down toward her again, voice low and soft as he mocked her.

She poked him in the chest with her finger, drilling into his sternum firmly until he relented and straightened back to his full overwhelming height.

"I'm being perfectly friendly, all things considered. And it's *Miss* Mason," she corrected.

"Oh?" He smiled at her, sudden dimples flashing in his cheeks that made him far more boyish and charming than he had any right to be. The way his eyes traveled from the top of her head and down over her body to her bare feet left little room for his meaning to be misunderstood. "Well, in that case, would you like to—"

Considering that she was wearing baggy pajamas that hung on her slender frame, her hair was pulled hastily and messily back into a low ponytail, and she had taken her makeup off hours ago, she had the distinct feeling that it was done more as a deliberate insult than an actual expression of interest.

"No," she said firmly. "Absolutely not. I don't make a habit of dating men like you. Please get your car off my lawn and turn your music down." She turned to go, glaring at the men that shuffled off the porch steps to make room for her to pass. "*You* owe me a new hydrangea," she said, pinning the guilty one with a firm look.

Dylan winked at her as she passed and called out, "Think you can handle living next door to her, Ethan? Not sure the stick could get much farther up her ass."

They all laughed again, but she ignored it, determined not to acknowledge them or give them more ammunition to use against her.

"Hey, sweetheart!"

Unable to resist, she stopped with one foot on the bottom stair of her own front porch, turning to find him leaning against his railing, lit cigarette in one hand and a bottle of beer in the other. "Dating wasn't exactly what I had in mind!"

She slammed the door behind her.

Two

The sight of her mangled hydrangea the following morning sent Eloise into another rage spiral. It was framed perfectly through her bedroom window, easily visible as soon as she opened her eyes, and it looked even worse in the creeping light of the spreading dawn. Petals and leaves were scattered haphazardly in the street, stems snapped and broken at unnatural angles that made her want to weep in frustration for the senseless loss of it.

And maybe *that man*—what had he said his name was? Ethan?—hadn't personally caused its destruction, but he was behind it nonetheless, with his careless behavior and nonchalantly irresponsible attitude.

He had probably floated through life on his intimidatingly large presence and his ridiculously good-looking smile. There had probably been no one to tell him no or hold him accountable for his actions, no one to explain to him that he was recklessly endangering the peace and order that other, *more sensible* individuals, such as herself, had worked so hard to achieve.

He was *infuriating*.

Most of the night had passed with her imagining his too-handsome face with its maddening little smirk and plotting her revenge. She'd never considered herself a vengeful person, but something about Ethan left her angrier than was reasonable. After a restless night led to sleeping through her alarm, she found herself rushing to get out the door on time, bitter about the lack of time for coffee and stewing over the memory of her flowers.

She had barely made it to the end of the driveway—wearing a wrinkled skirt and with wisps of hair slipping out of her hastily scooped up ponytail—when she spotted him. The car came to a sudden stop as she pressed down hard enough on the brakes to make her head bob.

Ethan stood on his porch holding a cup of coffee like he didn't have a care in the world. He was leaning against the railing, shirtless and wearing black pajama pants that sat low on his hips. His chest was even broader than she remembered and his right arm was covered from wrist to shoulder in the tattoos she had noticed the night before—a multicolored tapestry on a canvas of skin that was golden from the sun.

Clearly, he needed a stern lecture on the risks of sun exposure and the benefits of sunscreen, but before she could spend too much time dwelling on his chances of lasting UV damage, her attention had already wandered to take in the rest of him. Dark blond hair, rumpled from sleep and the glide of his fingers. The flat plane of his stomach. The lean, corded muscles in his forearms. The knowing tilt of his lips as he looked up and caught her staring.

Her cheeks heated, and she scowled at him, trying to school her features into an expression of disapproval as she stared him down. He lifted his coffee cup in a mock salute, and she set her teeth as she fought against the urge to respond to his taunt with a very uncharitable hand gesture.

She pulled out of the driveway without giving him the

satisfaction of flipping him off or rolling down her window to complain about how his car was still parked on her grass. He was *horrid* and she *hated* him. She ran the interaction over and over in mind as she drove, trying to figure out where, *exactly*, he'd gotten the upper hand and how she could have prevented it.

By the time she arrived at work—hastily parking her car in the lot beside Sun Valley Financial's five story building with its glittering glass front—she was almost late. *Late.* A state of being which would have surprised anyone who'd known her since she'd first toddled out of the playpen and into her daycare classroom. Everyone knew Eloise was always punctual.

Fortunately, the rest of the employees were already inside the building and there were only a few raised eyebrows from passersby on the sidewalk as she tried to jog across the parking lot and up the front walkway in heels.

She had nearly been *late*—for the first time ever—and it was all *his* fault.

There was a low, surprised whistle as Eloise pushed open the sparkling glass front door and dashed into the lobby. It was mostly empty, nothing here at this time of morning but a polished gray floor, some decorative plants, and the day's stragglers. She was intensely grateful that this building only housed the offices for the behind-the-scenes paper pushers, and she wasn't dashing into a functioning bank branch and past a crowd of customers as witnesses.

"No offense, Eloise, but you look like shit."

Eloise huffed and rolled her eyes as she turned toward the sound and spotted her three best friends standing in a small group beside the elevator. They were obviously waiting for her and she felt another burst of annoyance at Ethan for disrupting her predictable morning routine. She hadn't even had her coffee yet, something she already knew she was going to feel as the day wore on.

"Thanks, Chloe."

"Anytime." Chloe shot her an unrepentant smile and a wink. Artfully tousled brown curls fell halfway down the back of her dark blue suit and her makeup was habitually flawless. Simple gold jewelry glinted at her ears and throat, the metallic sheen a well-chosen complement to the outfit and her skin tone.

Normally, Eloise wouldn't have given Chloe's attire a second glance but this morning, wearing wrinkled clothes and nothing on her own face but a few swipes of mascara and some lip gloss, she felt unkempt and out of sorts in comparison. It added another layer of irritation to her already sour mood. There was always a light feeling of competition between them all, but Eloise occasionally felt like it was less friendly with Chloe than the others. There was never anything specific she could put her finger on, just a tug deep in her gut.

Beside them, Kim shrugged. "Chloe's right. Your freckles are showing and I've never seen you with a hair out of place before. It's like you're ... almost human." She reached up to tug on a piece of hair that had escaped Eloise's ponytail and laughed when Eloise gently slapped her hand away.

Kim was a petite redhead with an elegant pixie cut and a sweet smile. She was more timid than the rest of them, and shorter at barely five feet in her heels, but even she occasionally joined in on the group's good-natured teasing, especially when Eloise was the target. Eloise had never seen her without her signature red lips and a cardigan and often wondered if she might not have been happier as an elementary school teacher than working in finance.

"Stop that." Eloise tucked her hair back into its elastic band and smoothed out the wrinkles in her clothes as well as she was able.

"No, no, they have a point," Sarah said with a grin, holding up a steaming cup of coffee and waving it under Eloise's nose. Her smile was bright, and her eyes were full of faintly amused mischief. She had a chin length bob of straight black hair and wore four-inch heels the same bright white as her breezy silk blouse. None of the rest of them ever looked quite as much the part of a professional businesswoman as Sarah. She effortlessly was what Chloe tried so hard to be. Pretty, polished, and faintly predatory. "What happened to you?"

Eloise grabbed the coffee gratefully and took a quick sip, ignoring the burn on her tongue. No cream and very little sugar—Sarah always remembered how she liked it.

"Thank you, you're a goddess among women," she said gratefully, taking another sip. "And my new neighbor is what happened to me. Parking his car on my lawn, revving up his motorcycle and letting his buddies do the same. They destroyed my hydrangea! And then he had the nerve to hit on me."

Sarah laughed as they all turned toward the elevator. "Hasn't he only been there for one day?"

"Yes! Can you imagine how much worse it's going to get?"

The elevator dinged as the door opened, and they stepped inside. Luckily, it was late enough in the morning to be empty except for the four of them. They were all headed to different floors, all worked for different departments, but finance was still a boys' club and hanging on to the other women that worked there had been the only thing keeping most of them sane.

Eloise had been the last to join the group but they'd rallied around her on her first lunch break and swept her away to a café down the street. She'd been fresh out of college and new in town, prepared to be lonely because she'd never been comfortable making new friends. Sarah had taken one look at her and decided she was going to be one of them after that, whether she wanted to be or not.

She was Eloise's best friend, though Sarah managed to balance Eloise and Chloe on a fine line, her attention and status as her closest confidant switching between them. Perhaps suddenly having to share was what had made Chloe's attitude a little more sour.

"So, everyone's all set for a productive day except me?"

Sarah smiled, teeth a bit too prominent for it to be genuine. "Just another day working for the asshole who stole my promotion. Everyone knows he's useless and has the moral backbone of a limp noodle, but, hey, let's give the job to him because he's got a dick."

The rest of them all nodded sympathetically. Sarah had been furious for more than six months about that promotion, but it was hard to blame her. She'd worked here longer than any of them and had easily made her mark in the accounting department but then she'd stalled out at the next step, none of the higher up executives willing to promote a woman into a position that held any kind of real authority.

"And not just *any* asshole," Chloe added with a delicate shudder. "Dwayne."

"Fetch me my coffee, Ms. DeWitt," Sarah mocked, her voice dropping several octaves as she pretended to scratch a nonexistent beard.

"Lookin' mighty fine in those pants today, Ms. Torres." Chloe joined in with an even more on point imitation, mimicking his exaggerated southern drawl and pretending to scratch at her belly.

Kim cleared her throat, took a second to gather her courage, and then pretended to scowl down her nose. "Ms. Sloane, I need you to fetch me those papers, even though you don't work for me or even on the same floor as my office."

Eloise was laughing so hard she was nearly in tears, the

problems of the night before practically forgotten. "Ms. Mason, I realize I have never worked in the same department as you and have no training in your area of expertise but, if you will only stand here and let me look at your chest for the next half hour, I think I can explain the best way for you to do your job."

"Let's all just run away." Kim wrapped her arm around Sarah's waist to give her a quick hug. "To hell with him."

"We could live on the beach somewhere tropical," Chloe agreed. "If we had the money for it."

Eloise snorted. "Where are we going to get that kind of money? Tropical islands are notoriously pricey."

"Take it from here," Sarah said with a grin. "Six months of skimming off the top would let you live on an island for the rest of your life. A year would let you *buy* an island and never have to worry about anything again."

The elevator slowed to a stop on Eloise's floor and she stepped out, shaking her head at all of them. "You all have fun with that, and don't forget to put me on the visitor's list so I can come see you in prison."

Sarah smiled and waved when the door closed and Eloise made her way quickly and quietly to her desk, sipping coffee as she went. Every head turned as she passed, taking the opportunity to look at her figure while they thought she wouldn't notice. It happened every day and, like always, she ignored them.

She settled in , meticulously straightening the supplies and tidying the little box that held her incoming paperwork before she sat down to go over her daily tasks. Investment banking hadn't been her first choice of career, but it paid well and her parents approved so she'd done her best to make it tolerable.

She felt guilty for not being as passionate as Sarah—she knew what her parents expected of her and she did try her best despite knowing her heart wasn't in it—but even if she had been, she knew it would likely end with the same result. Without some sort of miraculous intervention, she'd find her own career stalling as well. It was not a comforting thought with her mother breathing down her neck about the speed of her advancements.

Eloise had never been much of a rebel but the frustration of working in a system that was never going to let them succeed was getting harder for all of them to ignore. As a matter of fact, if it wasn't for her determination to stay on the right side of the law—which she suspected at this point was at least partly motivated by a fear of spending several unpleasant years in an orange prison jumpsuit—she might have given in to the wild urge to try and convince Sarah and the others to take that island money and run. She could open a restaurant on a tropical island, couldn't she? If she pretended not to get phone service that far out at sea, she wouldn't even have to answer to her mother about it.

Of course, her friends would all think she was a bit unbalanced if she said that out loud and she supposed she might be. She'd never actually want to leave her quiet house and her neat office and her steady routine. Thoughts of abandoning it all jumped into her mind sometimes, but they were easily put back into place by clear, logical thinking.

She finished the last of her coffee, tossed the empty cup in the bin beside her desk, and started responding to her emails.

<hr>

She was too tired to care about the car or the hydrangea by the time she made it home. The other neighbors shot her sympathetic looks as she drove by, especially the ones who lived directly across the street from her and had to look at the mess. Jackson and David were a lovely couple, and she was sure they didn't appreciate the sight that now faced them when they walked out of their own front door. She waved as she stepped out of the car, and they waved back, but they were watching the house next door skeptically and she wondered what her new neighbor had been up to while she was at work.

Unfortunately, it didn't take her long to find out.

"Welcome home, sweetheart," he called, and she took a deep breath to brace herself against a surge of fresh anger.

She shoved it down, unwilling to put on another show for the neighbors, and bit back a sigh as she turned to face him. He was back on the porch, leaning against the railing and smiling at her, dimples showing full force. At least this time he was wearing a shirt.

This one, too, was black—she wondered irritably if he owned other colors—and it was stretched tight across his chest. She looked him over, gaze following the path of his tattoos from his wrist to where they disappeared beneath his sleeve. She knew how far up they went now, how they played vibrantly over his muscles.

It was a pity he was so arrogant and rude and so ... not her type. Not her type at all, despite the objectively attractive nature of his form. She ignored the low swooping pull her observations caused in her belly and frowned across the yard at him.

"My name is Eloise," she called back, curt voice just loud enough to be heard across the yard.

He bounded down the porch stairs, legs long and impossibly thick in black pants and heavy black boots and came to a stop just in front of her, blocking her from her own porch unless she wanted to step off the driveway and onto her grass. He smiled, revealing a flash of white teeth behind the quirk of his lips and in the brighter light of day she could tell his eyes were blue. Not the soft powder of her own, but dark and sapphire deep.

"Eloise." He repeated her name back to her, giving it a

seductive drawl she'd never heard before. "That's a nice name."

"I'm sure my grandmother would agree since she had it first."

"A family name." He glanced over her skirt and the ponytail she'd tried to fix in the bathroom at work. She had been only partially successful and she curled her fingers into fists to keep from trying to smooth it down as he evaluated her. "It suits you."

"Thanks, I guess." She edged toward the front door, trying to put some space between them. It wasn't a subject she was comfortable discussing.

She'd never really known that particular grandmother or any of the rest of her grandparents. Her parents hadn't been the sentimental types that made a lot of room for time with her extended family and her grandparents weren't any better. They'd dropped a present in the mail for Christmas and her birthday if they happened to remember, but that was the extent of their involvement. The name had been given more out of tradition and obligation than genuine connection.

"Listen, I'm sorry for the whole flower ... bush ... thing." He ran a hand over his hair, the nervous gesture drawing her attention back to the patterns inked into his skin, following them from wrist to the line of his T-shirt across his bicep. The colors were now close enough to form shapes- snakes, spiders, and skulls danced eerily up his arm, a silent testament to a life she understood nothing of.

She sniffed and tightened her mouth into a firmer line. Let him do his best to intimidate others with those displays. She wasn't the kind to back down from a confrontation when it was well deserved, no matter who the recipient of her ire was.

"I loved that hydrangea." She tore her gaze away from his skin to look back up at his face. If her mother had taught her anything useful while she was growing up, it was the power of a pointed statement followed by expectant silence.

"It *was* an accident." He tapped his fingers against his thigh and there, too, she found suggestions of violence, as a ring of silver crafted in the shape of a human skull glinted in the sunlight.

"Does that change the outcome?" she asked. Then, said even more pointedly, "Your car is *still* parked on my lawn."

He rolled his eyes and broke into a light jog to get ahead of her again when she stepped around him. "Come on, sweetheart, work with me. I don't need my neighbors hating me already and calling the cops every time I have friends over and, no offense, but you seem like the type."

"I'll 'work with you' when your car isn't still parked where it shouldn't be."

He huffed, cheeks puffing out with the air that escaped from between barely parted lips. "Listen, I'm trying to be nice here, but you don't want to get into this type of pissing contest with me."

She froze, body rigid as the implications of his words hung between them. The air nearly crackled with tension when she turned slowly to face him. "I'm sorry?" Her tone was glacial and she was *not* sorry.

"I'm a pretty laid-back guy but—"

"But?" She took a few steps forward, her heels making her eyes just level with his chin when she drew herself up to her full height. Even in her tallest shoes, she had to tip her head back to meet his gaze, but she didn't look away.

"Some of my friends aren't as friendly as I am."

"Are you threatening me?" She took a deep breath, puffing up and crowding into his space as he had crowded hers the night before.

He looked down at her, lips twitching as he tried to hold back a smile. "I wouldn't dream of threatening you, sweetheart. I just didn't want to see you tangle with someone more stubborn than you are. You might get hurt."

"There is no one more stubborn than me and if you're talking about those buddies of yours from last night, I handled them once and I'll handle them again if you don't stay off my lawn and keep the noise to a reasonable level. Now, *stop* calling me *sweetheart*."

She stepped around him again, intent on dismissing him from her mind as well as she was able as soon as she made it inside. The sound of his laughter followed her and she had nearly made it to the front door when he was able to breathe well enough to answer her.

"What about 'darling'?"

She slammed the door again, but she could still hear him laughing from the other side.

Three

The flat, empty sound of a car engine *not* starting was not the way Eloise wanted to start her morning. She sat in the driver's seat and glared across the front lawns at Ethan's empty front porch. Her car issues weren't his fault, but surely she would have been less stressed by the problem if she hadn't nearly been late once already this week because of him.

She tried the key again, wincing at the grinding sound that accompanied her fruitless attempt. "Damn it!" Her voice echoed in the small space as she hit the steering wheel hard enough to make her palm ache.

There was no way around it. She was going to have to call an Uber and wait for someone to show up. She was *definitely* going to be late this time. Her whole lunch break would likely be wasted trying to set up an appointment with a mechanic so they could tell her what the hell the problem was with her car. Then she'd have to take another Uber home or ask one of her friends to drop her off.

Damn it.

She dropped her head to the steering wheel—deciding to

take a moment to curse the internal workings of every combustion engine ever made by man since she was going to be late anyway—and jumped at a soft knock on her window.

"Need a hand?"

Ethan.

Of *course*, it was Ethan. It couldn't have been one of her other neighbors. Of course not. It would have been too easy if it had been any of the ones that were nicer and less obnoxious. They were definitely less attractive—even the most stubborn part of her mind couldn't deny the low swoop and flutter of her stomach when she'd realized he was standing just outside the car—but that was another point against him. She didn't have time to waste on fluttering stomachs and clenching thighs.

Not that her thighs were clenching, of course.

She made a conscious effort to relax her legs as he bent down to peer at her through the passenger side window, waiting patiently for her to answer his very simple question. She sighed, embarrassed and frustrated and slightly aroused despite her best efforts to pretend otherwise.

His hair was tousled from sleep and the shirt he was wearing did not do enough to hide the muscles of his arms from her gaze. She was nearly certain she could feel the heat of his body through the window, but surely that was her imagination. Maybe it was just the blood rushing to the surface of her skin in a horrible flush she hoped he couldn't see in the dim interior of her car.

"Do you know how to fix it?" She had to raise her voice so he could hear her through the glass, but she wasn't going to roll down the window and encourage him unless he actually knew what he was doing.

"Maybe," he said, tapping a finger where his hand rested on the car door. "Won't know till I get inside to take a look at the engine. I can't see what the problem is from out here."

"Right." She huffed, eyes wandering over the car's interior as she muttered to herself. "I just need to open the front part of the car. How hard can that be?"

"Can you pop the hood for me? Do you know how to do that, sweetheart?"

Her face was painfully hot as she shook her head. It was miserable having to admit that she had no clue what she was doing. If it was more complicated than putting gas in the damn thing she was useless, and somehow this, too, felt like his fault. Maybe he wasn't directly responsible, but he didn't have to stand there all smug and knowing while he witnessed her shame.

"That's fine." He walked around the front of the car and gently opened her door. "Let's just get you out of there and I'll find the lever for it."

"Fine." She swung her legs out—glaring as she had to stand up far too close to him—and crossed her arms over her chest as he pulled the small lever inside that released the hood of the car with a small *pop*.

He came up with a small case in his hand from under her seat. An emergency kit, she remembered. She'd stuffed under the seat when she bought the car and then promptly forgotten about it. It had a few small tools—the essentials according to the box—and she congratulated herself for her excellent foresight in purchasing it.

He ignored her petulance as he wandered back around the front and opened the car up to stare intently at the engine. "Let's see what we have here," he muttered.

It was tempting to wander closer and try to see what he was touching under there, but it would mean voluntarily putting herself closer to him *and* taking a risk of getting engine grease on her delicate pink blouse. She stayed where she was but stretched uselessly up on tiptoe to try and get a closer look before settling back down to wait and tap her foot impatiently.

"Well?"

"It's a car."

If he'd told her he could hear the noise her teeth made as she ground them together, she would have believed him. "I *know* it's a car. What's wrong with it?"

"Don't know yet." He leaned around the hood and smiled, easy and relaxed as a Sunday morning. There was a smear of grease on the bridge of his nose but it didn't make him any less charming ... or any less infuriating. "It takes a minute."

She dug her fingernails into the palms of her hands and returned his smile. Her mouth was tight and stiff enough that he clearly didn't believe it was genuine and he laughed before ducking back out of sight. He might be fixing her car, but he was also clearly enjoying her helpless dependence on him.

Bastard.

"Get in and try to start it up now," he instructed.

She sighed again—surely no one in history had sighed as much in a single week as she had since she'd met Ethan—and sat back down in the driver's seat. The car sputtered once and then the engine turned over with a nice, steady purr. "Huh," she mused. "What did you do?"

"Do you really want me to explain it to you?"

"I ... actually do not," she admitted. "Cars aren't exactly my area of interest. Should I take it to a mechanic for a more permanent fix?"

"Shouldn't need to." He wiped his hands carelessly on the black pants he wore as he stepped around the car to look down at her and hold out the emergency tool kit for her to take and stuff back under the seat. "Just a minor thing that had wiggled loose and it's tightened up now."

She didn't like the disadvantage of being so much below

him and he took a step back to make room for her as she stood up again. "Well, you saved me an expensive commute and a trip to the mechanic. What do I owe you for your help?"

"Nothing."

"Nothing? I would have paid a few hundred dollars if I'd had to call a mechanic or get the car towed."

"You would have but then I wouldn't have been a very good neighbor, would I?" There was a smirk playing at the edge of his lips and she wanted to wipe it off his face, possibly with her mouth.

It startled her, how much she wanted it, and she could feel the heat of that traitorous blush working its way up her chest again and her cheeks were on fire. It had been a long time since her body had reacted like this to a man and it didn't help her rising concern that it happened with this man in particular.

What was wrong with her? She shook her head slightly to clear her mind before she did something she'd regret. Women with ambition didn't let men with pretty mouths turn their heads like this. She knew it. Could nearly hear her mother saying it again and again, even after all these years. The space she'd put between them hadn't kept the lessons from sticking.

"Is this your attempt to make up for what happened to my flowers?" Better to keep that at the front of her mind. Irritation was a safer emotion and it wasn't as though he didn't deserve it after the way he'd behaved.

"You know, you're obsessed with those damn flowers."

"Maybe I should come over there and kick the stand out from under your motorcycle and see how long it takes for you to forgive me."

He shook his head, but she saw his lips twitch. "You're something else but I get your point."

"Good."

He rubbed at the back of his neck, his usual smirk

morphing into a more cautious smile. "Listen, let me make it up to you. I can take you to dinner or—"

"I thought dating wasn't what you had in mind?" She crossed her arms triumphantly as he gave her a short, surprised half laugh and continued before he could try to argue. "I appreciate the offer but no. I mean, thank you. You know? For the car? But I don't think that's a good idea."

"You don't think so?"

"Like I told you before, I don't date men like you." She hardly dated the men that weren't like him, either, but she knew what he'd say if she admitted to that. That she was frigid. A tease. A prude. She'd heard it all before and she'd become mostly numb to it, but somehow she didn't want to hear it from his lips.

"Men like me," he said slowly, weighing the words. "What's that exactly?"

She dropped the hood of the car with a thump, narrowly missing his fingers as he snatched them back. "The kind with friends that destroy my flowers."

She'd let him think it was because of something he'd done. Most men simply refused to take the hint that she wasn't interested, so she'd stopped trying to explain to them that her career had to come first. If she made it personal, they tended to take it personally and stop asking.

"Ah." He shook his hand, wincing at his fingers and their near miss. "What if I find a way to make that up to you?"

"I doubt there's any way you could do that."

"We'll see."

He closed the car door for her when she got inside, and she only looked back twice in the rear-view mirror before she turned the corner.

"Again?" Sarah looked up from her phone as Eloise sprinted toward the elevator with as much dignity as she could manage in heels. They all usually went up together, it was nice to start the day with friendly faces, but the others were nowhere in sight and it looked like Sarah had been about to give up and decided to head up alone.

Eloise slid through the closing doors of the elevator with an irritated scowl and less than an inch to spare. "My car wouldn't start this morning," she explained. "This week has been a nightmare."

"Sorry we didn't wait for you. Kim and Chloe both had to be in early and I was just getting ready to text you." She dropped her phone into her bag and smoothed down the lace of the red lace jumpsuit she wore beneath a trim black blazer. "Dwayne is on some kind of new power trip and he's making our lives hell if we're even a few minutes late."

"I guess there's no point in being bad at your job if you can't also make everyone around you miserable."

Sarah snorted but the look on her face was not amused. Her hostility toward Dwayne had increased with every week that went by after the promotion and she was bordering on plain homicidal. "I'm tempted every day to poison his coffee."

"I'd be your alibi."

Sarah smiled, and this time there was genuine humor in her eyes. "You wouldn't. There's not a rule-breaking bone in your body. I'd call you for a lot of things but not that."

"Let's hope we never have to test it."

"Hmm."

The elevator doors opened, and Eloise stepped out.

"Do you need a ride home?" Sarah asked, checking the time on her watch and tapping her foot at the slow elevator doors.

"No, the car's fixed now."

"You?"

"I'm afraid that's something else that's beyond my capabilities."

"Oh? You had a mechanic look at it already?"

"No, I didn't have time for—"

"Oh ..." Sarah's eyes popped wide. "Wait, did you have a man fix it? Did you have company last night?"

Eloise laughed as Sarah tried to question her through the closing door, and her good mood lasted all the way through until it was time to meet up with the others for lunch. Most days she ate at her desk, but they had a standing lunch date at the little café down the street on Fridays.

Fridays were for the girls, and they huddled together in the shade at the outdoor tables and sipped on iced coffee as they waited for salads with a tart raspberry vinaigrette or chicken salad sandwiches with slices of pistachio. It would be too warm to sit outside soon, but for now they were content to sweat a little to enjoy the little courtyard with its happily bubbling fountain and sweet-smelling flowers.

"Sorry we missed you this morning." Chloe popped a blueberry into her mouth and relaxed against the back of her chair. It sounded mostly like she meant it. "It's been a miserable day."

"Not so wonderful for Eloise, either," Sarah informed her.

"Just a little bit of car trouble," Eloise said. Her eyes were back on the menu, trying to decide if she wanted a chocolate éclair or a strawberry tart with her salad. She needed a little sweetness after the day she'd had.

"You never told me who managed to get it fixed for you in time for you to drive yourself to work and not be late?" Sarah had been fanning herself with the drink menu and casually fighting a bee for ownership of her glass of lemonade, but she sat forward in her chair, eyes suddenly calculating.

Eloise shot her a meaningful glance. "My lovely new neighbor."

"Ugh." Sarah deflated back into her chair; the hope gone from her eyes. "I was hoping you'd had a man over last night." She was comfortable with men in her bed and was always looking for some sign that Eloise had found one for herself, at least temporarily. It was a running joke between them that Sarah fully believed Eloise would be less uptight if she got laid more often.

"No, not this time." There was nothing more to say about that since they all knew she dated so rarely it bordered on never, even though they'd given up on asking her why. She'd never been able to put into words what it felt like to have your mother wind you so tightly men tended to practically run in the opposite direction.

Controlling women with mommy issues weren't exactly hot commodities on the dating market even *if* she'd been willing to put herself out there, which she absolutely wasn't. No dating until she was as firmly established in her career as possible or she'd never hear the end of it. It wasn't worth the hassle for the inevitable heartache.

"And I didn't ask my neighbor to come over and save me," Eloise added after a moment of silent contemplation. "He just showed up with his self-satisfied little smirk and waited patiently until I admitted I didn't know how to open the hood of the car."

"The worst possible thing that could happen around a man that already thinks he's a gift to women." Sarah said. She'd gone back to fanning her face, slightly damp dark hair stirring lazily in the artificial breeze. "Bastard."

"He *did* help," Kim observed. Her hands were busy dipping a slice of lemon into her own drink and setting it on a napkin, a sweet temptation for Sarah's buzzing foe. She always looked for the good in everything. People. Situations. Lemonade thieving bees. "Even if he was smirky."

"Exactly," Eloise agreed. "He's smirky! That's exactly what

he did! He came. He saw. He *smirked*. He was a condescending witness to my humiliation. And *then,* as if that wasn't insulting enough, he saved me a bunch of time and money so I can't even be mad about it."

"A bastard," Chloe agreed with a nod. "But is he a hot bastard?"

"Who knows? It's hard to tell beneath all the smirking and the irritating attitude." It was a lie but Eloise decided it was a harmless one. If she admitted what he did to her insides just by standing there, they'd never stop teasing her about it.

"Fair point." Chloe glanced at her phone and made a disgusted face. "If you're going to buy that dessert you've been drooling over in the menu for the last ten minutes, you'd better do it fast."

Thankfully, that was enough for them to all drop the subject of her new neighbor. Eloise was still licking chocolate off her thumb as they waited for the elevator, having been forced to eat her melting eclair on their way back to the office. It was a short walk, but summer was coming, and the heat and humidity rose with each passing day.

"Glad to see you found a way to keep that pretty mouth of yours busy over lunch, Ms. Mason."

Eloise flinched, quickly pulling her thumb away from her mouth and trying to paste a smile on her face as Sarah's boss stopped beside their little group. The rest of the office might be full of men who did little to hide their biases and their objectification but few of them were *that* bold. Being pals with the head of the HR department had some pretty disgusting perks.

Dwayne had always brought to mind every stereotype Eloise had ever heard of used car salesmen. He was deceptively attractive for an older man, dark hair swept back from a well-sculpted face with a practiced smile that she imagined he thought was charming.

"Excuse me?" she asked, tipping her head to the side and feigning ignorance as embarrassed heat burned all the way down to her chest.

He stepped to the side slightly until he was close enough to brush against the sleeve of her blouse with his elbow. "Oh, was that inappropriate? You're not going to go running to HR over a little joke, are you?"

She wished she could, wished it would do any good at all instead of getting her lectured over another apparent *misunderstanding*. "I—"

"Ms. DeWitt can tell you I'm a good guy, can't you Ms. DeWitt?" He took his eyes off Eloise just long enough to look pointedly over at Sarah. "You'd believe your friend if she told you I was a good guy, right?"

Eloise hated that. The way he hid behind a veneer of sweet southern manners and called them 'Ms. Mason' and 'Ms. DeWitt' while being a sleazy lowlife that made her skin crawl.

"Yeah, Dwayne's really something." Sarah's voice was high and friendly, but she was staring at the floor, her jaw tight and her hands clenched in front of her at the waist.

"I believe everything Sarah's told me about you," Eloise assured Dwayne and he smiled placidly, unaware of how many times a week Sarah called him a disgusting fuckface behind his back.

The elevator doors opened, and Dwayne walked on confidently as all four women hung back, each of them uncomfortably aware of how close they would have to be to him once they were inside.

Eloise was the last one on since she needed to be the first one off and she held her body as rigid as she could to keep from bumping the others into Dwayne. She didn't want to give him any excuse to be closer to them than necessary.

She fled as soon as the doors opened, shooting a quick apologetic look over her shoulder as she went. When Sarah texted her a picture of a steaming cup of coffee a few minutes later, she snorted. Maybe she *would* be willing to provide an alibi if someone poisoned Dwayne's coffee.

After everything that had happened that day, she held her breath when she left work that evening, fingers crossed as she turned her car key. The engine roared to life without issue, and she was briefly, improbably, grateful for Ethan and his presence next door. Whatever he'd done, it *had* saved her a lot of money and headache.

It was a pity he was so … so … *difficult.*

At least that was what she told herself when she got home and found a new hydrangea waiting for her on the front porch. It was smaller than the one that had been destroyed but the leaves were healthy, and the blooms were a lovely pink. He'd tied a bow around the plastic nursery pot, pink to match the flowers, and there was a small white card attached. The writing on it was hasty and almost unreadable, but she squinted at it in the dim porch light until she was able to make it out.

Sorry about the flowers
-Ethan
Well, that was *something.*
Definitely better than *nothing.*
She glanced at his darkened windows several times as she set the pot back on the porch, careful to place it in the best possible place for the right amount of sunlight until she could find time to plant it and dipping a finger into the soil to see if it needed to be watered.

It was a pity that someone with such a handsome face and who seemed capable of the occasional moment of surprising sweetness, had to be so smug. And condescending. And *difficult.*

Four

Ethan kept his car off her lawn and—more importantly—kept his distance, but she couldn't deny her curiosity about him grew the longer he lived next door. Apparently, it was harder to hold onto a grudge when he was behaving himself.

She watched him slyly from the windows of her own house, her face hidden behind the curtains as she leaned forward onto her tiptoes to get a better look, and within a few weeks of his arrival, she was sure of several things.

The first was that he didn't seem to work a normal job. He kept no regular hours and seemed to have no determinable schedule. When he left his house, it was nearly always in the company of one or more of the men she'd encountered that first night. More often than not it would be the pair she thought were brothers. Myles, the shy young man that had destroyed her flowers, and Dylan, the irritating one with a bad attitude that made her teeth clench every time she saw his cruel, arrogant expression.

Her second observation was that he was unusually secretive about his activities. All the men were preoccupied with looking over their shoulders, taking furtive glances around them whenever they were outside. Despite that, Myles had a habit of speaking too often and too loudly that had gotten him chastised many times by the others, with Dylan going so far as to slap him in the back of the head to silence him while muttering savagely under his breath. So far, little of Myles's ramblings had been particularly useful, but she had heard bits and pieces of conversations about a job they were working on.

"What do you think he's doing over there?" Eloise asked, unceremoniously dropping the question on her favorite remaining neighbors, Jackson and David, one Saturday several weeks after Ethan moved in. She was standing at their living room window, a cup of tea in her hands as she stared intently at her own house across the street.

"What?" They both looked at her blankly and she gestured with her cup to the house across the street. Not her house. The one beside it. The one where Ethan lived. He needed to trim his grass and his flowers were wilting in the late spring sun.

Neglectful, as she'd suspected he would be. She sniffed, trying to summon the proper amount of disdain, as her neighbors blinked at her slowly.

"Ethan?" David asked, his tone bewildered.

They continued to stare at her without making a sound when she nodded a confirmation and huffed a little in embarrassment. "He doesn't seem to have a job. I just wonder if maybe he's dealing drugs or something. He has to pay for that car somehow."

"In *this* neighborhood?" Jackson seemed to come back to himself, the shock of her question wearing off enough for him to ask his own with a shake of his head. He was leaning on the arm of their sofa, a dark blue button-down shirt with a chaotic pattern of hot pink flamingos opened to mid chest and a long-stemmed wine glass cradled between graceful fingers. "I doubt it."

Jackson was in his early fifties, blunt and colorful in a way that she normally appreciated, but she scowled at that, tipping her head to take in his patient smile and his husband's reproving look.

"Okay, but you've seen the way he goes in and out of there. He's obviously up to something." She looked meaningfully at David, hoping for support and, ideally, confirmation that she wasn't the only one who couldn't seem to keep her eyes off the house. Surely, it was suspicion that drove her, more than her own desire to watch the way Ethan's body moved as he crossed the lawn from front door to car and back again. It's not like she was *looking* for reasons to dislike him.

David, in his late thirties, was younger, quieter, and more introspective than his husband. He was stricter about rules and order—even at home his shirts were always ironed and his slacks crisp and perfectly tailored—but he was too polite to echo Jackson's doubts directly. Even if he disagreed with her, he was far less likely to be so open about it.

"This is a pretty safe area," he hedged gently.

"But it's possible," She tried not to wince at the stubbornness of her own voice. "We don't know anything about him really, so we don't know what he might be up to over there."

David clucked his tongue at her and the two men shared a meaningful glance, but his hand on her arm was gentle. "He's been nice to everyone since he moved in. That bit with your yard was unfortunate but he replaced what was damaged, right?"

She shrugged but she couldn't deny it. She'd planted her new hydrangea lovingly in the place of the old and it was thriving.

"It's not like you have to date him," Jackson began with a shrug, "but—"

"Date him?" Her heart seemed to slow down and restart all at once with a painful thump. "Who said anything about dating him?"

David lifted an eyebrow at the unusual forcefulness of her tone. "I think Jackson's just trying to say that you don't have to like this guy or spend time with him if he makes you uncomfortable, but maybe you should give him a chance. You've always been a little quick to assume the worst until you're proven wrong, but I've never seen you *this* determined to jump to the worst possible conclusions about someone before."

"You weren't all that fond of us, either, if I recall correctly," Jackson said without taking his eyes off his wine glass. At least he had the decency not to look directly at her when he made a valid point she couldn't dispute. Her immediate love of the house and neighborhood hadn't transferred over to the neighbors. It *had* taken her a little while to warm up to them. It had taken her a little while to warm up her friends at work, too. Maybe, just maybe, she *was* being a little too hard on Ethan, as well.

She took another sip of her tea without commenting on their observations because she couldn't bring herself to deny *those*, either. "So, you think I'm overreacting?" She squinted at his house, the car was parked in the driveway, but the motorcycle was gone. He wasn't home and she was tempted to go over and peek through his windows.

Jackson shook his head and David gave her a patient smile before answering. "I know you don't really care for the man and he *does* keep odd hours but it's not unusual to work from home these days. Don't you think that makes more sense than having an actual drug dealer living in the house next door to you?"

It was a reasonable explanation for Ethan's behavior, and it was obvious they thought she was paranoid. Maybe she *was* but, too hard on him or not, there was something about Ethan that made her uneasy. It went deeper than her normal reluctance to get to know new people or her mother's meddling insistence that men were nothing but trouble.

She was still stewing on it when she got home from work the next evening. She'd had Ethan on her mind all day and her eyes went automatically to his house when she pulled onto their street, noting with a frown that his bike was back in the driveway. He wasn't outside, but he was almost definitely home.

Not that she *cared*, she assured herself. She was only checking to see where he was so she could make sure to stay out of his way. He was keeping his distance, and she would keep hers. She would stop trying to catch a glimpse of him and his activities out of her windows—probably—because Jackson and David were likely right about her being paranoid, but she didn't have to be any more involved with him than necessary.

Eloise froze, key still in the front door lock, when a small blur darted her way from the shadows. Her heart was pounding before she recognized it for what it was and she laughed weakly as a wrinkly brown and white puppy jumped against her thighs. She knelt and ran a hand over the dog's back, noting that it was apparently clean, healthy, and well fed. Someone's escaped pet then, poor thing. It leaned into her hand, and she rubbed a silky ear between her fingers. She had always wanted a dog growing up, but her mother had never allowed her to have pets.

"Where'd you come from, sweetie?" she asked, cooing to the pup as it snorted and licked at her fingers. "You shouldn't be outside alone."

"Hey!"

She looked up and rolled her eyes as Ethan bounded up

the front porch steps. She was not in the mood to deal with him. "Yes?"

"That's my dog," he said, waving a hand at the animal, who wagged an unrepentant tail at him and made no move to return to its owner as it sat for Eloise's attentive stroking.

"Is it? Then you should keep him inside unless he's on a leash."

"I *do* keep him inside. He's started making a break for it every time I open the door and making me chase him around the neighborhood."

She shrugged, determined to blame him despite his excuses. "What's his name?"

"Winston," Ethan said with a grin.

She stood up and eyed him suspiciously as he lifted the puppy into his arms. "Are you serious?"

He chuckled, flashing his dimples and making her stomach flip pleasantly. "Doesn't he look like a Winston to you? You know? Bulldogs and Winston Churchill?"

"Hmm." She knew nothing about World War II beyond what little she'd learned in school and then promptly tried to forget, and she knew even less about dogs.

The pup was curled contentedly in Ethan's arms, sharp looking puppy teeth gnawing on his fingers, and she shook her head in bewilderment. She didn't want to encourage him by laughing at the absurdity of him holding a dog like a baby, but her lips twitched involuntarily as she reached for the doorknob again.

"Do you want to have dinner with us? We owe you for reuniting us after his escape attempt."

The question stopped her before she could open the door and she looked back at him, equal parts surprise and exasperation warring in her chest. "You're just going to keep asking me aren't you?"

"Maybe." He shrugged and settled the pup more firmly

against his chest as it began to wiggle. "Before you answer, just know you can hang out in the living room and pet the dog while I cook if that's what you want to do. Feeding you is the least I can do to say thank you."

She glanced at Jackson and David's house, remembering what they'd said to her about giving him a chance. They were so certain that she was overreacting, overthinking as always, and Ethan was being unexpectedly pleasant, his thumb stroking the neck of his dog as she thought over his offer.

She looked from him, his lips tipped up in challenge, to the dog in his arms. Surely, she could trust the dog's judgment. Her experience with them may have been limited but that's what others had always told her about animals, that their intuition about people's intentions were stronger than a human's and more reliable. The dog looked like he trusted Ethan implicitly, like he knew he would be cared for and protected despite the man's immense size and intimidating appearance.

She sighed, shoulders slumping in good natured defeat. "What are you cooking?"

Triumph flared in his eyes as he held out his free hand, waiting for her to take it. "Spaghetti."

"Now?" She looked from his outstretched hand to his dimple and back down at his dog. It felt like some sort of dream. The unsettling kind where you know you're dreaming but you can't change the outcome. He showed up and smiled at her and the next thing she knew she was petting his dog and agreeing to eat his spaghetti. None of which had been part of her plans for the evening. In the back of her mind, an alarm was blaring, but she couldn't seem to remember what the danger was when he looked at her like that.

What harm could spaghetti really do, after all?

"Did you have other plans for tonight?"

She thought of her empty house, her strict routine, and shook her head.

His hand was warm as it closed around hers, and nearly twice the size. The ring he wore brushed against her fingers and she trembled, remembering the way the skull had glinted in the light—a clear warning that she ignored as she followed him across the yard.

He didn't let go of her hand like she expected, instead keeping a light grip on her like he thought she might change her mind and run back to her own door instead. Her cautionary nature warred with the comfort of letting him hold her in even such a simple way. When he finally let her hand drop so he could let her inside, she wasn't sure if she was more relieved or disappointed.

The house was much the same as it had been when old Mr. Callaghan had lived here, but the furniture was different —a black leather couch and a large polished wooden coffee table instead of the pastel fabrics and white wicker that Mr. Callaghan had kept after his wife passed away. The biggest flat screen TV she had ever seen dominated one wall and the others were empty, with no trace of family photos or any personal touches.

"The house looks different," she mused, watching him set Winston on the floor and give the puppy an affectionate pat. It was sad to see all the traces of her friend erased. She'd missed him more than she'd realized and she wiped a subtle hand over misty eyes.

"You've been in here before?" Ethan asked.

"I used to visit my neighbor," she explained, her fingers drifting over the edges of the furniture as she explored the once familiar space. "His home health nurse found him passed out in his chair one morning and they took him to the hospital but he didn't make it. He was a sweet old man and liked my cookies. I probably didn't come by as often as I should have."

"A sweet old man." His lips turned up slightly at the corners, a sardonic twist, as he echoed her words. "That's not exactly how I remember him."

"You knew him?" She flicked her gaze to his face, her hands stilling on the arm of his couch as she watched an echo of old pain flit across his face.

"He was my grandfather," Ethan said with a jerky shrug as her jaw dropped open. "It's not a big deal."

"I guess that explains why the house never went up for sale," she mused, trying to see some resemblance between the lines of his face and the old man in her memories and finally settling on the height of his cheekbones and the length of his nose.

"My inheritance," he confirmed.

"I guess that's something." It was but she knew very well how poor a substitute money was for love, especially from your family. She would have given a block full of houses to be more than an obligation to her own, after all.

He looked over his shoulder as he wandered to the fridge and looked inside. "You want a beer?"

"Ah, no thanks," she said and wrinkled her nose as she followed him into the kitchen. "Beer isn't really my thing."

"You don't drink?"

"Wine, occasionally." She was only half paying attention as she tried to subtly take in the rest of the house. It was bare and unadorned, but tidy. He wasn't big on decoration and his space only looked half lived in but at least he wasn't a slob. "I won't turn down a sweet and bubbly white if it's offered."

"I'll get some," he said. "In case you decide you still want to come back after you taste my spaghetti."

She leaned on the counter and eyed him skeptically. "Can't you cook?" Her eyes wandered over his tattoos as he took a quick drink of his beer and her fingers itched to touch them. She wanted to ask him what they meant and why he'd chosen them, but she wasn't sure she was ready to hear the answers.

"In theory?" he asked, bringing her attention back to the question she'd asked. He lifted the beer to his lips but failed to hide his smile. "No, not really."

"So you were just gonna toss a jar of cheap sauce on some noodles and hope I didn't notice?" She raised an eyebrow at him but he didn't look ashamed of himself and she was less annoyed than she should have been that she'd been tricked.

"Something like that," he admitted.

"With noodles that were still a little crunchy?"

"Probably." He looked over once, assessing her reaction to his confession. "But offering you dinner *did* get you here, so I don't feel too bad about it. To be honest, I should have just asked if you wanted to have something delivered."

She laughed, relaxing even as her instincts warned against trusting him too much and too quickly. "Well, everyone should know how to make at least one basic meal and there's no time like the present to learn. Turn on some music and we'll make spaghetti."

"You're not supposed to be the one cooking dinner."

"Maybe not," she acknowledged, shamelessly opening the doors to his cabinets, and hunting for ingredients among the boxes and bags of prepackaged food, "but I would like to be able to eat it."

He had the sense to look embarrassed as he walked away to turn the music on, and it only took five minutes of quiet arguing for them to decide on a compromise on the radio station.

"You really listen to classical?"

She turned the water on to boil and smiled at the horrified tone of the question. "Yes, it's soothing. Better than that noise you blast out of here every day."

He grunted. "We're gonna have to agree to disagree on that one, sweetheart."

"Why do you *insist* on calling me that?" She blew out a quick, hard breath to get the stray hair out of her eyes as she worked and pinned him with a look.

"Sweetheart?" He seemed surprised, thumbnail picking at the label of his beer bottle.

"Yes, you call me that every time I see you." Sometime since she'd met him it had lost the original mocking tone but he still persisted. It was almost absentminded, like an endearment you used on a long-term lover. Did she remind him of an ex-girlfriend, perhaps?

He lifted a shoulder, more to hide his face than to shrug, and kept his eyes firmly away from her. "One of the few things I remember about my dad is that he always used to call my mom that. I guess I picked it up from him. Now I use it on pretty women with a tendency to bust everyone's balls."

She paused, pleasant heat rising to her cheeks as she watched him clumsily chop vegetables for a salad. There were so many questions about his past she could have asked him just based on that one small piece of information but everything felt too personal, too much after such a short acquaintance. Instead she settled on the other part of what he'd said. "Is that how you see me? A ball buster?"

Her cheeks flushed harder–almost painful now—from saying that out loud. Her mother would have washed her mouth out with soap for such language and she'd never developed much of a cursing habit—but he didn't seem to notice.

"Is that not how you see yourself?"

"No," she said flatly. The idea would never have occurred to her and even hearing it from him, it felt alien and unobtainable. She was too anxious for that, too easily twisted by her fears and worries, by other people's opinions. There was a standard, a level of achievement she needed to obtain and boundaries for her behavior that she had been conditioned to follow. Moving here, settling for a small house in New Orleans instead of staying at home or getting an apartment in a bigger city like New York or LA, had been the biggest rebellion she'd been able to muster in her entire life. It had taken all of the fight she had to do that relatively small thing and she had nothing left.

"How do you see yourself?"

She frowned, but he was watching her curiously, calm and patient, and the truth bubbled up inside her. "Frightened," she admitted. "Like I have to control everything all the time or something terrible will happen."

"That sounds tiring."

She swallowed, letting the unexpected understanding of that settle over her. The tension in her shoulders, her unconscious flinch as she waited to see how he'd respond, evaporated. "It is."

"What do you do when you're not busy trying to control everything?"

"I cook," she said, waving a hand at the stove, "listen to classical music, read … Nothing exciting."

"Hmm," he said, tossing tomatoes in a bowl and glancing at her out of the corner of his eye. "Watch your neighbors through your windows?"

She looked away, torn between guilt and embarrassment, but he was smiling, so she settled on a lighthearted response. "Only the suspicious ones," she teased.

He winked at her, and heat skimmed its way under her skin, unfamiliar in its intensity, and the blood rushed to her cheeks. The control she clung to so tightly, the iron grip that she held over herself and her more vulnerable emotions, wobbled dangerously and her heart stumbled in its place.

What was it about him that made her feel so off balance?

The edge of danger that she couldn't quite pin down or the boyish charm that she couldn't quite ignore?

The question lingered in her mind as they ate, Ethan keeping the conversation flowing by telling her how he'd picked Winston because he'd been the smallest and weakest, the runt of his litter. Jackson and David had been right, he was kinder and less difficult than her first impressions of him had led her to believe. It softened her, the unexpected gentleness of him, and she was reluctant to leave when the time came.

He seemed relaxed when he walked her back to her door, but her heart was fluttering. She'd been comfortable with him, content to watch the way his mouth curved around his words when he talked, and the connection between them had been easy and immediate.

It wasn't easy for her to admit, but as he walked up the steps toward her front door she was forced to consider that maybe part of the reason she had been determined to dislike Ethan was because a small piece of her really *wanted* to like him. It was a worrisome thought, one that kicked off all her heightened warning instincts again. She'd never been quick to like or to trust and Ethan wasn't just a stranger with mysterious habits and, perhaps, dangerous friends. He was an attractive man that didn't back down from her prickly exterior and was persistent in flirting with her.

It wasn't that she *never* entertained men. Certainly she had for a night or two when the opportunity presented itself for something safe, with a man that seemed as boring as he was trustworthy. But Ethan wasn't safe—he wasn't boring *or* trustworthy—and the excitement that ran along under her skin when he looked at her made her wary. Better to think he was a threat than to think too hard about what else might be going on.

She paused with her hand on the knob, ingrained manners taking over and causing her to fight the urge to run inside. The longer she stood here, the greater the chances one of them would get some bad ideas about how to say goodbye, but she had never been the kind to be rude when it wasn't called for. "Thank you for dinner."

"Thank you for rescuing my dog," he said with a grin, stepping closer until she was peering up at him from under her lashes and she could smell the gentle waft of cologne and the unique scent of his skin.

Her eyes fluttered down to settle on his mouth and instead of stepping back to safety and sanity, she tipped her chin up in welcome. Her heart was pounding and her breath was painfully shallow, all her attention focused on his lips and their slow descent ...

She jumped when a car door slammed, both of their heads turning when a cold voice shouted, "Callaghan!"

Dylan and Myles stood beside Dylan's sleek black car, which she knew cost at least three times as much as her own, more sensible sedan.

Ethan rocked onto his toes, a dangerous look crossing his face before he turned back to smile down at her, his face softening again as he stepped back. "They've got the worst timing. I guess I've got to go. An appointment I forgot about."

"This late?"

He flashed her a smile as Dylan called his name again. "Just a little bit of business."

"Business? Is this about that job you and Dylan keep talking about?"

His eyes darkened and flashed menacingly toward Myles, before returning to meet her gaze intently. "I told him to keep his fucking voice down," he muttered. "What do you know about that?"

"Nothing really," she said, her hand tightening on the doorknob. "Just that you were working on a job together."

"Stay away from Dylan," he demanded. The soft, easy-going man she'd had dinner with was gone. His eyes were like ice and his voice was just as cold. "Don't go snooping in his business, either. It's not safe for you."

"I wasn't *snooping*." She glared up at him, refusing to back down in the face of his sudden bad temper. "Besides, if he's so dangerous then why do you still work with him?"

"I don't have time to explain this now. Just go inside and remember what I told you." He looked like he wanted to say more, but she folded her arms across her chest and turned away, refusing to look at him. "Damn it," he swore. "We'll talk about this later." With that he was gone, striding quickly across the yard, every line of his body tense as he closed the distance between himself and the others.

Five

Ethan dropped his keys on the table beside the door and made his way to the fridge. "Beer?" He didn't know why he asked when he already knew the answer and he handed two over his shoulder before grabbing one for himself. There was still almost a full twenty-four pack in there, but the rest of their crew for this job would be arriving any minute—distant friends of some guy Ethan had known for a bit in high school—and they'd have him cleaned out before the night was over.

Between him and Dylan they had enough friends of friends they'd grown up around to keep from having to reuse the same people too often. A perk of staying close to your childhood stomping grounds, he supposed, though that wasn't the reason he stayed. He may have lost the only part of his family that mattered when his mom died, but he'd still managed to put down roots. New Orleans was home and he couldn't imagine living anywhere else. He was protective of home and family and everything that it stood for.

It was one reason he would've preferred they had this meeting anywhere else instead of at his house, but he'd been outvoted. The bar Dylan owned—a run-down hole in the wall place called Tough Break—was off limits for planning sessions because there were too many prying ears and Ethan's new house, though a bitter inheritance, was a better choice than Dylan's.

Cops were nosy in lots of places but quiet, gently prosperous neighborhoods like this one weren't usually on that list. They wouldn't be drawing any attention to themselves here, and that was one less thing they had to worry about. Bad memories aside, the house was useful enough that handing it down to him was one thing he could be grateful to his grandfather for.

Ethan wasn't particularly sorry he'd had to die to do it.

Dylan settled on the couch, his boots on the coffee table as he eyed Ethan with a speculative look. "I see you're getting friendly with that mouthy neighbor of yours."

Ethan sat down beside Myles on the other couch, carefully keeping his expression light and carefree. Personally, he liked Eloise. She was a knockout to look at with all that blonde hair and those icy blue eyes. Long limbed and graceful, she gave the impression of soft elegance until she opened her mouth. Sure, she had a lot of long pretty words, but a little nudge or a poke and she was fit to be tied.

He was amused by her feisty attitude and complete lack of common sense when it came to assessing danger. She charged in headfirst like a pissed off chihuahua and it was fun to watch. At least it would be, until she inevitably ran up against a bigger dog.

Dylan was a really big dog and his bark was nothing compared to his bite. He wouldn't find her snooping funny or her uptight attitude a challenge to explore. Ethan had plenty of reasons to be grateful to him, but Dylan could be a powder keg under the best circumstances. Eloise, despite the tight grip she tried to keep on herself, was a firecracker ready to go off and Ethan had no intention of bringing the two of them anywhere near each other if he could help it.

"Not really," Ethan said. He caught Myles giving him a speculative look out of the corner of his eye and grinned back at him like he didn't have a care in the world. Myles was a good kid but he was terrified of Dylan. Better to have them all fooled than to betray he'd given Eloise anything more than a passing glance.

"Oh?" Dylan glanced around the living room, gaze lingering on the pair of still half full glasses on the table in front of him. Eloise's lipstick was clearly visible on the rim of the second glass. "Sure as hell looked like it."

"Winston got out," Ethan explained. "She came over to bring the dog back."

"Just being a good neighbor, then?" Dylan obviously didn't believe a word of Ethan's excuse, but he smiled as he took another drink of his beer. After all the years they'd known each other, he was as comfortable here as he'd be in his own house and took up half the couch like he owned it.

"Something like that." Ethan met his gaze evenly, unbothered by Dylan's cool evaluation or Myles' uncomfortable shifting in the seat beside him. He'd known Dylan for half his life and as vicious as Ethan had seen him be, it had never spilled over onto Ethan himself. They had discovered long ago that bonds written in blood were not easily broken. After so many years, the two of them were practically brothers.

Dylan had certainly been there for him in ways most of his own family never had been. You couldn't choose your blood or the way they treated you—a hard lesson Ethan had learned right there in the room they were sitting in—but you could choose to surround yourself with people that mattered. Dylan had become his family and through him, Ethan had gained a little brother in Myles, and a purpose. He owed his current life to Dylan in more ways than he could count.

"Fuck her if you want," Dylan said after a moment of hesitation, "but don't let her become a distraction. That last job wasn't as lucrative as we'd hoped, and we need to keep our heads in the game."

Ethan winced and got up to grab another beer. "No worries there. I'm pretty sure she's not gonna talk to me at all after tonight."

"Losing your charm, Callaghan?" Dylan cracked a mocking laugh. "Pity, she's pretty enough to be a good fuck if you could get her to relax long enough to spread her legs. Is she as frigid as she looks?"

Ethan shrugged and tried to hide an unusual ripple of annoyance by popping the top on his second beer and taking another drink. Ethan had mostly learned to ignore Dylan's attitude toward women, but he found he didn't like the idea of anyone talking that way about Eloise.

She was a pain in the ass, sure, but she was independent and funny, and she liked his dog. He'd started out with the intention of irritating her as payback for her bitchy attitude, and he'd enjoyed getting her under skin and watching her fume, but damned if he hadn't also enjoyed the scrunch of her nose when she laughed.

He was tempted to tell Dylan exactly where he could shove his opinion, but if he said anything about it, it would only make Dylan that much more determined to continue. He was perverse that way, another thing Ethan had learned to ignore.

"I guess," he said instead. "She works for some kind of financial place downtown. Sounds like some kind of real fancy shit, so she's probably used to all those rich trust fund brats in their slick three-piece suits."

"She works at a bank and you're just now mentioning

that?" Dylan's boots thumped on the hardwood when he dropped his legs off the coffee table and leaned forward to rest his elbows on his knees. His eyes were lit with a calculating light that Ethan knew all too well.

"Not really a bank," he corrected. "Not like you're thinking anyway. According to her she handles investments or some shit. I asked her about setting up an account, made it seem like I was just looking for an excuse to run into her, but she said they don't do that kind of business in her building. Basically, she works at the regional headquarters and they don't have any customer facing operations, it's just a place where they do the paperwork and administration duties for the smaller branches."

He waited until Dylan sat back, disappointment on his face, before propping his own feet on the coffee table and pointing at him, beer still in hand. "And I didn't tell you, because I just found out."

"The paperwork places probably know how everything works at the branches." Dylan said slowly, the calculating look returning after a few moments of thought. "What she knows might still be useful. We've been playing in the minor leagues, trying to keep Tough Break off the cops' radar by dabbling in petty shit and hitting up convenience stores and check cashing places. You wanna live that way for the rest of your life? Because I don't, and she could be just what we need."

"Maybe," Ethan admitted reluctantly, "but she doesn't seem like the type to be careless with what she lets slip."

Dylan gestured at Ethan and swung his gaze hard to his little brother. "You see this shit, Myles?"

Myles swallowed and his eyes were wide. "I—"

"Forget it," Dylan interrupted. "You're both useless."

Ethan dropped his gaze to the beer hanging between his fingers. *If Dylan had been anyone else* ... No, there was no point in imagining what he'd do. Ethan was a laid-back kind of guy overall, but his size and appearance were usually enough to keep people respectful. He also wasn't above using his fists if it came down to it, so his reputation as a brawler would often do the rest. No one but Dylan would've had the balls to sit in his living room and insult him to his face.

"What do you want me to do? I told you she probably isn't speaking to me now. Y'all scared her off a minute ago." Not entirely true. He had been the one threatening her about minding her own business and as long as she'd taken to unwind a little around him, he figured she'd be unlikely to do it again after that. He'd started to make a little progress and now he'd lost it. A fact that he resented but what else could he do? She needed to stay the fuck away from Dylan and how else was he supposed to have made sure she got that message loud and clear?

"Get her to forgive you for whatever you did to piss her off tonight. She must be into you or you wouldn't have gotten her over here in the first place. Be your usual charming self and let the rest work itself out. If you fuck her good enough, she'll probably tell you the vault codes."

"She handles investments," Ethan repeated, more firmly this time. He wanted out of this conversation and for Dylan to never have Eloise's name in his mouth again. "And since she spent most of the time she was over here talking about work, I happen to know her friends probably don't know that shit, either. They all work in accounting or auditing or—"

"Figure it out." Dylan was already pulling out his phone, the conversation over as far he was concerned. He'd given an order and he expected Ethan to get it done, come hell or high water.

"Why don't we just find a bank teller and fuck the vault codes out of someone who actually knows them?" Myles, timid though he was, spoke up from his spot beside Ethan, and Dylan looked at his brother the way a man might look at a worm wriggling on the sidewalk.

"Kid's got a decent point, Dylan. If you're serious about hitting up a bank—an actual fucking bank—wouldn't it make sense to go for someone closer to the source?" Ethan jumped back into the conversation automatically, not so much because he thought Dylan would go for his suggestion, but as a reflex to take the heat of Dylan's attitude off of Myles. The kid was quiet and jumpy, as opposite of Dylan as it was possible to be, and he didn't handle his big brother as well as Ethan did.

Myles caught his eye, and a knowing look passed between them. He was grateful for the intervention and Ethan was happy to provide it. He'd never had a little brother of his own, but Myles was about as close to it as a man could get.

"That's how you get caught." Dylan leaned back and dropped his boots back on the coffee table. "If you're going to do an inside job, you have to stay a step removed. Everyone at the branch is gonna be looked at real hard when the cops show up."

That made a kind of sense Ethan couldn't argue with, and he didn't like the way this conversation was going. Not that he had an objection to the idea of getting more than friendly with an attractive woman, but he knew Dylan well enough to recognize when he was dreaming up something unusually reckless, even for him.

Ethan had been part of those plans since he was sixteen and he knew how they usually went down. There was more than a slight chance that if Eloise was involved, even without her knowledge, she'd get hurt.

"It won't be a problem for you, will it?" Dylan was staring at him, eyes narrowed, and Ethan felt Myles shift uncomfortably again. They both knew it wasn't a good idea to say no to Dylan once his mind was set on a plan. He sensed money like a shark sensed blood in the water and there was no getting around him. "You know how much I depend on you, right? We're family."

Ethan tightened his jaw, his initial resistance fading away beneath memories of being sixteen and terrified, still bruised from that last confrontation he'd had with his grandfather and then the cops. He'd been big, but young and wet behind the ears when they'd tossed him into juvie and left him there to rot till he turned eighteen.

He didn't know what would have happened to him if Dylan hadn't decided to give him a chance. They were the same age, but Dylan was more than just big. He was mean and calculating, years of experience being bounced from abusive dad to foster homes to juvie and back again having sharpened all his broken edges.

There was nothing Dylan wouldn't do to get ahead, and he had taken Ethan with him. That two-year stint had flown by and when the system had spit him back out again, Ethan was a different, more violent man than he would have been otherwise. He had Dylan to thank for that transformation.

And for his survival.

Whether Eloise deserved what he'd unintentionally dragged her into or not, he wasn't going to step away from what had been asked of him. He couldn't. It wasn't the first time he'd had to ignore his reservations to do what was required for a job and Dylan had no reason to believe Ethan would fumble instructions now. Current personal feelings aside, and he had more of those than he probably should have, he owed Dylan too much to let him down.

"No problem," he said, his gaze level on Dylan's. He could handle this. He *would* handle this because he had no choice. As long as he was careful, he could manage Dylan's demands and keep him far from Eloise at the same time. "I'll get whatever you want from her."

Six

"Eloise? Are you listening?"

Eloise jumped, the background noise of a crowded Friday night restaurant rushing back as the voice cut through her thoughts. The air was heavy with the sound of music and the scent of frying onions but she had been oblivious to all of it. It was rare for her to go out on the weekends, especially to a place with twinkle lights on the wall and a brightly colored plastic menu, but Chloe had chosen the location, insisting that the fishbowl sized margaritas and excellent food would make a fun night.

She flushed and turned to look at Sarah. "Sorry," she mumbled, a guilty flush rising to her cheeks. "Just a bit distracted."

"What could be so distracting that it takes away from my birthday dinner? And does he have a set of gorgeous bedroom eyes?" Sarah waggled her eyebrows suggestively and leaned in to put her hand on her chin. She'd let them put a small, sparkling pink birthday hat on her head but she managed to remain dignified. They were two margaritas into her special evening—the regular kind, thankfully, not the fishbowls—and there wasn't a single dark hair out of place, not a smudge of lipstick or shadow of mascara anywhere she hadn't intended it to be. She was a queen holding court in a party hat instead of a crown.

As always, it was just the four of them—herself, Kim, Chloe, and Sarah—and they were all looking at Eloise now. She wasn't sure how to answer Sarah's question. He *did* have gorgeous bedroom eyes, but she hadn't mentioned the dinner she'd had at his place to anyone else or the way he'd left so abruptly, words of danger and warning on those soft pink lips.

He was an enigma she couldn't quite unravel, this man that held squirming puppies and worked magic on a car engine but clearly had plenty of dark secrets to hide. She didn't like riddles and her temper hadn't cooled in the days that had passed since then.

Sarah spotted the flush on her cheeks immediately and clapped a hand to her mouth. "It *is* about a guy, isn't it? Spill!"

Eloise hesitated, looking away and focusing her attention on the paper straw wrapper she was busily winding around her finger. She'd still rather not tell them—it was easier to pretend it hadn't happened that way—but Sarah knew how to read her better than anyone. She'd already spotted Eloise's blazing cheeks and guilty expression. There was no way to hide it from her now and trying would only make Sarah that much more determined to get to the bottom of it.

"Remember that new neighbor I have?" Eloise glanced up once, quickly, and then back down at her straw paper. The tip of her finger was turning a little purple from lack of blood supply but she wasn't ready to give up her grip on it just yet.

"The flower destroyer who fixed your car?" Kim asked. Her eyes were wide and slightly glassy. She rarely drank and was more than a little tipsy. Her cardigan had slipped down off of one shoulder and her short red hair was disheveled from running her fingers through it.

Eloise nodded. "That's the one."

"Wait," Chloe said, leaning forward eagerly, margarita clutched in her hand. She had been only half paying attention, turned around in their booth to flirt with a man behind them, but Eloise had her full interest now. "The bad boy next door that you hate has hot bedroom eyes? You didn't tell us that part!"

"It's a long story," Eloise hedged. Long and embarrassing. "Apparently he has this really cute dog and we made spaghetti and after that I thought he might kiss me. Strangely enough, for one very brief moment I thought that I might be okay with that, even after everything that's happened, but *then* his buddies showed up and he got all bristly and threatening and ..." She trailed off, sucking in a deep breath and shrugging. "I don't know what's happening, but I know I don't like it."

"He made you spaghetti?" Chloe asked. She finished her drink and started looking around the crowded restaurant for a waiter. He wasn't immediately visible and she drummed her fingers impatiently on the tabletop and grinned knowingly at Eloise. "Sounds like a date."

"No, I made the spaghetti. He was going to make me dinner. I even went to his house but it turns out that he's not a very good cook."

Sarah swirled her straw in her margarita and gave her a pointed look. "He let you cook in *his* kitchen? That's definitely a date."

"You're all focusing on the wrong thing here." Eloise huffed, expelling a deep breath and wrestling with her own impatience. "Did you hear what I said? The part about his friends showing up and him getting all 'tough guy' on me and telling me to mind my own business?"

They frowned at her in unison, and she took another long sip of her drink.

"Hmm." Kim leaned back and crossed her arms protectively over her chest. "That does sound suspicious."

"Oh, come on," Sarah said, shaking her head. Her party hat tipped dangerously to one side and Chloe reached across the table to fix it. "That could be because of anything. Maybe this guy stole his last girlfriend or something and that's why he wants to keep you far away from him."

Kim shook her head, always cautious, but Chloe jumped at the chance to agree with Sarah and nodded enthusiastically. "Yeah," Chloe said. "I mean, sure, it's a little strange, but he seems like a nice guy when he's with you, right? A little gruff, but maybe a bit of a tender side under there? Sounds like a dream guy to me."

Kim frowned. "So, she's just supposed to pretend that whatever was going on with him that day didn't happen? It sounds like he could be up to something illegal. What if he's involved with something really dangerous?" She slipped her cardigan back onto her shoulder and tried not to make eye contact after she was done talking. It was rare for her to argue, especially with Chloe or Sarah, but the margaritas seemed to have given her a boost of liquid courage.

Chloe twisted a lock of her long, brown hair around her finger and cast a sidelong look at Sarah as Eloise's stomach turned sour. They all got along well enough but Chloe didn't like being contradicted and they had all been drinking just enough to loosen their usual inhibitions. "Involved with something? Like what?" Chloe asked. "Insurance fraud?"

There was an unpleasant edge of sarcasm in the question but Kim's eyes narrowed. "I watch a lot of true crime and you'd be surprised what a seemingly normal person can be involved in."

"I told Jackson and David I thought he might be dealing drugs because he keeps such odd hours and is always looking over his shoulder." Eloise waved a salsa covered chip at them, anything to draw their attention to her and away from each other, before biting into it.

Kim snorted. "Dealing drugs? That's the best you could come up with? What if he's a serial killer or running a human trafficking ring to steal people's kidneys? Or *worse*?"

"Worse?" Eloise asked, but no one was paying attention to her again.

"As if something like that would stop me from finding the man of *my* dreams," Sarah said. "Sometimes you have to take a chance on love."

Kim pointed a finger at her. "That kind of reckless attitude is exactly how you ended up dating your last boyfriend and that guy was—"

"Yeah, yeah," Sarah said, one hand waving to dismiss the rest of whatever Kim had been planning to say. "But you have to try, don't you? I have a goal. I'm gonna be one half of a power couple, find somebody with *ambition*, and I am not about to let something that's probably not true anyway get in the way of my dreams."

"Ethan is *not* the man of my dreams," Eloise reminded them. "I barely know him. Jackson and David don't seem to think he's that bad but—"

"I agree with Sarah," Chloe said, and Eloise barely resisted the urge to roll her eyes. "You're always so ..."

"Picky," Sarah supplied when Chloe struggled to find the right word. "You barely date and when you do, you tear the guy to pieces in your mind. You look for flaws so of course you find them."

Eloise looked away, running one finger down the condensation on the side of her glass and avoiding their eyes as they watched her. She *was* terrible at dating but only because she had never really *tried*. It wasn't like she was defective. It was just that she knew where her priorities were supposed to be until her career was established.

Career first, that's what her mother had always told her. Eloise was starting to think she'd really meant *career only*—she was twenty-seven and still dodging lectures about her career and her dating life during their monthly phone calls, after all —but even if that wasn't the case ... Well, if she ever *was* successful enough in her career for her mother to stop nagging her about avoiding men, she was going to start her romantic life with someone more respectable than *Ethan*. Someone with a good job, health insurance, a 401K ...

She'd have to go into it *sensibly*, with someone that checked all the boxes for a long-term life partner. Ethan didn't check any of them, as far as she could tell.

God, what had she been *thinking* even going to his house? Maybe she should stop being mad at Ethan for just being, well, *Ethan* and start being mad at herself for getting distracted by a pretty smile and a pair of dimples.

"You should at least let him explain what happened." Chloe's expression was caught somewhere between pity and condescension. She never seemed to have trouble attracting men so Eloise supposed she shouldn't be surprised that Chloe wasn't the most empathetic person to her struggles.

"It *has* been a long time since you were even interested in anybody," Kim agreed reluctantly. It looked as though it pained her to say it and Eloise thought it probably had. Any hint of possible conflict was more than she would want to be involved in. Kim was so timid she would probably have run from Ethan on sight and never looked back.

"I'm not interested in him," Eloise insisted. It wasn't entirely a lie. She had her priorities and that was more important than her skyrocketing blood pressure and odd urge to lean into him and find out what he *tasted* like. A small shudder ran through her at that mental image and she hoped the others didn't notice. "I'm just mad that he got me to feel sorry for him and his ridiculously named dog and *then* he had the absolute nerve to get a bad attitude with me."

"You wouldn't be this mad if you didn't think he was hot." Sarah smiled, lips curving like a cat that had finally caught the canary. "And maybe you like that he's a bit unpredictable. You can't figure him out and it bothers you just enough to keep your interest. Opposites attract and all that," she said with a nod, twirling the little umbrella in her drink with a knowing wink.

"I've never been into bad boys," Eloise grumbled, unwilling to admit that her friend had made several very accurate points.

"You've never found a hot one who looks at you with bedroom eyes. Ten bucks says he's itching to get under your skin and ruffle those perfect feathers of yours."

The image that conjured, of Ethan's hands and his mouth disrupting the tight grip she kept on her life flashed tantalizingly across her mind and she shrugged helplessly. She wanted it—her physical reaction to him was stronger than it had ever been for anyone else—even though she knew very well that she shouldn't.

She'd never been this at odds with herself before. It was as though, somehow, in the course of a few offhand meetings and one disastrous spaghetti dinner he had cracked her open and all the carefully concealed urges she'd been refusing to acknowledge all her life had come spilling out. She was trying to shove it all back in before anyone noticed but it was sliding through her fingers and making a mess of things.

Maybe *this* was what her mother had always warned her about. You could build a life and a career for yourself, put all the blocks in place with years of work and consideration, and someone could waltz in and disrupt it all on a whim. One flashing dimple and an attractive body and she was dangerously close to losing her focus.

"I can see the wheels turning in your head," Chloe observed. "I know you're not usually one to jump into a situation without thinking it through, so I get it, but consider this ... The more you try to make him off limits, the more tempting he is. Maybe, instead of fighting the attraction we *know* you have for him, you should just let him take you to bed and get it out of your system."

Eloise opened her mouth to object before slowly closing it again as the idea began to take root. It wasn't something her mother would ever have approved of, but it did have a certain appeal. Not that she had to jump into bed with him, of course. Surely, just spending more time in his company would be enough to rid her of this fascination. Men tended to reveal their worst selves pretty quickly, and it wouldn't take long for his irritating habits and demanding ways to take some of the shine off of his physical appearance.

"Chloe has a point." Sarah was already looking around, joining Chloe's hunt for their missing waiter, but she paused long enough to pin Eloise with a stern look. "Think about it, okay?"

Eloise found that she couldn't think of anything else as the meal progressed. She was lost in thought as they left the restaurant and barely remembered the conversation where they all decided to stay at her house that night, hoping to get a glimpse of the mystery man that was causing her so much trouble. They were disappointed when they got to Eloise's house—tumbling out of an Uber to giggle and shush each other in the driveway—to find out he wasn't home.

"I can't believe he's not here." Sarah was already rummaging through Eloise's kitchen drawers for a corkscrew, bottle of white wine in hand.

Kim had gone straight to the pantry and now was trying to hit the popcorn button on the microwave with one eye closed.

She had started leaning precariously to the left but she was determined. "He probably would have been asleep anyway."

Chloe had gone straight to the bathroom to change and emerged with her hair in a loose bun and dressed in Eloise's pajamas. She headed straight for the couch, reaching for the remote as she tried to peek out the living room windows. "If he's not here now, that just means he has to come back sometime, right?"

Sarah finished unscrewing the wine and started pouring it into glasses. "Right."

They were still awake, wine drunk and laughing at the romcom playing on the TV, when he came back hours later. Everyone rushed to the window, all peering out at him with bleary eyes as he parked the bike and turned toward the front door.

Sarah whistled softly. "Tall, tattooed, and *very* hot? I'd let that man dick me down in a heartbeat."

Eloise choked on her wine. "Sarah!"

He stopped suddenly, narrowing his eyes as he stared at the window, and they all squealed and ducked down. Eloise was the first one to have the nerve to peek back above the sill, her heart hammering with a mix of humiliation and thrill. He was still standing in the same place, waiting. When he spotted her again, he winked, not at all bothered.

She wished the floor would open up and swallow her.

Her head was pounding when she woke the next morning, bright light streaming in through the window announcing that she had slept in far too late. An unfamiliar weight on her legs had her lifting one eye open cautiously, but it was just Chloe, sleeping sideways across the foot of her bed, arms thrown wide, and face pressed heavily into a stolen couch pillow.

Eloise winced as bits of last night's memories flitted across her mind. Ethan had caught her—*them,* all of them—staring at him at 3 am. He had winked at her, that smile that made her knees unsteady and her pulse hammer flashing languidly at her in the darkness.

She wiggled out from under Chloe, whose right arm had been thrown haphazardly over her face, and wandered downstairs. She found her phone on the floor of the hallway, a new voicemail from that morning, reminding her that she was overdue to call her mother. "Eloise, are you ever going to pick up this phone when I call ..." She deleted it, ignoring the guilt that twisted hard in her stomach. Dealing with that would have to wait until later, when she wasn't hung over.

She'd moved a thousand miles away, traded in hard northern winters for sweltering southern summers, and the sound of mother's voice always sucked her right back in. She was ten again every single time and there was no escape. It was hard enough to deal with without a dry mouth and a headache hammering away behind her eyes.

The kitchen counter was littered with empty glasses and several open wine bottles, and she shook her head a little when she found Kim curled up on her couch, one foot peeking out from under the living room's throw blanket and snoring softly.

She checked the rest of the downstairs—the bathroom, the little reading nook with built-in bookshelves—but there was no sign of Sarah.

The porch creaked under Eloise's feet as she stepped out, glancing around to search the yard and finding Sarah sitting on the porch step with a bottle of water in her hands.

Sarah glanced over her shoulder with a wide smile when

she heard the front door open. "Finally! I thought you were never going to wake up."

"Is everything okay?" Eloise wrapped her arms protectively around her middle and glanced nervously at Ethan's house. He'd gotten home late, and was likely still asleep, but she felt exposed with her unbrushed hair and baggy pajamas.

"I'm fine. Just had a few words already this morning with your neighbor's big, broody friend. Dylan? He was out here at an indecent hour with that bike of his, trying to wake the neighborhood."

Eloise narrowed her eyes. "He didn't give you a hard time, did he?"

Sarah shook her head, lips twitching. "I don't think he quite knew what to make of me, so he left."

"Good."

"But not before he hit on me," Sarah said with a laugh, her eyes full of mischief. "He's cute, maybe I shouldn't have run him off."

"There's something off about him," Eloise cautioned. "Apart from what Ethan said, he gives me the creeps."

"But he's *hot*," Sarah said, her grin entirely too wild for that early in the morning, even one without drunken antics the night before.

"Hmph," Eloise groused. "The others are still passed out, but we can go ahead and start whipping up some muffins if you're hungry."

"I never turn down muffins," Sarah agreed. "Especially your muffins. Blueberry?"

"Always."

The smell of breakfast in the oven and coffee brewing brought everyone to the kitchen, all of them lounging around and leaning on the counters as they waited for breakfast to be ready. Sarah entertained the others with a repeat of her story about encountering Dylan, and Eloise shook her head in amusement as they all cheered her on when they found out that he'd hit on her.

"So, Eloise's not the only one with a cute bad boy love interest now?" Kim asked, half her face hidden behind the rim of her coffee cup. "I'm glad he'd already left by the time I woke up and went out this morning."

Eloise frowned and pointed a butter knife at her. "You wouldn't have had to risk it if you'd quit smoking last month like you promised."

Kim winced. "I *tried* but they're doing some sort of restructuring at work and there are rumors they're planning to downsize my department so of course everyone is fighting to put in more hours. Have to prove you're useful and committed to the company, right?" A muscle twitched over her left eye and her laugh was bitter. "I just couldn't give up the only thing that calms me down. I hate it and God forbid my mom ever finds out about it, but it's my one little guilty pleasure."

"If you'd woken up sooner, you could have been the one meeting Mr. Tall, Dark, and Cranky and then maybe you'd have *two* guilty pleasures." Sarah laughed when Kim's cheeks turned a vibrant, horrified shade of pink.

"I can't believe you're interested in him," Eloise said as she popped her head out of the oven with her hands full of muffin tin. Her memory conjured a clear picture of Dylan's eyes, and a shiver ran through her. "He's so ... cold."

"I'm not really interested," Sarah picked at a blueberry on top of a muffin, her eyes suddenly wistful. "Not for anything serious. I just ..."

"What's wrong?" Kim asked when Sarah fell silent and plucked the muffin from the tin, tossing it back and forth in her hands to cool it as she frowned.

"I just need some distraction from work stress," Sarah admitted. "Working under Dwayne is a fucking nightmare and it's even worse knowing that should have been my job. I *earned* it."

"You're right," Eloise said readily. "It would be nothing more than what Sun Valley deserved if you quit and took your considerable talent somewhere else. They don't deserve you if they can't appreciate you."

Sarah sighed, deep and sad. "I know but if I do that, I feel like I'm just giving up. It's like admitting that I can't get the respect there and I hate it."

"You want them to know how good you are before you leave," Chloe said with a shrug. "Really rub it in."

Sarah nodded fiercely. "Exactly, I'm tired of people feeling like they can walk all over me."

"You'll get your chance," Eloise said. "I know you and if you can't find a way then you'll make one."

Sarah smiled ruefully, her finger tapping restlessly on the side of her coffee cup. "Thanks, it's good to know that I'll always have all of you, even if my job is shitty and my dating life is shittier."

"If all else fails, you can always move in with me and adopt a dozen cats," Chloe said with a grin.

"That would be truly living the dream," Sarah said, shaking her head and rolling her eyes.

"I'll have you know that my cat lady house will be very desirable real estate." Chloe sniffed. "At least six cats per old woman and how can you beat that offer?"

"Then let Kim live there," Sarah said with a smirk.

"Hey," Kim protested, tossing a piece of muffin at Sarah. "What about Eloise?"

"Eloise has her mystery man from next door," Sarah said, tossing the muffin back at Kim and missing by a wide enough margin to send it sailing past her head and into the living room.

"He's not my man," she muttered, chewing morosely on

her own muffin as she made a mental note to sweep up all the muffin crumbs after everyone left.

"After that smile he gave you last night I'd say he wants to be," Chloe said.

The doorbell rang and Eloise was spared having to think of a response to that as she straightened up and tried to smooth her hair into place.

"It might be Ethan." Sarah's voice followed her as she left the kitchen and the others laughed when Eloise frowned over her shoulder at them.

"It's probably Jackson or David," Eloise said. "Ethan doesn't have any reason to come over here."

"You're over here," Chloe called, but Eloise ignored her and scurried for the door. She yanked it open as the bell rang again.

Ethan was standing on her front porch with tousled hair and a sheepish smile. Her embarrassment from the night before and the anger she'd been carrying around since their almost-date dimmed at the sight of him, leaving her once again unsettled at how quickly her common sense vanished when he looked at her.

"Hey," he said quickly, hands up like he thought she might close the door in his face. "I know you're probably pissed at me about what happened the other day but ..." He trailed off, his eyes widening as he stared over her right shoulder into the house behind her.

She already knew what she'd see if she turned to look, and she gave him an exaggerated, long-suffering sigh. "They're behind me, aren't they?"

"All three of them," he confirmed, shooting a charming grin in the direction of her living room. "I thought you weren't alone in the window last night and I'm glad it was a sleepover with the girls and not a date."

His gaze was suddenly warm, possessive, and it was

enough to remind her why she had been irritated with him in the first place. She leaned on the door frame, arms crossed over her chest and determined to ignore that he was seeing her in her pajamas again. "How do you know it wasn't a date?"

"Oh," he said, looking from her to the living room and back. "You and … all of them, huh? Well, aren't you just full of surprises?" He let the words linger in a deliberately speculative drawl that did nothing to conceal the humor in his tone.

She knew he didn't believe her—she was clearly too tightly wound to regularly participate in orgies—and shook her head, an unwilling smile tugging at the corners of her mouth. "What do you want, Ethan?"

"To apologize for how I handled things with Dylan," he said. "And then maybe I could give you that dinner I owe you? I'll take you out this time, so you don't have to cook for me. Just as friends," he added quickly, holding up his hands to stop her from voicing the rejection already forming on her tongue.

"I don't know," she said slowly. Chloe's idea was still tempting—even more so now that he was standing on her doorstep with that charming grin and she hadn't melted onto the floor in a puddle of shame—but everything about her life had been exactly the way she liked it before he'd showed up.

Clean.

Orderly.

Predictable.

His presence had upset her balance and it frightened her. What would she do, if instead of getting the itch out of her system, spending time with him somehow made it worse?

"We can go anywhere you want," he said, taking a step closer until he was crowding her space and she could feel the heat of his chest, "even if it's just out for coffee and then afterward you could come over and visit Winston."

She squinted up at him, a frown twisting her lips as he

winked at her. "Tempting me with a cute dog isn't fair," she protested.

"You know what they say," he mused, twisting a lock of her hair between his fingers. "All's fair in love."

"And war," she retorted. "Which one is this?"

"I think that depends on which one of us you ask," he said. "Maybe a bit of both?"

She huffed at him and gently swatted at his hand until it fell away from her hair. There was absolutely no chance that she was not going to regret what she was about to say, but the will to resist him melted away every time she looked into those blue eyes of his.

She hesitated, standing in the doorway of her tidy little house as Ethan waited for an answer. It seemed to her that she was standing at the edge of some intangible precipice, poised breathlessly to fall or fly if she were foolish enough to jump.

"We can go to dinner but that's it. *And*," she rushed to add, "just as friends."

"Just friends," he agreed. His face was stoic but the look in eyes was unsettlingly triumphant.

"Oh, and I want an explanation for whatever that was that happened with Dylan. I admit I jumped to the worst possible conclusion, because that's what I do, but I still think I deserve to know what is actually going on."

He winced but nodded reluctantly. "I was hoping you'd forgotten about that but, yeah, sure. We can talk about it at dinner, okay?"

"Okay." He perked up again at that, the glint back in his eye, and she sighed. "I'm going to regret this, aren't I?"

His dimples flashed and he chuckled, low and satisfied in a way that made her stomach flip. "Not if I can help it, sweetheart."

Seven

She'd agreed to go to dinner with him.

Just as friends.

She'd meant that, she really had, but the idea of going to dinner with him still tied her stomach up in knots and she wasn't sure if it was mostly him that she didn't trust to stick to that rule or herself.

She knew she shouldn't be this nervous, she'd spent years navigating around men without becoming entangled, but it was hard for her to keep her focus when he was around. If her mother lived close enough to get so much as a look at her face when Ethan was in sight, she'd be lectured for a month. Eloise could hear her mother's shrill voice in her head, the refrain from her childhood never quite fading away.

"Keep your mind where it belongs," she'd said when Eloise had come home from school with her first harmless crush. *"Don't let some boy turn your head,"* she'd said when Eloise had been asked to go to prom. *"You don't want to end up like me, do you?"* she'd asked when they'd dropped Eloise off at college.

But would that really have been so bad? Eloise had always wondered what was so terrible about having a solid career *and* a family. Had a husband and child really interfered with her mother's life so much? Or had her mother simply not wanted those things and resented having them pushed upon her?

"You can keep it fun," Sarah reassured her. Eloise had spent the first ten minutes of their Friday café lunch panicking about her casual Sunday dinner plans with Ethan and Sarah was ruthlessly taking the situation in hand. If Eloise hadn't been so embarrassed about reacting like a lovestruck teenager she might have even been grateful. "Just a bit of light conversation. Nothing too serious. You're going to dinner with him, not getting married."

"Which isn't to say that you can't sleep with him," Chloe added, her smile like that of a cat proposing a raid on the milkman's cart.

"It's not even a date." Eloise had already lost count of how many times she'd said it and the response was wooden and automatic, tasting like cardboard on her tongue.

"It *sounds* like a date," Kim said. Her shrug was apologetic as she sipped her lemonade but the others both nodded.

"Whose side are you on?" Eloise grumbled. They'd gotten an indoor table this time, but the sun shining in through the glass was still hot on her cheeks. She hoped it would help disguise the blush she knew was rising on her face. Maybe they would mistake her constant embarrassment for heat stroke.

"She's on the right side of this little disagreement," Sarah said firmly. "The *winning* side. Right, Kim?"

"I mean—" Kim began.

"Exactly," Chloe interrupted. "She wants to go down on the right side of history once you end up sleeping with Ethan."

"I'm *not* sleeping with Ethan."

"I'll bet you a month's worth of desserts that you do," Sarah said. "You can have your pick every Friday if you make it through the full week after this date without sleeping with him."

"Deal," Eloise agreed. "I'm going to start with a blueberry scone." She wasn't as confident as she tried to sound and something about the way Sarah's lips turned up at the corners told her they were able to see right through her to the heart of her conflict.

By the night before their not-quite-a-date, Eloise had almost convinced herself that she hadn't made a mistake with their bet, that she could enjoy his company for this one meal and then put him out of her mind. She gave herself a firm pep talk as she stood in front of the tall mirror in her bedroom, holding a pink floral dress beneath her chin as she considered whether it was an appropriate outfit for something that wasn't a date. It was cute, but not really sexy. A little jewelry would make it seem put together without looking like she was trying too hard.

She tossed it into a growing pile at the foot of her bed just as the doorbell rang. She hesitated—it was late and she wasn't expecting company—but it rang twice more by the time she'd grabbed a light silk robe and hurried down the stairs. "I'm coming," she panted, belting the robe sloppily before reaching for the doorknob. She pulled it open without looking through the peephole and found Ethan standing on the porch, a bag in his hand and a deep scowl on his face.

"You didn't check to see who I was before you opened the door." It was clearly meant to be scolding, and he waited for her to answer in a disapproving silence.

"No one ever knocks on my door this late except David or Jackson," she explained. "This is a safe neighborhood."

"No neighborhood is that safe."

She wanted to argue, wanted that idea to be as ridiculous as she'd convinced herself it was during the years she'd lived here, but a sweeping glance over his set face and the tattoos that crawled over his skin changed her mind. If either of them was going to be an accurate judge of how dangerous a place might be, it would be Ethan. If he saw a threat, it would be a legitimate one.

She crossed her arms over chest, guarding against an imagined chill. "Did you want to come in? Our date isn't until tomorrow." She flushed at her slip of the tongue, but he didn't seem to notice.

The scowl disappeared, replaced by an embarrassed smile as he held the bag up. "I stopped and grabbed something to eat on the way home and I thought, maybe, it would be enough to get me in the door a day early? I had PB&J in the pantry but eating all by myself ..."

She sighed, her heart squeezing with an echoing pang of loneliness, and pushed the door open wider. "That's manipulative, you know?"

"But it worked." His grin was smug and just a little wicked, enough for her to roll her eyes but she couldn't quite control the twitch of her own lips or the swoop of her stomach.

"It worked this time, but it won't work next time unless you brought something good." She reached for the bag as he held it just out of reach, wrinkling her nose skeptically at the scent of something unfamiliar and spicy. "What did you bring me?"

"Take out," he said. "Gumbo, mostly, but I grabbed a few other things since I wasn't sure what you liked."

She dropped down off her tiptoes, mouth twisting into a skeptical frown. "I'm not letting you in next time."

"What?" He looked genuinely offended. "You don't like gumbo?

"I've never tasted it," she admitted.

"How long have you lived here?" It was almost cute how baffled he looked, like the idea that she'd never tasted gumbo had rocked his entire world view. There was a crease in the center of his forehead that she wanted to smooth with her thumb.

"How do you know I haven't always lived here?"

The crease vanished and his worried expression turned amused. "You don't sound like you're from around here. Not enough drawl in that prim little accent of yours."

"I guess that makes sense." He paid more attention to her than she'd realized and she wasn't sure how to feel about that. She felt vulnerable around him, not just because she was wrapped in nothing more than her undergarments and a thin robe, but because he always seemed to see and know things that others missed. He was constantly watching her, assessing what made her tick with heated eyes.

"How long have you lived here? However long it was, it was too long to have never tasted gumbo."

"Five years," she said, chin coming up to look at him more fully. "I've never gotten around to it." Not that she really wanted to, but she had been busy, and it wasn't like anyone had ever offered to feed it to her before now. Not specifically. She'd glanced at it on menus but nothing more than that.

He brought a hand up and let his fingers skim across her jaw, hot and feather light against her skin. "You keep tipping your chin up like that when you argue and someone's gonna take it as an invitation to clock you in that pretty face of yours. You've got a fighter's spirit and your mama should have taught you not to square up to people like that."

"People don't hit others over minor disagreements in the neighborhood where I grew up." It came out as a whisper and she fought against the urge to lean into his hand the way she had seen Winston do when he wanted more affection.

"Lucky you." His eyes were locked on her face and she didn't remember moving so close to him.

She coughed a little and stepped back, warnings racing

through her head. She tried to fill her mind with images of blueberry scones to remind her of her bet with Sarah. She and Ethan were just friends, nothing more. "So, about that gumbo."

He let her change the subject without mentioning her sudden flustered tone. "I guess it's not your fault you've never had it," he conceded, turning away and setting out the contents of the bag on her table while she watched from a safe distance. "Your friends talk like they're from around here so they should have been feeding you."

"It's not their job to feed me—" she began but he shook his head.

"It's hospitality," he explained. "You moved from somewhere up north," he said it like a dirty word, "where they don't know anything about cooking or comfort and when you move down here it's our duty to teach you how to eat grits and greens and gumbo."

"Well, that doesn't make sense." She sniffed the air and crept a little closer when he took his first bite and didn't immediately fall over dead. "I ate perfectly fine growing up."

"Mmm hmm," he hummed. It seemed deliberately neutral, a polite void instead of an opinion. "Open up."

He waited patiently, eyes locked on hers as she weighed her choices. Her trust in him pitted against the unfamiliarity of what he was offering. He smiled when she stepped closer and parted her lips slightly, eyes twinkling with triumph as she accepted the smallest bite possible.

"It's ... good."

He laughed at her surprise and leaned down to give her a quick kiss on the cheek. The absentminded press of his mouth was enough to make her heart skip, to stop completely and then thump madly in her chest. Heat shot through her from her lips to her fingertips as she leaned into him, unconsciously chasing his warmth. It had been thoughtless, a brief burst of affection that seemed utterly fitting for a man with his effortless charm, but it nearly knocked her off of her feet.

The smile on his face vanished and she watched, breath suspended, as he seemed to catch the change in her expression and paused, eyes going dark, before he lowered his head again. This time his mouth caught hers, warm and soft, with none of the rush and the roughness she'd been anticipating. His thumb brushed over her cheek, light and reassuring, and she stepped closer until she was molded to his chest. She fit against him like she belonged there, and a tremble ran through both of them at the contact.

Thoughts of bets and blueberry scones and *just friends* were incinerated in a rush of hot desire. Shaky and adrift on the feel of him, she didn't hesitate when the silken slide of his tongue along the seam of her lips asked her another silent question. She answered with her mouth, opening to his exploration as she let her hands roam up his chest. One found the steady beat of his heart and the other the soft curling ends of his hair where it lay against the nape of his neck.

He made a low, desperate sound that skated over her skin and set off an answering echo inside her. A thrill rushed beneath her skin, a potent mix of fear and heady confidence. It was intoxicating to be wanted with such intensity.

The breath whooshed out of her when he scooped her up, broad hands cupping the backs of her thighs as he pressed her against him. "Wha—"

"We're just going in here," he explained, already carrying her to the living room as her head found its spot against his neck. He maneuvered her easily as he sat down on the couch and settled her on his lap. "Comfortable?"

She shouldn't be, with one knee on each side of his thighs and chest heaving just in front of his eyes, she should be over exposed and vulnerable, but there was no room in her mind for the sharp edges of her usual fears. She'd forgotten them and her determination to keep him at arm's length. "Yes."

"Good." He kept his eyes on hers as his hands began to wander, tracing the tops of her thighs and the lace edges of her underwear, following the silken lines of her robe up her stomach and over her chest, leaving a trail of scorched skin behind him.

She was the one that leaned in, offering her mouth and pressing herself against him, breasts rubbing his chest and hips shifting to get closer as he tangled his fingers in her hair. He was still slow and methodical, stripping her of her inhibitions with his tongue and his lips and the gentle scrape of his teeth. She'd been kissed before but nothing like this. Never this thoroughly or erotically or with as much naked and undisguised enthusiasm.

She let him kiss her until she was writhing on his lap, grinding against the hard bulge of his arousal like a hormone crazed teenager, before she pulled away for a shuddering breath. He turned his attention immediately to the curve of her neck, lips moving down the column of her throat and scrambling her thoughts. "Ethan."

He froze, pausing for the space of only a few heartbeats before pulling back to meet her eyes. "Do you want me to stop?"

She didn't, not really, but she knew she'd regret it if they went any further. "I'm sorry," she said quietly. It was difficult to shift off his lap without making the whole situation more awkward than it already was and she wasn't convinced she'd pulled it off as she settled onto the cushion beside him.

"No reason to be sorry," he said and the hand he put on her knee was soft and reassuring. "I didn't plan any of this when I came over tonight." He took a steadying breath, fingers working absently as he softly stroked her leg.

"I know," she said after a moment of silent contemplation.

"It's just ... Intimacy, physical or otherwise, is not something I take lightly."

"I don't think you take anything lightly, sweetheart." His lips twitched at her indignant frown before he continued. "I did *not* expect you to tumble into bed with me over a bowl of gumbo."

Her breath came out with a shudder as she relaxed, the tension draining out of her. "Okay," she said slowly. "So, we'll just forget this happened and—"

"You can try but I don't plan on doing that, either."

"I said we could be friends, Ethan, and this isn't what I had in mind." She kept her gaze down, focused on the skull ring he wore, a glint of silver against the rough skin of his hand. He'd put that hand on her and she'd liked it. Liked it enough to be frightened of it and what it could mean to her.

"I'll tell you what," he said, tipping her chin up with his finger until he was looking her in the eye. "You still come to dinner with me tomorrow and I promise to behave. I'll be a perfect gentleman and I'll keep my hands to myself."

"That's—"

"Wait," he cut in, finger lifted to indicate he wasn't done. "I'll keep my hands to myself *until* you want me to touch you. If you want to be more than friends, you'll have to tell me exactly what you want. Out loud."

The idea of that was humiliating, which made Eloise absolutely certain she'd never be willing to do any such thing. Sarah was going to owe her a whole month of pastries. Maybe she'd start with a cream puff, instead of a blueberry scone.

She held out her hand for Ethan to shake. "Deal."

Eight

His car smelled like leather and the faint hint of his dusky cologne as he pulled out of his driveway with her in the passenger seat. Summer nights meant late sunsets, and the horizon was a riot of pinks and oranges beneath the deeper purples and blues of the night sky. The first stars were winking to life and he had put classical music on the radio.

"We don't have to listen to this," she said, waving her hand at the dashboard before settling it uncomfortably back into her lap. She wasn't sure where to put it. Sitting with her hands clasped in front of her seemed too formal, too stiff, but she didn't know what else to do, so she gripped her fingers together and hoped he wouldn't notice how rigid her posture was or how tensely she held her muscles.

"I know you like it."

"I do." They lapsed into silence as she picked at the fabric of her dress—she'd decided to go with the pink floral after another two hours of worrying over her choices—and wracked her brain to think of something to say. The night before, and the odd agreement they'd come to, weighed on her as he turned the car toward the highway.

He wasn't looking at her, his eyes on the road as he drove them toward whatever destination he'd picked for dinner. He'd claimed to know the perfect place and she had to admit he'd been right about the gumbo. She'd relaxed a little, letting him handle the details and take control in a way she normally avoided. It was hard not to, when he seemed so casually sure of himself, so confident. She often managed to fake that sort of energy, but it never settled as well on her as it did on him.

She took the opportunity to look him over, his focus on the road giving her a few uninterrupted minutes to drink in the details of his appearance without embarrassment. He'd opted for casual—jeans and his boots with a nicer black shirt with the sleeves rolled up to reveal his forearms—and he'd taken the time to comb his fingers through his hair and make sure his short beard was neat and tidy.

She wondered if it would feel as scruffy under her fingers as it had against her cheeks the night before, and she tightened her grip on her own hands to keep from reaching across the car to find out. There wasn't much to distract her from the impulse. The familiar town visible through the windows was certainly nothing new and the inside of the car offered only a monotone gray interior. The dashboard was polished and free of dust but something caught her attention as she focused on the instrument panel.

"Ethan?"

"Hmm?"

"Please tell me you're not actually doing nearly a hundred miles an hour." Her tone was carefully blank, but her mind was screaming.

He glanced over at her and flushed. "Sorry."

She knew her eyes must have been comically wide, her knuckles white where she was clenching them, but she didn't relax until he slowed the car to somewhere closer to the speed limit.

"Well," she said slowly, "Remind me not to ride in the car with you again after tonight." He chuckled and she crossed her legs, pressing her thighs together at the sound of his laugh as it rolled over her. If she'd expected her response to offend him, it seemed she'd been off the mark, though, to be honest, he usually did seem amused when she was at her most uptight and inflexible.

"Come on," he urged. "It wasn't that bad."

"Okay, *maybe* I didn't even realize how fast we were going *but,*" she said, before he could gloat, "it's dangerous to do that. You're speeding and if you crash, you take out all those other drivers. Just look at that minivan. Are you going to take out a minivan?"

He frowned and muttered, "I bet you're fun at parties."

"I only got invited to parties so I would be there to clean up the mess." It popped out before she could stop it, leaving her wondering not for the first time why she was so willing to let her guard down around him. It was true enough, but not the kind of information one usually shared voluntarily with others.

"Seriously?"

"Not anymore." She hurried to explain, before he had the chance to feel sorry for her. "Not since I moved here and met Sarah and the others."

He turned on his blinker, slowing as he exited the highway. "Those are your friends from work?"

"Yes." She tried to ignore the embarrassed flush she could feel rising on her cheeks. She was sure he hadn't forgotten them after their antics the first time they'd been introduced. "The ones you met the other day."

Thankfully, he didn't tease her about their spying again

and seemed content to turn the topic to less humiliating subjects. "What kind of work do you do there anyway?"

"Nothing interesting." He clearly wasn't the type to find an office job tolerable and she forced a smile when he glanced curiously in her direction. "Just working with numbers all day."

"I think you'd be surprised what I find interesting about you."

"Hmmm." She was sure she should have said something, really anything would have been sufficient, but her cheeks warmed again when he stole another meaningful glance in her direction. Even with just a passing gaze of his eyes, he managed to convey a wealth of passion and intention.

It left her frozen, heart pounding and mind unusually muddled, until they finally pulled off the road and into a crowded parking lot.

"Wait there," he told her, putting the car in park and pocketing the keys before getting out and walking around the front to open her door for her.

She laughed, startled and oddly charmed. "Do people still do that?"

"Maybe." His grin was infectious. "I mean, someone has to, right?"

"Right." The nervous smile he'd given her stayed on her face as she let him take her hand and lead her toward the building.

The pizzeria wasn't one she was familiar with, and she glanced around curiously after Ethan opened the door for her and they stepped inside. Low music was playing and patrons were chattering at the small tables. It seemed like the kind of place that had been there for a while—the chairs looked worn and there was wood paneling on the walls that made the decor look dated— but the smell of pizza sauce and spicy pepperoni made her mouth water.

Some of the people at the tables nearest the door quieted when they caught sight of them standing at the entrance. Eloise frowned, puzzled, but the hostess bustled over before she could mention the strange reaction to Ethan.

"And there's my boy," she said, rapping Ethan on the arm with a menu. She was several inches shorter than Eloise and stocky. There was still some black in her white hair and her round cheeks were pink with pleasure. "What brings you in tonight?'

"Paula," Ethan said, turning that grin on her while Eloise struggled against a sudden and uncomfortable surge of envy. "I need to charm my date with pizza, and for pizza—"

"For pizza you always come to Paula! Good pizza, anyway!" The other woman—Paula, it seemed—finished her declaration with a short, loud laugh and turned to Eloise with a bright smile. "I'll take good care of you."

"Thank you," Eloise said but she leaned close to Ethan as they followed Paula to their table. "This isn't a date, remember?"

"Do you want to tell that to Paula?" he whispered back. "You saw how excited she got when we came in. If I told her you weren't my date, she'd spend all night trying to convince you to date me."

"How do you know her anyway?" Eloise knew she sounded peevish and that it was beyond ridiculous to be jealous of a woman that was probably twice her age— especially when this was most certainly *not* a date—but she couldn't quite swallow down the odd feeling after he'd smiled so warmly at their hostess.

"Dylan owns a bar nearby and I happen to work there," Ethan said. He didn't elaborate and for once he was oblivious to the undercurrents in Eloise's tone. "Drinks at his place are decent but the food is shit and I like pizza, so I escape this way as often as I can."

It was odd to think of Ethan having a job—she suspected he used the phrase *work there* pretty loosely— but it was even more odd to think of Dylan doing anything as respectable as owning a business, even if it *was* a bar. Eloise mulled it over as Paula got them settled at a table for two in a quiet corner and handed them their menus.

"Drinks?" Paula asked.

"Um," Eloise mumbled, flipping to the back and searching for the right section.

"Wine?" Ethan asked.

"You're driving," she reminded him.

"Of course," he said, exchanging a look with Paula that she couldn't decipher. "Glass of wine for you and for me..." He trailed off, eyes scanning the menu.

"Lemonade for you," Paula declared. "Freshly squeezed and non-alcoholic. White wine or red for the lady?"

"White," Ethan said. "Red is better for pizza but the lady has a preference for sweet and bubbly white wine."

"You remembered," Eloise said when Paula had left to get their drinks, impressed despite herself.

"You're worth remembering." His voice was husky and full of meaning and his eyes were hot.

Eloise ripped her gaze away, feeling stripped and laid bare under his stare in a way she hadn't been prepared for. She needed a distraction and turned her attention to the red, plastic menu. It listed offerings of pizza and salad and calzones. "So, you eat here often?"

He was unfazed by the abrupt change of subject. "A few times a month," he agreed. He was watching her instead of looking at the menu.

"What do you recommend?"

"Everything."

She barely resisted the urge to roll her eyes. "I'm sure it's all *good*, but you have to have a favorite."

"I do." He leaned over and tapped the menu. All of the pizzas had fun, oddball names and the one he indicated had a long list of ingredients that matched the one it had been given. "Everything but the Kitchen Sink. It's one hell of a pizza."

Eloise scanned the list of toppings. Ham, bacon, sausage, onions, peppers—both green *and* banana—plus tomatoes, black olives, green olives, pepperoni, several kinds of cheese ...

"Green olives?" she asked, brow lifted skeptically. "On pizza?"

"Everything but the kitchen sink," he confirmed. He looked over his shoulder and waved an arm to get Paula's attention, already indicating they'd like a number seven. "Best pizza I ever had in my life."

"Okay." She tipped her head and considered him. He'd already ordered it so she might as well get something out of it. "New deal. I'll eat this pizza ..."

"And?" His eyes lit up with interest at the possibility of an interesting trade.

"*And* you tell me about this bar Dylan owns. I don't see him as the type to tend bar and balance the books."

He hesitated and then shrugged. "Not much to tell. His dad owned the place until he died and now Dylan does. He hires people to tend the bar and balance the books so he doesn't have to. No real mystery there."

"What kind of bar is it?"

He waited to answer as Paula bustled up to the table with their drinks and patted his shoulder as she left. Apparently she'd already informed the kitchen about their order and asked for it to be bumped up the line. Flirting with the restaurant owner had its perks and Eloise was amused despite herself.

"The rough kind," he said, when Paula was out of hearing range. "Dylan's dad was a big part of some old biker gang that used to hang out there. That was years ago but the reputation as a dangerous hangout stuck. It's empty more often than it should be and the crowd that does come in is just looking for cheap beer and a place to lay low."

That seemed like something she could imagine from Dylan and she pondered it as she took a sip of her wine. It was bright and sweet, bubbles dancing over her tongue. There were many questions she wanted answers to, but it was probably best to start simple.

"Does it have a name?"

"You ask a lot of questions for a deal over pizza." He leaned back, fingers tapping on the table as he looked at her with a heavy-lidded gaze.

"Green olives on pizza is a lot to ask," she said brightly, her smile sweet and challenging. "Besides, I'm a naturally curious person."

"Tough Break Bar and Grill," he said, "but the *grill* part is honestly more wishful thinking."

"Hence the pizza?"

"Hence the pizza," he agreed. "And the sushi bar around the corner and the Indian restaurant down the block and—"

She laughed and held up her hands in surrender. "I get it. You don't like to cook, and Dylan won't feed you properly, so you make yourself a nuisance everywhere else."

He laid a hand over his heart, his expression comically wounded. "Paula loves me."

That much was obvious, more so when Paula came bustling out with their pizza herself, no waitress in sight. "Enjoy your date and keep the table as long as you like," she commanded as she slid the pizza onto the table and placed a hand on top of Eloise's. "Maybe you can be the one to charm him away from his mess, huh?"

"Mess?" Eloise asked.

"Paula," Ethan said, his voice a warning Eloise had heard only once before.

Paula wasn't impressed and the smile on her face never wobbled as she winked at Eloise. "He deserves better than the life he's made for himself. Remember that and trust an old woman who's seen too many things in this neighborhood."

She didn't stay to see Eloise's reaction, leaving them alone with their pizza and questions Ethan didn't want to answer. "Is that why everyone looked at us funny when we came in? People are scared of you around here?"

"You've run out of pizza questions." He wasn't looking at her now, his attention directed at their dinner instead of her face.

"Hmm, I haven't tasted it yet." She glanced pointedly at her still empty plate and waited.

He sighed and dropped a slice on each of their plates. "They're not scared of me, necessarily. Dylan's dad didn't have the best reputation, remember? I guess people around here figured the apple didn't fall from the tree, especially when he was sent to juvie as a kid. Not long before his dad died, actually."

"*Did* the apple fall far from the tree? Is that why you didn't want me around him?"

"Take your bite, Eloise."

She wrinkled her nose, eyeing the pile of toppings skeptically before taking the smallest bite possible. The little moan was involuntary, and her eyes slid closed with pleasure as she chewed. "This is incredible."

"Told you." He smirked as she took another, much bigger bite. "So, what are you going to trade for answers to your last question?"

"Hmm," she hedged. She couldn't think of anything else to offer. "I'll answer a question from you for every one of mine?"

"Deal." His smile flashed again, and she was again aware of a subtle undercurrent in his response that she couldn't quite identify, like he'd scored a point in a game she wasn't aware they were playing. "Dylan took over the bar and never got involved with that biker gang. He's a shitty businessman but he hires enough people to handle it and doesn't have to run drugs out the back or whatever other shit his dad was into."

Something about that didn't quite add up in Eloise's mind. They all drove nice cars and had plenty of money. If Dylan was so bad at running a business and the bar was usually empty, then where were Dylan and his employees getting all that cash? Ethan was never going to answer that question if she asked it flat out, so she went at it sideways. "Then why didn't you want me talking to him?"

He shook his head. "My turn, remember? When was the last time you went on a real date?"

She frowned and took another bite, ignoring his amused look. So what if he knew she was stalling? "At least a year," she admitted. "Probably closer to a year and a half."

He lifted a brow and opened his mouth for a follow-up question, but she held up a finger to quiet him. "Dylan?"

"I don't want you around him because he might not be as openly dangerous as his dad but he's still an asshole," Ethan said shortly. It was an interesting choice of words but he asked his next question before Eloise could dwell on it. "Why?"

Eloise paused with a bite halfway to her mouth. "Why is he an asshole?"

"No." He laughed, a little huff of amusement through his nose that Eloise almost didn't mind was at her expense. "Why haven't you dated?"

"I should have offered to trade something else." She hadn't expected him to dive into questions about her love life, or rather the lack of it. It rankled, having to admit she wasn't exactly heavily experienced in that area. He seemed like the kind of man that left a trail of broken hearts and satisfied bodies so he wouldn't be able to understand her difficulties.

"Probably," he agreed. "Too late."

Yes, it was, but what was she supposed to say to that? That she hadn't dated much at the age of twenty-seven because her mother had told her not to? It sounded ridiculous when she put it that way, but she hadn't even been able to convince herself to call her mother back yet. Ethan's presence in her life hung over her like a guillotine over her neck. She'd never been any good at lying, unless it was to herself, and her mother would hear the guilt in her tone as she picked up the phone.

"I have a very demanding career," she said slowly, giving him a fraction of the truth if not the whole of it, "and I was trying to keep my attention on that."

"So do a lot of people and they still manage to date."

"Yes, but ... I don't know." She faltered and dropped her gaze to the tabletop.

"Nobody impressive enough to distract you from your ambitions," he finished, apparently filling in her absent reasoning with the nearest thing he thought might make sense.

"I suppose so."

"But you have your friends."

She looked back up at him with a genuine smile. "Sarah, Chloe, and Kim," she confirmed. "We work together at Sun Valley downtown. I think I mentioned that the night we had spaghetti? It's ... hard sometimes to be a woman in that environment and they've been amazing."

"Boys' club?"

She nodded and reached for another slice of pizza. "Yeah, it's nothing like I expected. More stressful, less fulfilling, and some of the men I work with ..." She shuddered, the memory of Dwayne still lingering too close to the surface. "What about you? Do you date?"

He blinked at the change of topic but didn't object. "Sometimes, but nothing serious."

She lifted a brow at the vagueness of his response, and he

shrugged. "Let's just say my lifestyle hasn't been great for serious relationships."

"Well," she drawled. "I guess it's a good thing this isn't a date."

"Maybe I'd be willing to change that lifestyle for the right woman." His eyes twinkled and she knew he was teasing her. It lightened the mood enough for the tension between her shoulder blades to ease some and she was grateful.

"And this would be me?" She batted her lashes at him as he grinned. "I assume this lifestyle of yours has something to do with the questionable company you keep?"

He smiled, the twist of his lips a bit wistful. "Yes."

"Have you considered keeping other company?"

"You don't leave your family."

"I didn't know you were related." He'd mentioned Dylan's father, but no connection to him. Actually, he hadn't told her anything at all about how they'd come to know each other, so maybe it was a possibility.

"Not by blood, but some things are thicker than that." He paused like he was searching for the right words to answer her question without revealing too much. She'd done the same when he asked why she hadn't dated so she kept her silence and waited for him to finish.

"Dylan was there for me when no one else was," he said finally. "I owe him."

"It seems strong friendships are something we have in common."

"Hopefully not the *only* thing." He winked at her and made her laugh again.

They finished out their meal with lighter conversation, but she wondered about it as he drove her home. Was that the only thing they had in common? They lived very different lives, knew very different people. They didn't share a love of the same music or read the same books. He was laid-back and charming while she was tightly wound and often unapproachable.

There was nothing to indicate they would get along at all except for a mutual adoration of his dog and one evening of ill-advised kissing. Maybe she had been right in the restaurant. Maybe it *was* a good thing it hadn't been a real date.

But when he walked her to her door and then left without kissing her, she was rocked by the strength of her disappointment. Maybe he had *also* been right. Maybe she just hadn't found quite the right person to distract her from her ambitions or motivate her to finally deal with the pressure of her mother's expectations.

She wasn't sure how she felt about that, but she knew the way she reacted to him was different than anything she'd ever experienced before. It was odd to go to bed wishing she wasn't alone, and her fantasies involved a great deal more than just having him in bed beside her.

They hadn't made any specific plans to see each other again after their dinner, which had been another small disappointment. Eloise had to admit, if only to herself, that if she won that bet with Sarah, it would be more to do with not seeing him than the strength of her own self-control.

Nine

Tough Break Bar and Grill was a real shithole. Dylan knew it, the patrons that stumbled in the door every night knew it, and Ethan knew it. He suspected the cops knew it, too, but they'd stopped actively poking around years ago. Dylan didn't use it as a not-so-secret base for a large criminal operation anymore, so they busted patrons on the way out for DUI and possession and whatever else and left Dylan alone.

Ethan was well aware that Dylan *preferred* for the bar to remain as worthless and rundown as possible while still keeping the doors open. As far as Dylan was concerned, his dad's mistake—apart from being an abusive asshole who couldn't keep his kids out of foster care—had been having too many loose lips running around the place. He wouldn't have gotten shot over some deal gone sideways if he hadn't put his trust in so many people that didn't deserve it.

Dylan's dad had surrounded himself with a whole gang of accomplices and had his fingers in many criminal activities. Dylan, smarter and meaner than his old man had ever been, relied almost entirely on Myles and Ethan. Sure, some jobs required a carefully chosen skeleton crew that would bring in a few more faces, but Dylan didn't brag about his business dealings all over town. He broke the law often, but he broke it well. No sloppy mistakes. No rushed decisions.

Ethan looked around at the peeling paint, the stained carpet, the air hazy with smoke from cigarettes and whatever they were burning in the kitchen. There was a single bartender behind the bar, nose buried in her phone as she ignored the handful of people nursing drinks and leaning dangerously on their barstools. Dark hair curled riotously around a heart shaped face and her lips were painted a vivid red. There were no uniform requirements at Tough Break and she took advantage of that to pour her body into a tight, white shirt. It was sheer enough so the patrons could easily see the red bra beneath and hugged every curve. She'd cut the front so it dipped dangerously low over her breasts to reveal the angel wing tattoos that spanned most of her upper chest. Her tip jar was always full and it certainly wasn't from her bartending skills.

Sunny was a pleasure to look at—pretty enough that he'd made the mistake of indulging in a brief but intense physical relationship with her—but she was barely competent at the job she'd been working at for over a year. If Dylan had cared at all about the actual success of his business, she would have been fired months ago and Ethan wouldn't still be dodging her killer glare every single time he had to make an appearance.

As it was, Tough Break's general vibe was one of unkempt neglect—of a place that barely scraped by on cheap beer, overpoured drinks, and Sunny's tits—and it was a ruse. Dylan let them all see him as a careless and incompetent man because it suited him for people to believe that. People weren't suspicious of you when they thought you didn't have two decent brain cells to rub together. If Ethan had stood up in the middle of a Friday night rush and announced a list of their crimes, they would have hesitated to believe him no matter how much they feared Dylan's temper.

Dylan? The mastermind behind a lifetime career of illegal activities? They would have laughed in his face. Cruel? Yes. Selfish? Undoubtedly. Smart and disciplined enough for criminal success? He couldn't even keep his father's interests—legal and otherwise—properly afloat. Absolutely not. He had the willingness, they all knew that, but he had them convinced he lacked the ability. It was one of his more brilliant cons, as far as Ethan was concerned.

"How's your dating life, Ethan?"

He had just managed to settle at a back table with a cold beer and already Dylan had found him. He'd slid into the chair across the table, his own beer in hand, and was watching Ethan with that flat viper's gaze, a dead giveaway that he was thinking about a job. The question seemed personal at first, but Ethan knew better. If Dylan's mind was bent on work, there were no emotions involved. Just business and profit.

"It's coming along," he said. "I took her out to dinner last night but—"

"You came through," Dylan finished. His face relaxed, taking on a less severe expression that wasn't quite a smile. "I knew you would. What did you find out?"

"Nothing yet."

"Nothing?" Dylan hesitated and glanced across the bar, but everyone was involved in their own conversations, and no one was close enough to overhear them. "Are you not trying hard enough or do we have to go about this the hard way?"

"There's no need for that." Ethan saw the way Dylan's lips thinned but he didn't backtrack. "She may not know anything useful anyway."

"We won't know if you don't ask." Dylan set his beer on

the table in front of him with a thump that set the glass bottom to wobbling. "Are you trying to protect her from me?"

Yes.

Ethan was surprised how quickly the answer came to him. For one wild moment he thought he'd spoken the traitorous thought out loud, but Dylan's face didn't flicker, there was no response written in the icy depths of his eyes. There'd never been reason for Dylan to question his loyalty and Ethan wondered what his reaction would have been if he'd admitted to his sudden unexplainable urge to keep Eloise safe, even if it compromised Dylan's plans.

He'd always kept women at arm's length because he knew Dylan considered anyone in his sphere as a tool at his disposal. Drawing Eloise into that had been a mistake, but it had also put her in unusually close proximity to a part of him he'd never let anyone else see. She was bright and perceptive, her questions cutting to the heart of his motivations and forcing him to examine them in a way he hadn't in years.

There was no way he was going to let Dylan do anything to cause her harm or interfere in her life any more than absolutely necessary, but he knew the best way to do that was to never let Dylan know it was happening.

"I'm protecting *us*," he said, leaning into years of friendship and Dylan's expectations. "If she does have information we can use, it will be worth the wait and if she doesn't then we don't want anyone to have any suspicions about why I was hanging around."

Dylan nodded slowly but he kept his eyes locked on Ethan's. "You know how important you are to me. You've had my back for more than a decade and I've had yours. I kept you safe when you needed me and gave you a place to go when you got out of juvie. Don't forget those things because of some twit with perky tits."

"I'll get it done," Ethan said flatly. Guilt and rage coiled inside him, but he let none of it show. "I've never let you down or failed to pay back what I owed you. Do you really think that's going to change after all these years?"

Dylan paused, leaving the question unanswered, when Myles came out from the back, arms loaded with boxes and a line of sweat down the back of his T-shirt. If Dylan ever worked as hard at the bar as his little brother did, it would have been a thriving business. It had the potential but Dylan was too lazy to put the work in. It wasn't as thrilling doing inventory as it was planning a robbery.

Myles spotted them and set the boxes on the bar, pinning Sunny with a hard look and indicating she needed to put away whatever was inside. She rolled her eyes when he turned his back, which made Dylan laugh as Myles headed their way, wiping his forehead with the back of his hand and grabbing a beer as he went.

"Ethan." He sat in the chair beside Dylan, reaching across the table to shake Ethan's hand. "You look like shit."

"Thanks." The kid was probably right. He'd been up most of the night wondering if he'd done the right thing by leaving Eloise standing on her doorstep looking disappointed at the end of what was absolutely a fucking date, no matter what she said about it.

"If you're done?" Dylan's meaning was clear as he stared down his brother and Myles, smiling and happy a moment before, diminished under his glare. He mumbled a barely audible apology that Dylan ignored. He turned his attention back to Ethan and continued where they had left off as though Myles didn't matter and his presence didn't warrant an acknowledgement.

"You've never given me a reason to doubt you," Dylan shifted in his seat, looking over his shoulder again before continuing, tone colder than anything Ethan had ever heard aimed in his direction before, "but I was assuming you'd have something for me. Are you losing your touch or just enjoying the piece of ass and paying no attention to what the bitch says otherwise?"

Ethan flicked a glance at Myles and found that both men were watching him carefully. Myles had always been quiet and timid, following in Dylan's footsteps without question and with such devotion that Ethan had often wondered if it was due to loyalty or fear. Either way, no matter how often he jumped in to protect him from Dylan, he was unlikely to find support in that corner.

"I didn't find anything because I doubt there's anything to find. She doesn't know anything about the local branches and it's a waste of time for me to keep pumping her for information when she doesn't have any."

"Are you going to stop fucking her?" Ethan's emotions, usually so carefully controlled, must have shown on his face. "You haven't managed that yet, either? Well, I doubt you're going to walk away and leave that well untapped. As long as you're sniffing around, you might as well keep trying. We've got other options but you know they're risky. This would be easier and help maximize potential profits."

"I don't know what you want me to do." This time Myles shot him a surprised look at the aggression in his tone. He didn't know if she had anything they could use but he did know she'd get suspicious if he pushed her about it and he didn't want her to have any more to do with this if he could figure out how to get her out of it. Convincing them she was worthless was probably his best bet, though it made him sick to lie to Dylan. "She doesn't know anything."

"I want you to figure something out." Dylan spoke slowly and showed no outward reaction to Ethan's outburst. "Everyone knows something, right? If she can't access work schedules or vault codes, maybe she can work some fancy magic on those ledger books."

Ethan snorted. Dylan must really be frustrated if he was talking out loud at the bar about vault codes. Usually those conversations were carefully saved for safer locations. "Auditing would catch her before we had enough to pay next month's bills."

"You always see obstacles and not opportunities" The bar door swung open and momentarily bathed them all in light from outside. Two people strolled up to the bar and Dylan sniffed and lowered his voice. "If you need someone in auditing, then figure out a way to convince them."

It seemed simple enough. Ethan had to admit it was a better idea than any he'd had, but it would involve putting Eloise directly into the mess unless he could work out a way to go around her completely, which was unlikely. Finding someone else to work with that would be willing to take such a risk wouldn't be an easy task, but it would be worth it to keep her away from Dylan.

"I'll try."

Dylan seemed pleased with that, and he smiled as he downed the rest of his beer. "In the meantime, don't let her distract you from the job we're doing tomorrow. This one's dangerous and it's going to take everyone at their best if we're going to pull it off."

Ten

A loud banging pulled Eloise out of a restless sleep. She picked up her phone, turning it over and blinking against the sudden burst of light to find it was nearly midnight. She'd gone to bed almost an hour ago and had yet to fall into anything deeper than a light doze. It was shaping up to be her third night without sleep, her dinner with Ethan playing through her head each time her head hit the pillow. She had tried everything from warm milk to counting sheep but she still tossed and turned.

The banging came again, louder and more desperate this time, and she grabbed a robe to toss over her pajamas as she hurried down the stairs. She tried to reassure herself that it was probably just Jackson or David but there wasn't any reason for them to be coming by this late unless it was an emergency. She sped up as the pounding started again, loud enough to vibrate the pictures on her walls.

She wrenched the door open and stumbled backward, a cry of alarm on her lips as a hard, hulking body pushed inside and quickly closed the door behind them. She sucked in a deep breath, preparing to scream, and a large hand closed forcefully over her mouth.

"Shhh, it's okay! It's just me!"

"Ethan!" His name came out garbled behind his hand and she swatted it away. "What the hell are you doing? You scared me half to death."

"You should always see who it is before you just open the door," he advised, turning away to slide the locks into place. "I'm sorry. I know it's late."

"What are you doing here?" She was already backing away from him, stepping into the dining room to put some space between his body and hers until she could figure out exactly what was going on.

"I need help," he admitted sheepishly, pulling his other hand away from his side and showing her a bloodied, crimson palm. It was hard to see under his black shirt, but a patch of damp fabric clung to his side and the wound he'd been concealing there. "I didn't know where else to go."

Eloise's stomach turned over in one slow moving, graceful loop and she felt her own blood drain from her face. She reached blindly for the chair beside her, knuckles whitening as she gripped it for balance.

"What happened?" she asked, trying to focus on his face as her tingling lips formed words that she didn't remember her brain making. "You should go to the hospital."

"I can't," he said quickly. "I can't go to a hospital, and you can't call for help, okay? Promise me?"

"Ethan..."

He grabbed her arms, warm wetness sliding over her skin as she recoiled. "You have to promise me, Eloise."

"Is that ... Is that *your* blood?"

"Most of it," he said, lifting the hem of his shirt to show her the seeping wound in his side. "Lucky enough, the bullet just grazed me, and it's not buried in there somewhere."

"What the fuck?" Her voice was unnaturally high pitched and she winced at the tone and the swear, swallowing hard to try and get it under control. She was teetering on the edge of hysteria and neither of them needed her fainting at his feet. "You *have* to go to a hospital."

"Eloise, look at me," he insisted. "If I go to the hospital, then I'm going to jail. If you call an ambulance, I'm going to jail."

That sobered her a little and she looked at him, swallowing thickly. They'd have to deal with that—he couldn't just show up and say that to her and expect her not to have questions—but getting him appropriate medical care took priority. "Isn't there someone else? I mean, couldn't Myles or Dylan do something? Don't any of you know how to treat injuries?"

"Dylan already poured part of a bottle of vodka on it, and I didn't appreciate it," he said, and looking at him a little closer she had to admit that he did seem a lot paler than usual, his skin sweaty and green with pain.

"What do you expect *me* to do?" she asked, voice rising again and hands shaking. "Sew it back together?"

"Do you have a needle?'

"No! I mean, *yes*, I do have a needle but *no* I will not be sewing up gunshot wounds in my dining room. I don't know anything about first aid." Her head was swimming and she thought she might throw up if she had to look at the wound again.

"Butterfly bandages? I can't reach it, or I swear to you I would do it myself," he said, looking down at her with pleading eyes.

"Just what the hell are you into anyway?" If he wasn't going to go to the doctor, he could answer her questions. "You just *show up* here and *bleed* all over my floor ..." Her words faded away when he wobbled a little on his feet, his eyes momentarily losing focus as she reached for him and struggled to keep his body upright. "Damn it," she grunted, her back protesting under his weight. "How much blood have you lost?"

"More than I would have if I hadn't gotten shot," he said unhelpfully. "And Dylan gave me the rest of the vodka before they dropped me off."

"No honor and no help among thieves I see," she said irritably, guiding him the rest of the way into the dining room and pushing him down into the nearest chair. She hadn't expected better behavior from Dylan—dropping his friend off to fend for himself or die was pretty much what she would have bet on from him—but it surprised her that Myles hadn't done something. She supposed you had sunk to the level of the lowest of your companions. "Sit here and don't move while I look for a first aid kit. I don't even know if I *have* butterfly bandages."

But she did, of course, because she was always prepared for everything. A frantic rummage through her bathroom cabinets produced a sizable first aid kit with antiseptic, gauze, butterfly bandages in several sizes, and some over the counter painkillers. The last weren't advisable considering how much it seemed he'd been drinking, even she knew that, but maybe he could take them in the morning to take the edge off.

She hurried back into the dining room, arms stuffed full of towels and medical supplies, to find him sitting in the same chair, his head tipped back and his eyes closed. She stepped forward cautiously, her heart a shallow beat in her ears as she listened intently for the sound of his breathing, her eyes focused in silent terror on his chest as she watched for the rise and fall that would indicate he was alive.

"Ethan?" She wasn't sure the sound of his name would even carry far enough for him to hear her. It was thin, thready, and full of quiet fear.

"Hmm?"

"Damn it," she said, stomping the rest of the way into the room and dropping everything onto the table beside him. "I thought you were dead."

"Not quite," he said. "Honestly I think it mostly just hurts like hell."

"It probably wouldn't have bled so much if Dylan hadn't decided to use alcohol as a pain killer. I know nothing about medical procedures but even I know alcohol is a blood thinner."

Ethan just shrugged. "Maybe you aren't the only one that's shitty at first aid."

"Well, thank you so much," she said, voice dripping with sarcasm as she lifted the hem of his shirt—tugging it up until he lifted his arms with a grimace and let her slide it off over his head—and started poking around the wound. Anger made it easier to separate herself from the situation and her nausea faded away. He had a jagged edged red line across the side of his torso, but the bleeding had nearly stopped, and it wasn't as serious as she'd originally thought.

He was wincing when she stood back up to assess her supplies, but he seemed to know better than to complain about her fumbling bedside manner. "You did say that you weren't any good at this," he said, waving a hand to indicate his wound. "It doesn't seem like it's anything vital, so I should be fine regardless."

She snorted and started laying supplies on the table in a tidy line. "You still look like shit."

"You should see the other guy."

His attempt at humor fell flat and her fingers stilled on the gauze in her hand. She didn't want to ask, but she had to know. "Did you hurt anyone tonight?"

"I can't say I wouldn't have hurt someone if I had to—I value my life enough to shoot back when someone takes a chunk out of me—but it wasn't necessary this time."

He was so close to her, his eyes dark and serious as he watched her preparations. She knew he didn't want her to ask questions, but she had to know. "What happened?"

He hesitated a beat too long before answering. "Bar fight."

"Bar fight?" It was possible, but that pause made the hair on the back of her neck stand up. He wasn't being honest about it and she crossed her arms and stared him down, daring him with eyes to lie to her again.

He shrugged, wincing when it pulled on the wound and sent a fresh rivulet of blood running down his side. "I told you, it's a rough crowd. The cops don't tend to come running when someone starts fucking up the place so we handle it ourselves."

It made sense, in a very Ethan-esque kind of way, and without further proof that he wasn't telling her the truth she could only shake her head in disappointed bemusement as she went back to work again. They'd have another talk about it once he was patched up. She started to unroll the gauze as she glared at him over her shoulder. "You need a new job."

"My mother would've agreed with you, but sometimes it's just not that simple." He sounded so tired. Not just physically but mentally and emotionally, as well.

"So what happens the next time someone shoots at you? You shoot back? You might kill them." Her fingers were shaky as she tried to estimate the amount of gauze she'd need and prepare the white medical tape. How close had he already come to hurting someone? Closer than they'd come to killing him tonight?

He reached out and caught her arm in his grip, turning her until she was facing him, her eyes nearly level with his while he was sitting. "Or they might kill me," he said. "I can't leave, and I do what I have to."

"Why? If you're in danger or, God forbid, if you're doing

something illegal like I think you are, then *why* can't you leave?"

He shook his head and tugged her hand, drawing her forward until she was trapped in the space between his thighs. "I can't talk to you about that—I shouldn't even be talking to you about *this*—but I couldn't stay away from you."

"Ethan ..."

"No," he said, tipping his head until his forehead rested on the curve of her shoulder. "I'm sorry. I'm so sorry that I couldn't stay away."

Would she have been happier if he had? If he had stayed on his porch and been nothing to her but an annoying neighbor?

"I'm glad you didn't stay away," she said, her voice so low that she wasn't entirely sure he could hear her. His body shuddered, the words rolling over him and creating a visible effect as he pulled her closer, hands tightening on her hips.

"You should let me bandage this," she said tightly, swallowing hard against the rising nervousness in her throat. She'd been so focused on the blood and the wound that she'd forgotten for a short time how dangerous it was to be so close to him. It had been foolish, and the heat spreading through her from every place his body was touching hers was a potent reminder of her error.

"Yeah," he agreed, turning to nuzzle his face into the side of her neck. "I should let you do that."

Her skin came alive under the simple touch, aching for even the soft breath that caressed her as he worked his way up her neck and across her jaw with a gentleness that seemed at odds with the kind of man that showed up to a woman's house in the middle of the night nursing a gunshot wound.

She grabbed for his shoulders, her knees weak beneath her, and met nothing but skin. It was jolting, disorienting until she remembered that she'd taken his shirt off to examine his side.

She hadn't paid attention then, hadn't even really looked at him when she'd done it, but her eyes flew open at the feel of hard muscle and hot flesh under her hands.

She whimpered, horribly and humiliatingly *whimpered*, when her gaze met a wall of pale skin and vibrantly inked colors. The tattoos on his arm snaked up over his shoulder and across one side of his chest. His skin jumped slightly under her fingertips as she traced the lines, and his eyes were dark and dangerous as he watched her.

She felt powerful, truly bold for the first time in her life.

When his hand cupped the back of her head and pulled her lips down to his, she didn't hesitate, leaning into him with a pounding heart and parted lips.

His tongue swept inside, hotly possessive and tasting of vodka, and she was lost. The final threads of rationality and control that kept her safe snapped under a surge of desire and she tangled a hand in his hair, pulling him closer as he rumbled in satisfaction, the low and satisfied sound sending a rush of heat straight to her core.

She might have embarrassed herself further by climbing into his lap if she hadn't accidentally bumped his side with her knee in her clumsy attempt.

"Shit," he swore, taking great, gasping breaths as she pulled back quickly, wincing at the fresh drops of blood that were dripping onto the floor.

"I'm sorry," she whispered, horrified at the result of her own foolish eagerness.

"Don't be," he said. "I want to do that again as soon as this is taken care of. We can throw some tape on it or something and I'll be good to go."

She laughed, a breathless and disbelieving little giggle that sounded foreign to her ears. "No. I'm going to try and tape you up and then you're going to go home and sleep till you feel better."

"I can stay," he offered, pressing a quick kiss to the corner of her mouth when she hesitated.

"What about Winston?"

He frowned and ran a hand over the hair on his chin. "I don't suppose you'd let him sleep over, too?"

She glanced around at her spotless rugs and the cream fabric that draped her elegant chairs and streamlined sofa. The man had a perfectly good bed at home and a puppy still in the potty-training phase. She knew precisely what her mother would have advised her to do in this situation and looking back on it later that was exactly where she'd put the blame for her sudden rebellious impulse. "Bring him over," she agreed.

"Can I kiss you again in the morning?"

He was persistent and irresistibly charming, flashing her a boyish smile that made her own lips twitch in response. "I suppose you can," she agreed, "if you're feeling better."

"With that as a reward?" The humor in his eyes faded, replaced by something hungrier. "I'm feeling better already."

Eleven

He was still there the next morning, his face relaxed and surprisingly boyish as he slept on her couch with his long legs extending over the armrest. He'd brought over Winston and a plush dog bed and then fallen asleep while they watched couples search for houses on some HGTV show.

He didn't stir as she crept around the kitchen, keeping an eye on him through the doorway as she mixed the batter for pancakes and added bacon to a skillet. The routine of it was soothing and it helped calm the surging feeling of panic she'd been trying to battle back since he'd shown up bleeding on her doorstep. She still couldn't quite figure out when he had gone from irritating neighbor to something more, but the sight of all that blood and the thought of losing him ... well, she was just glad it hadn't come to that.

The strangeness of it all seemed less overwhelming in the fresh daylight. He was fine and no one had gone to the hospital or to jail. She hadn't even thrown up on his shoes, despite the brief moment where she'd thought she might. He really needed a new job, if customers at the bar were this dangerous and unpredictable, but that was a concern for another time.

She was humming happily as she added a pancake to the pan and jumped when her phone rang. A quick glance at the name on the screen was enough to have her tensing up again. The timing was terrible but she'd avoided it as long as she could. If she put it off any longer, she was likely to find concerned police on her doorstep making sure she hadn't drowned in her own bathtub or some other tragic mishap. Ethan hadn't moved from his position on the couch and after peeking her head around the corner to make sure his eyes were still closed, she took a deep, centering breath and answered.

"Hello?"

"There you are." Her mother's voice was curt. "This isn't the first time I've called."

Eloise clenched her teeth and put the phone on speaker so she could slide the spatula under the bubbling pancake. She flipped it with one smooth motion and tried to keep the irritation out of her own voice. "I've been busy, Mother."

"Busy?" There was a soft scoff. "You're always busy with work and those little friends of yours but you still answer my calls. I do hope you're not dating."

Eloise glanced at Ethan's sock-covered feet, just visible from her spot at the stove. "I'm twenty-seven," she said simply. "I have a home and a successful career." She could have said more. That they were demanding. Unfulfilling. Empty. But she had learned years before that her mother had little patience for such things.

"All the more reason not to waste time."

Deep breath. Flip. "Is that why you called?"

"Of course not. Can I not call just to see how you're doing?"

"You never have before," Eloise reminded her.

"I'm certain that's a lie, Eloise. Why would you say such a thing to me?"

"I'm sorry, Mother." The apology was routine, a flat gesture of habit devoid of any remorse, but even if it hadn't been she knew it wouldn't have been enough. No amount of sincerity would do once Deborah Mason decided she was the injured party.

"You always were an ungrateful child," she said with a sniff. "You're coming soon to visit? Your father misses you."

He didn't, but there was no point in mentioning it. "When I can," she said. "Busy, you remember?"

"Career first," her mother said, as she had nearly every day of Eloise's life. "Very sensible of you."

"Always," she agreed. "You've made it clear what's expected of me."

"You make it seem like such a burden." Her voice returned to its previous pouting tone. "Would you rather I'd raised you to spend your life barefoot in the kitchen?"

Eloise curled her bare toes against her kitchen rug as she turned her bacon. "Of course not," she said. "Though maybe it doesn't have to be one or the other."

"You're better off," Deborah said firmly. "I never made up the difference in my career after you were born."

Eloise pressed her fingers to her temples, rubbing circles in an attempt to ward off the gathering headache. "I know how much you sacrificed for me," she said. Another platitude. When had Deborah ever allowed her to forget? "I need to get ready to go into the office this afternoon," she lied.

"Make sure you're careful. You know I keep track of the news in that part of the country—though why you felt the need to move there is quite beyond my understanding—and that little town of yours is overrun with crime. Did you know that just last night someone got shot robbing—"

"No, mother, I hadn't heard about a robbery."

"You should watch the news, Eloise. They didn't even catch the people responsible, so they could still be out there."

"I doubt they'd have any reason to bother me if they are." Eloise was only half listening, her frustration mounting with each minute. "I really need to start getting ready."

"Well, I won't keep you then. I'll tell your father you said hello."

"Thank you," Eloise said. "Goodbye, Mother."

There was a click followed by still silence, and she looked down to see that Deborah had already ended the call. "I love you, too," she said under her breath, a lifetime of bitterness a dull ache in her chest.

"She sounds like a real bitch."

"Ethan." Eloise fumbled the spatula, her gaze flying to meet his as he leaned against the door jamb. She hadn't heard him get up and her cheeks flooded with embarrassed heat as she considered how much he might have overheard. "She's my mother."

"Yeah, I gathered that much," he acknowledged. "Still a bitch, though. Reminds me of my grandpa."

Her fingers stilled, the bacon crisping too much at the edges as she stared at him. "Mr. Callaghan? Why?"

"He had certain things he wanted from my mother, from me. She was an artist, a single mom after my dad split. My grandpa resented her refusing to settle for a more practical career. He had aspirations, you know? Wanted her to be a doctor or some shit. They didn't speak after she got pregnant with me but when she died, I had nowhere else to go except to him. He was determined I'd turn out different than her, fulfill all the expectations she wouldn't, and when I didn't fall in line …"

"He was angry," she said, filling in the gaps in what he was reluctant to say. Her afternoons with him, the tea and the polite conversation, didn't seem like such sweet memories anymore. "He was always kind to me."

"You're exactly what he thought we should have been," Ethan said easily, nodding his head to remind her about her cooking. "Steady, career oriented, ambitious."

"I'm exactly what my mother thinks I should be, too." She stacked bacon, eggs, and pancakes on a plate and handed it to him. "I don't know how to be anything else."

"Would you want to be?"

She turned off the stove and slid the spatula into a sink of hot, soapy water as she contemplated. "I don't know," she said truthfully. "I never really let myself imagine what it would be like if my life was different. There was a line laid out for me and I had to follow it."

"You don't have to do anything you don't want to do."

She made a face, not bothering to hide her skepticism. "How do you do that? Just ignore everyone's expectations?"

He sat down at the dining room table with a wince and poured syrup over everything on his plate. "I decide what I want from my life, who matters to me, and everyone else just has to deal with their disappointment."

She sat down beside him, her legs tucked up in the chair beneath her. "Don't you think that's a little selfish?"

He paused with the fork partway to his mouth and shook his head. "More selfish than someone expecting me to live my life to their standards even if it makes me unhappy? No, I don't think that I'm the selfish one in that scenario."

"When you put it that way ..." she said quietly. Her fork scraped against her plate as she picked at her eggs. "I just never thought of it in those terms."

"I had my mother to give me perspective," he reminded her. "I don't think you had anyone to lift that burden for you when you were growing up."

"No," she agreed. "My grandparents were never around,

and my father would never stand up to her. He spent all his time at work, and he probably would have agreed with her anyway."

"You just need a little bit of adventure, a taste of something irresponsible to get you started."

She smiled at him over her coffee cup. "Maybe that's what this is? This whole thing with you might be my little rebellion."

"I don't mind showing you a little bit of fun," he said cryptically. "Do you own a pair of jeans?"

Twenty minutes later she was standing in his driveway as he adjusted her ponytail and set a helmet on her head. Somehow—and she could never quite figure out exactly how he did it—she ended up following him into one reckless situation after another. "Are you really asking me to ride this thing?" she asked, biting her lip, and shoving her shaking hands into her pockets.

"It's not hard," he assured her. "I promise you'll be safe with me."

"You can't possibly know that."

"I probably can't," he admitted, pressing a quick and surprising kiss to the tip of her nose. "But that's what makes it fun."

"Not fun," she said. "Risky."

He laughed, lines crinkling the skin around the dark blue of his eyes. "Life is risky. You can't avoid it. All you can do is decide which risks are worth taking."

She narrowed her eyes at the motorcycle. "But what if I hate this?"

"Then it's not the right risk for you," he said, all traces of humor vanishing from his face as his eyes flicked down to her lips. "You'll know when you find something else that's worth taking chances for."

"Right," she said, taking a step back and a deep wobbling

breath before looking skeptically at the motorcycle with its black paint and leather seats. She'd avoided kissing him again this morning, unsure she wanted a repeat of her response the night before. "How do I get on?"

He guided her through it, showed her how to swing her leg over and settle in behind him with her hands on his hips, careful not to hurt him with the one that rested just below his bandages. The engine rumbled to life and her hands tightened until they ached.

"Just relax," he instructed. "Let me do the work."

"I just have to trust you not to kill me?" She had to raise her voice to be heard and winced at the panicked squeak she hadn't been able to hide.

His chest rumbled with a laugh she couldn't hear over the deep purr of the machine beneath her and he turned back to shout over his shoulder. "I get the feeling trust doesn't come easy to you, but I promise I'll keep you safe."

"Sure," she muttered, her breath catching in her throat when he eased them forward and crept toward the nearest stop sign. She clung to him in terror, her fingers twisting the fabric of his shirt until she worried the thin material might give beneath the pressure, but he went slowly, circling the block to get her used to the noise and the lean of the turns before he took them out of the neighborhood.

"Are we going to go very fast?" she cried, hanging on to him as they stopped at a stoplight. She glanced around at the cars, so terrifyingly close to her exposed body. The helmet was paltry protection for her head, but what about the rest of her? She doubted her arms and legs, or the soft flesh of her torso would hold up against any kind of impact with a car. Ethan had some kind of death wish to do this all the time like he did.

"Not unless you want to," he answered. "We'll stay on the back roads where there's not much traffic and a slower speed limit."

"Okay," she agreed. "Just a short ride. I can't take very much of this."

She clutched at him on the turns and had to bite her lip to keep from gasping at each bump, but once they left the crowded streets behind for the empty lanes of the roads just beyond the city, she began to relax. It wasn't something she'd choose for herself as a hobby, but the wind was cool on her face and the sun warmed her shoulders. There was a freedom in it, and a charm in the country houses they passed, each cute with their wide porches and brightly colored flower beds.

He kept them headed west until they left even those houses behind and the road began to wind through cotton fields and the dark waters of the bayou. Spanish moss hung from the trees, creating a cathedral of gossamer green. Cicadas screamed from the branches loudly enough to be heard even over the rumble of the bike, a warning that the full heat of summer was well on its way.

"You okay?" Ethan turned his head at the next stop sign, his hand coming to squeeze her thigh in case she hadn't heard him.

"Yeah." She squirmed on the seat, shifting her weight slightly to the side. "I think I'm ready to go back."

He chuckled and patted her knee. "It can make your ass hurt when you aren't used to it," he admitted. "The seat's not the softest."

"Sorry."

There were no cars or other people around and he turned around to make eye contact with her over his shoulder. "You don't always have to apologize," he said. "You did better than I thought you would."

She sat up straighter, her chest puffing out a little at the praise. "Did I?"

"Well, you didn't cry all the way here," he teased.

"Oh, you're hilarious." She rolled her eyes, but there was

no malice in it. He *was* pretty funny, and she enjoyed this softer side of him.

They arrived back just after noon and the steady beam of the sun overhead and inescapable humidity had her shirt clinging to her chest like a second skin. She'd never regretted making the move to Louisiana. Getting away from her mother had made trading the cold snap of northern winters for southern heat seem like a good decision, but summer afternoons certainly brought air that felt like hot soup. She plucked at the fabric with one hand and used her wrist to push clinging tendrils of hair off her forehead.

"Want something to drink?" She was already swinging her leg over the seat, gripping his shoulder to steady her as she dismounted. He'd explained the importance of wearing protective clothing during the ride but she was eager to get inside and trade her jeans for something cooler.

"Sweet tea?" he asked, reaching to unbuckle her helmet as she paused beside him, wobbling a little on legs that had gone to jelly now that the vibrating engine was no longer between them. He dismounted enough to face her, then leaned back against the seat of the bike, his booted feet stretched out on either side of hers so she was wedged between his thighs. Her face was hovering just above his as he pulled her helmet off and his eyes drifted to her mouth.

"I have lemonade," she offered quickly. *Too quickly* and she saw the amusement flash in his eyes as she leaned her head back out of reach. "Water. I might be able to make up a cup of chamomile but it's—"

He shook his head, a grin tugging at the corners of his mouth as his fingers caught on her hips and tugged her closer. "What am I going to do with you?" he asked. His eyes wandered over her face, refocusing on her lips as she wet them with her tongue.

"Sweet tea wasn't exactly a popular drink where I grew

up." That wasn't what he meant, and she knew it. But she didn't have a coherent way to explain the constant push and pull of her emotions where he was concerned. She was a moth, drawn to him like a flame but driven back by the heat when she got too close. She danced at the edge of danger, unable to walk away and afraid to dive in.

"And where was that?" He brought one hand up to cup her cheek, his thumb drifting over her chin.

She'd avoided those discussions, tiptoeing around his questions about her parents, if she had any siblings, what her childhood home was like. The less anyone in her life knew about the tense relationship she had with her mother and the nonexistent one she had with her father, the further removed it felt from her new life.

It had embarrassed her that he'd gotten a glimpse of it in the phone call he'd overheard but the inescapable intensity of the look he was giving her now made her want to let him in, to let him see just a little behind the walls she hid behind. "Chicago," she said simply. "My parents live in Chicago."

"That explains—"

She leaned up, pressing onto the tips of her toes and sliding her hands over his chest as she closed the distance between them. The worries she normally would've had about the neighbors seeing them were drowned out by the pounding in her ears and the soft press of his mouth. She'd spent her whole life trying to be perfect, analyzing every decision until she was almost paralyzed with fear, but suddenly she didn't want to miss whatever he might have to give because she was too afraid to take a chance.

He needed no further encouragement; whatever he'd been about to say was forgotten as he deepened the kiss. He tasted of syrup and morning coffee, the sweetness of it dancing across her tongue as he drew her in until she was pressed tight to his chest, her knee on the seat beside his hip and her fingers tangled in his black T-shirt.

Something shifted inside her, a new need rising that made her body tingle and her head spin. This was wild and reckless. Risky. All the things she'd never let herself be … And she wanted it. Maybe she'd been right before and whatever this was between them was her own little rebellion. Maybe it was the lingering irritation from the phone call with her mother, or the heated way he looked at her, or the steady hum of adrenaline in her blood after her first motorcycle ride but whatever it was, she wanted to give in to it.

"Let's go inside."

Twelve

"Inside?" He'd frozen, still holding her against him as he looked down into her face and searched for confirmation. "We're not still pretending this is just us being friends?"

"Friends?" She tipped her head and considered him. "Not even friends. Just neighbors. I've done this with the whole cul-de-sac."

"Ah." He nodded, lips twitching. "I'm sure they were very grateful."

"Will you be grateful?" She pressed against him, unable to resist the urge to tease when his eyes were so hot on hers.

"You have no idea."

"I dreamed about you," she admitted. "When you first moved in and I hated you. I still wanted you, even then."

"Christ," he swore. "Your bed or mine?"

"Um."

"Let's go." He started toward her front door and changed his mind, pivoting toward his own closer door instead. He had to let go of her long enough to fumble with his keys and he shot her an apologetic look. "It's probably not as clean as yours but I know I have protection."

She laughed as he tugged her inside and closed the door behind her. "Good call. I don't think I have any and I didn't even think of that. I'm on birth control but—"

"You're not the kind to take unnecessary risks and in this area, I have to agree with you."

That soothed some of her nerves, the formalities settled and out of the way enough for her to refocus on the excitement and anticipation simmering under her skin.

He was close enough for her to touch and she was finally going to let herself do far more than just that. Her fingers itched just thinking about it and a slow heat was building between her thighs.

"Upstairs?" she asked, already backing across the living room to the base of the staircase.

"Yeah," he agreed. His eyes were tracking her movements, shadowing her steps as she climbed. "My bedroom is just down the hall."

His room was as sparse as the downstairs, dark colors and heavy furniture making the room feel far different than her own even though it was close to the same size. The white walls were just as bare as the rest of the house, no pictures or decorations except the flat screen that took up most of the wall across from the window.

She'd been brave downstairs, carried away by adrenaline from the terrifying thrill of the motorcycle ride, yet she felt the spark of that fade away now that she was faced with the wide expanse of his bed and her own uncertainties.

"I can see you thinking," he said, his voice still coming from a considerable distance behind her. "What are you worried about?"

She turned to face him and found him leaning against the

doorframe, his arms crossed over his chest and his eyes still on her.

"I'm not worried."

"Liar."

"I'm a little worried," she admitted. "I don't do this often and I may not actually be as confident as I just seemed."

"If you're not sure—"

She waved a hand to silence him. "It's not that."

"All right." He pushed off the door frame, towering over her even from across the room. "Let's start with this."

She was rooted to the spot as he crossed the floor until she had to tip her head back to look at him. Her breath shuddered out of her when he cupped her cheek in his palm and caressed her lips with his thumb. The gentle simplicity of the touch rekindled the desire that had gone dormant beneath her nerves and brought it roaring back to life.

Her lips parted in expectation but instead of kissing her as she expected he skimmed the skin of her throat with his fingers and traced the curve of her cheekbone with the tip of his nose.

"Ethan ..."

She wasn't sure what she wanted to say and whatever it might have been was lost to the baffled pleasure of his fingers in her hair, tangling in the silken strands to tug her head back and open her throat to the exploration of his mouth.

If he'd intended to begin with something less intimate than kissing, she feared he'd made a significant miscalculation. The softness of this and the focus in his gaze was every bit as devastating as the onslaught of his kiss would have been. Her knees trembled and for a moment she wondered if she was going to embarrass herself by falling at his feet.

There was a self-satisfied smile on his face when he steadied her and pulled her against him. It seemed he had enough confidence for both of them, but she wasn't going to let him leave this room thinking she was incompetent or fragile.

His smirk turned to amused surprise when she gripped the hem of his shirt and lifted it until he raised his arms and allowed her to pull it over his head. It was a stretch for her—even on her tiptoes she suspected he'd humored her and bent down so she could manage it—but the full view of his broad chest drove that little irritation from her mind.

She'd seen art—statues and paintings that were hundreds of years old, still revered for their quality and loved for their beauty. She'd stood at the tops of mountains and at the shores of seemingly endless seas while she marveled at the world's wonders.

Nothing had awed her quite as much as Ethan's bare chest.

The muscles in his stomach jumped when she touched them, and she smiled up at him. Knowing she wasn't the only one affected by whatever this was between them made her heart beat a little faster. It was like taking a curve on the motorcycle—wild and thrilling and empowering in a way she couldn't explain.

He watched her with a hooded gaze as she explored his body, making no comment as she followed the lines of his tattoos, skirting carefully around the gauze still protecting his wound, and discovered the puckered skin of his scars. The longest of them, thin and wicked as it curved around his side, was several inches long.

She tapped it with a finger and watched his calm expression briefly flicker with something unreadable. "What happened here?"

He licked his lips and sucked the bottom one between his teeth as she waited for an answer. "Run in with someone who didn't like me."

"Are you telling me you've been shot more than once?"

"Stabbed that time." He said it with such a lack of emotion that it took her several long seconds to realize he wasn't joking. "It was a long time ago."

"How long?"

"I was still a teenager."

Her heart ached at that and despite his intimidating size and somewhat sinister appearance she had no trouble imagining him as a scared, hurting young man. Her parents had asked a lot from her, especially her mother, but she'd never feared for her life, never worried for her safety. It was a miracle he had come through all of that as happy and whole as he seemed to be.

"Was it bad?" It was a foolish question—he'd been *stabbed*—but he seemed to know what she meant.

"Frightening more than anything. There was a lot of blood, but it wasn't life threatening."

"You've made a habit of that, haven't you?"

"It looks that way." He was smiling again, the shadows of past pain gone from his eyes. "It was better the second time around. All I had to patch me up the first time was Dylan and a cranky nurse that must have been at least sixty."

"Dylan was with you?"

He reached for her hand, pulling it away from the scar and pressing a kiss to her knuckles. "We were in juvie together and he made it clear after this that things wouldn't go well for anyone else who thought I'd make a good target."

She was quiet after that, trying to take in a story that made her grateful for Dylan and trying not to resent it.

"Where'd your mind wander off to?"

She flushed. "Sorry."

"I like watching you think. You wrinkle your nose just like this when you think hard about something." He scrunched his face in a comical imitation and she giggled at the accuracy.

"I'm not supposed to be thinking right now."

He lifted her arm again and pressed a kiss to the inside of her wrist, his smile turning wicked when she shivered at the contact. "You're always thinking."

"I can't help it."

"I know." He stated it as a fact, like he was reciting her height or the color of her eyes. A part of her, neither good nor bad, just something that was. He'd remained focused and undeterred by all the stops and starts they'd had since she'd first asked him to go inside with her. "Let's see what we can do about that."

Turning off the constant noise of her thoughts was never an easy task for Eloise, but she didn't voice her doubts when he dropped her hand and reached for the hem of her shirt. His fingers brushed against the skin beneath, and her thoughts, always so heavy and constricting, scattered like dandelion fluff on a warm breeze.

He stripped her down slowly, removing her shirt and then her bra, eyes and hands brushing over each newly exposed inch of her before moving on. Her pulse was pounding but she didn't move to cover herself. The rush of blood in her veins was anticipation for once and not nerves, leaving no room for modesty.

It only got worse when he dipped his head to kiss her again. His bare chest was flush against her and with nothing to shield her from the warmth of his skin, she feared he'd burned his way onto her permanently, remolding her until she would never fit against anyone else.

The idea flitted through her mind and was lost again when his mouth began to demand her full attention. He was patient and thorough, exploring her mouth before moving across her jaw and down her throat with his lips as his hands became familiar with the curve of her hips and the dips of her spine.

Her thoughts quieted, taking with them all her worries, and Ethan took full advantage of her relaxed state, backing her the few remaining steps until her knees hit the bed behind her, and then followed her down when she allowed herself to be spilled over onto his soft sheets.

She'd known he was large but having him pressed between her thighs and looming over her made him seem suddenly impossibly big. He enveloped her, wrapped himself around her as she lost herself in the taste of him and the delicious hardness of his body where it met hers.

Eloise knew she was shaking, trembling already with a level of want she'd never experienced and didn't have the ability to hide, but instead of rushing now that he had her in his bed, Ethan kept his same stubborn, tantalizingly slow pace.

Sunlight shimmered on the walls and behind her eyelids as he moved down her body, teasing her breasts with his lips and teeth before moving down her stomach. There was nothing here to hide her, no shadows to shield her flaws from his gaze, but every new bit of her that he encountered was given such attention that she held no doubt that he liked what he saw.

She'd never been entirely comfortable showing herself to a man, but she'd live the rest of her life as naked as the day she was born if there was only Ethan there to see her.

He peeled her out of her jeans, nipping at her thighs and making her squirm. "Ticklish?"

"Don't you dare." She tensed her muscles, prepared to fight, and glared at him until he chuckled, fingers skimming her knee, threateningly close.

"Wouldn't dream of it."

She eyed him suspiciously until he laughed again and made the motion of a cross over his chest. "I swear I won't," he promised, leaning up to kiss her hard on the mouth. "But you're beautiful when you look like you're ready to fight me. I wanted you the first time I saw you, standing on my porch in your fucking pajamas looking like you were about ready to chew glass."

"You were rude."

"And you were amazing." He kissed her again, more demanding than before. "You're better than anything I could have dreamed up."

She smiled, willing to let him flatter her even if she didn't believe a word of it. "Now that you've got me here, what do you intend to do about it?"

He needed no further prompting and she watched with interest as he stood and pulled off the rest of his own clothes, leaving them in a heap on the floor beside hers. Sometime soon she'd have to analyze why she wasn't bothered by that, why she hadn't given even a passing thought to picking them up and folding them neatly on a nearby dresser, but there was no time for those concerns now.

The awe she'd felt at the sight of chest paled in comparison to the sight of him nude. She'd seen plenty of ancient statues, sculpted by masters with an eye for male beauty, and he could easily have been carved of marble with one rather large exception.

"What are you staring at?"

She pulled a pillow over her face, laughing with embarrassment. "I was just admiring your ... attributes."

"Oh yeah?"

"Mmm hmm," she murmured, rolling onto her stomach propping her chin on her hand so she could take in the glory of his naked body over again. "You look like a Greek god, one of those statues you see in museums." She waited for him to smile, let it run straight to his ego. "Of course, they have all that muscle and masculine prowess then ..." She glanced down and saw his head dip in response as he followed her gaze. "Tiny little penises."

His head snapped up. "What?"

"It's a good thing you don't have that problem," she said sweetly.

"That's the meanest way a woman has ever told me I have a big dick."

She shrugged. "You like it when I'm mean."

He didn't deny it, but he did give her backside a small slap as he climbed back into bed with her. "I should have known better than to tell you that."

"Definitely." She'd lost her desire to tease him now that he was back within her reach and she pulled him close before he could respond, parting her lips to invite him in as he settled again between her thighs.

Without words or clothes to distract them, the heat between them built quickly and before long she was writhing beneath him, wet and aching. "Ethan," she gasped, hanging on to the last little thread of her rational thought. "We have to—"

"Got it." He leaned over, rummaging around in a drawer beside her head and coming back with a condom in his hand.

"Hurry," she panted, and she expected him to tease her for that, but he was focused, as eager and determined as she was. It took only moments for him to accomplish his task, but it seemed much longer to Eloise as she waited, body tense and desperate.

One smooth push was enough to open her for him and she arched into it, satisfied noises pouring unchecked from her throat and her eyes locked on his.

He never looked away from her unless it was to kiss her again, and she found herself unsettled by the intensity of his gaze even as her body responded to his more quickly and overwhelmingly than she'd ever dreamed possible.

It had been difficult, almost impossible, for her to orgasm with anyone else in the past. With Ethan, it came more easily. The usual tension her body held was absent and she leaned into the sensations she was experiencing, chasing the orgasm as it built instead of wondering what he'd think of her. She let it take control and it crashed over her within minutes, shocking them both.

He followed her over the edge soon after, hiking her leg over his hip to drive deep and letting out a pleased grunt that made her smile into his shoulder. When he rolled onto his side, he tugged her with him, holding her close in the circle of his arms until he slipped out of her and headed for the bathroom to dispose of the condom.

She followed him, waiting beside the door until he came out and letting him kiss her again as he passed. It didn't take her long to clean up but by the time she returned to bed he was spread out across the covers, dozing with arms flung wide and just enough room for her to climb back in beside him. Surely, if he wanted her to leave, he would have said so before he fell asleep.

Eloise watched his face as he slept, the sun lighting the line of his nose and shadowing the dimples of his cheeks. She was happy and satisfied and it seemed that he was, too, but something at the back of her mind made her uneasy.

He'd been so wonderful with her, soft and understanding when she needed it and unafraid to give more intimacy in one afternoon than she'd ever experienced before, and a wave of uncomfortable guilt washed over her. She'd taken Sarah's words to heart and resolved to keep things light and casual, but had she forgotten to make sure Ethan knew that?

Thirteen

"Winston!" Eloise called the dog's name and followed up with a series of shameless kissy noises as Ethan's pup opened one eye and then returned to his nap. He was clearly unimpressed with the little collar she'd found, complete with a small plaid bow tie. Ethan had insisted the thing was ridiculous, but with a name like Winston, how could he not be dressed as a gentleman?

If Ethan didn't want Winston to wear it, then he shouldn't have left her alone with him while he ran to the store. After several weeks of being at her house more often than he was at his own, he knew what he was in for when he left the two of them together.

She wasn't sure what she was going to do about her growing feelings for him, but when he playfully accused her of liking Winston more than she did him ... Well, maybe it wasn't entirely true, but surely it was a near thing.

After a lifetime of wanting a pet of her own, Winston's little paws and sweet brown eyes had wormed right into her heart. Ethan reminded her often that he was going to be a big dog someday and she should stop babying him, but Eloise was convinced he would always be the perfect size for cuddling, no matter how fast he was growing.

Her attachment to the pup had become a running joke at the office ever since Sarah had discovered the background picture on her phone was one she'd snapped of Winston sleeping on her living room rug.

"Wait," Sarah had asked, snatching Eloise's phone and shaking it to get everyone's attention. "You're buying me dessert for a whole month because you're sleeping with Ethan and your new background picture is of his *dog*?"

"What's it supposed to be?" Eloise had made a grab for her phone, but Sarah's reflexes had always been quicker than hers and she'd dodged it easily.

"Ethan? The two of you together? Something couple-ish? Not his *dog*?"

Eloise sniffed, settling back in her seat with her arms crossed and ignoring the others as they laughed at her pouting expression. "I don't think we're at that place yet. Maybe not ever. We're just having fun, remember?"

"Uh huh," Sarah said with a wink. "Lots of fun."

"You were the ones who said I'd be able to keep it light and casual."

"Looks like you're doing a good job of it," Chloe said, collapsing into a fresh round of giggles.

"Your mom really should have let you have a dog growing up," Kim said. She was trying to keep her face expressionless, but her twitching lips gave her away.

"It's actually not that funny."

"It's just so ... *you*." Sarah took a bite of the muffin Eloise had bought her and shrugged. "You never want to really be involved in anything or with anyone and you fight it every step of the way."

"I do not."

"Do you remember how long it took us to convince you to spend time with us outside the office?"

Eloise had no answer to that, so she'd gone back to ignoring them until they'd quit teasing her. She loved them but sometimes it was hard being around people who knew you almost as well as you knew yourself. She wasn't just an open book with people scanning the pages. They'd worked their way down into the spine and found out what kind of glue was holding her together.

Somehow in the years since they'd met, the three of them had become more than just her friends—they'd become her family. The sisters she'd never been blessed enough to have. And with that came all the incredible and irritating things that families were good for.

They'd all been in a good mood that day, laughing and teasing her about Ethan and the dog. She wished it had stayed that way.

While her relationship with Ethan had become stronger and smoother, the same could not be said of her relationship with her friends. Eloise couldn't pinpoint exactly what the problem was or when it had begun, but after several weeks of increasingly short tempers and few words, there was no denying that something was definitely wrong.

Work had been even worse than usual with rumors increasing about company restructuring and potential downsizing, but somehow that didn't seem to be enough to account for their behavior.

Kim took every opportunity she could find to slip outside for a cigarette and had confided that she was up to almost a pack a day. Chloe had dark circles under her eyes and had gotten reprimanded for falling asleep at her desk. And Sarah, usually the most steel-spined out of all of them, was lingering over her phone calls and texts like a jumpy teen with a secret boyfriend. Eloise had tried to ask her about it but she'd been shut down every time.

None of them were willing to provide any reasonable answers and when Sarah did acknowledge the changes, she casually blamed Dwayne for a lot of what was happening, saying it looked like things that should have been taken care of in her department might have to get kicked to Kim in auditing.

Ethan kept trying to convince her that there was nothing to worry about, but if there was ever one thing Eloise was incredibly good at, it was worrying.

She dropped the collar on the table when her phone rang, pointing a finger at Winston as she picked it up. "Don't get comfortable," she warned. Ethan would end up taking it off but she wanted a few cute pictures before he got home.

"Hello?"

Eloise winced. She hadn't looked at the screen before she answered, making the foolish assumption that the only people that would be calling her this late on a weekend were ones she'd actually want to talk to. Her mother was not on that short list.

"Eloise?"

"Yes, sorry." There was no help for it now. She'd already answered the phone and was stuck with the consequences. "I'm here."

"Good." Deborah didn't ask if she was interrupting, a fact that set Eloise's teeth on edge. She didn't ask because she didn't care. Or perhaps because she assumed Eloise had nothing better to do on a Saturday night than indulge her. "I'm sure you know why I'm calling."

"I ..." Eloise frowned and ran the calendar of important events through her mind. It wasn't a holiday or her birthday. It wasn't either of her parents' birthdays, either. She knew not having an answer would result in another lecture, but she was coming up blank.

"Oh, for heaven's sake, Eloise," Deborah said after a moment of tense silence. "Do you still not watch the news?"

The news? She did not. Eloise got her news online like most normal people but she pretended she didn't have social media so her parents wouldn't start monitoring her accounts. "I'm sorry, Mother."

"Never mind that," Deborah dismissed. "If you watched the news, you'd know there are still no new leads in that robbery case I talked to you about last time."

Eloise thought back to their last conversation. She'd been distracted with Ethan stretched out across her couch, but she thought she vaguely remembered her mother telling her something about a robbery across town. It was exactly the kind of thing Deborah would seize onto. Something that truly had nothing at all to do with Eloise, but that she could use as an excuse to call and make demands about Eloise's behavior. It was nothing more than an excuse and a flimsy one, at that.

"I'm sure they'll find the people responsible," Eloise assured her. It was exhausting but the fastest way to get her mother off the phone was to agree with whatever she said and make promises she absolutely did not intend to keep.

She glanced up as the front door opened, her heart rate skyrocketing as Ethan let himself in, arms loaded with late night snacks and a relaxed grin on his face. If her mother heard him here at this hour, she'd know Eloise was seeing someone and the resulting guilt trip was something Eloise was certain she could live without.

She held a finger to her lips, pleading at him with her eyes to be quiet. "Listen, Mother, could I call you back tomorrow—"

"We'll be busy tomorrow," Deborah said, cutting over Eloise with a dismissive sniff. "I just wanted to call and make sure you were behaving sensibly. I've been thinking about how busy you've been, not answering my calls and such because of those friends of yours, and I think it might be a good idea for you to move home. It hardly seems like New Orleans is safe, what with the crime and all."

Ethan's eyebrows rose sharply when Eloise choked a bit on her own spit and made a strangled noise. "Mother, you know better than almost anyone how much crime there is in Chicago."

They'd been going around in this circle—Eloise trying to keep her distance and Deborah trying to reel her back in—ever since Eloise had first announced her intention to move out of state but somehow it always surprised her. Maybe it was the lengths Deborah was willing to go to, the wildness of the excuses she was willing to fabricate out of thin air.

"This is different. They tried to rob an armored truck, for goodness' sake. Next they'll be robbing banks and where will that put you? Half a step away from danger, *that's* where. If you were behaving sensibly—"

"I'm always behaving sensibly." Eloise's eyes were still locked on Ethan, and she saw him tip his head skeptically. "As I told you last time, I'm perfectly safe and perfectly boring."

"But—"

"I'm sorry, Mother, I really need to go. It's late and I need to wake up early in the morning."

Ethan managed to stay quiet long enough for Eloise to get her mother off the phone but the call made her jumpy. Just hearing Deborah's voice was enough to make her feel guilty about what she had allowed to happen between them.

"Your mind is a million miles away again," he observed, watching her closely as she hung up the phone and dropped her face into her hands.

"She makes me question every decision I've ever made,"

Eloise admitted. "Nothing I've ever done is good enough for her."

Ethan, already at home in his usual spot on her couch, pulled her into his lap. "Forget about her," he said. He kissed her once, firmly and decisively. "You can't live your life for her. You're enough for your friends. Enough for me. Enough for yourself. You don't need to be anything else."

They hadn't talked about what this was—what they were doing or what it meant to them—but his words were soothing. She meant *something* to him, there was no doubt in her mind that at least that much was true. It was in the way he looked at her, the way he pulled her close to him in his sleep and held her like she was something precious that he needed to protect.

It made it easy for her to sink into him, to find her solace in the taste of him and the warmth of his embrace. He was able to read her well enough by now to know when she needed him to be gentle and when she wanted to feel the scraping graze of his teeth on her as he nibbled at her lips and let his hands roam over now-familiar curves.

She didn't need kindness after dealing with her mother. She needed distraction and Ethan was happy to provide it. Every time before this, he had let her lead him upstairs and waited while she carefully closed the curtains before making love to her.

But not this time. Her eyes flew open when he began to work at the small buttons on her silk blouse.

"What—"

"No one can see you."

She glanced nervously over her shoulder at the windows facing the street. The blinds were drawn, and the curtains closed, but she still felt exposed in a way she never had in the bedroom. Kissing him on the couch had been one thing, but she knew they weren't in that place anymore. If he started touching her here, she knew where that would lead.

"Someone might come to the door."

He finished opening the line of buttons and pushed the silk down over her shoulders. One large hand came up to cup her breast as he shook his head. "Then we won't answer it. We're busy."

"*You're* busy," she protested, but it sounded weak even to her and her fingers were already fisted greedily in his hair. "*I'm* trying to get you to be busy in the perfectly good bed upstairs."

He flicked the clasp of her bra open in response and grinned at her small indignant huff. "Live on the wild side just a little and I'll show how perfectly good the couch downstairs can be."

Eloise chewed on her bottom lip as his thumb traced patient circles around her hardening nipple. If she really wanted to go upstairs, she knew he'd take her, but Ethan had a way of tempting her to push her own boundaries. She was a little scandalized, yes. Worried, certainly, about being seen and feeling a little guilty at the impropriety of being nude in any room that wasn't her bedroom or bathroom.

All the shame that she realized suddenly came from her mother.

He was giving her the chance to reject that small, judgmental voice in her mind that so often sounded like the woman who'd raised her, and instead listen to her own desires.

"Okay," she agreed quietly, nodding more to reassure herself than him. "We can stay here."

"Yeah?" His smile was mischievous as he waggled his eyebrows at her suggestively. "You're gonna let me fuck you here?"

"Ethan." She groaned it, his name an admonition as embarrassed heat flooded her cheeks. She should be used to it by now, but he always found a way to fluster her, like he could sense exactly what words would do the trick.

He'd managed it at least once every time they'd been together since the morning she'd woken up in his bed to find him already awake and watching her with lust in his eyes. Her vague plan to slip out unnoticed had been abandoned, a blush spreading rapidly as he described in detail how beautiful she looked in the early morning light. It had been impossible for her to leave after that, and she'd found she had no regrets when he'd started their day by pushing into her and driving her to two orgasms before she'd even had her first cup of coffee. She'd never let a man see her with her hair tousled or makeup smudged but it felt natural with Ethan.

She'd never let a man peel off all her clothes and pull her onto his lap in her living room either, but somehow this, too, seemed inevitable. He pulled things from her that she hadn't known existed and made it seem like they'd been there all along.

Ethan didn't seem to mind her distraction as he stripped her down to her bare skin. Her frequent glances over her shoulder and the warmth of her blushes only seemed to amuse him. He liked keeping her off balance and watching her squirm, something that might have bothered her if it hadn't been for her own arousal.

She worried for a moment that one of them would have to run upstairs for a condom but he pulled one out of his wallet. It wasn't the best storage place and she'd lecture him about that later, but for now she decided it was good enough. As sexually active as she'd bet he was before he met her, it was unlikely the thing had been in there for long. That caused a little twinge of jealousy but he was already moving to shift her into place and she forgot about anything but the press of him between her thighs.

He gripped her hips as she sank down onto him, already

wet and surprisingly ready from the thrill of what they were doing. The possibility of being seen was a rush she hadn't anticipated, but it was the look in his eyes that drove her higher. He was watching her like she was every bit as much of a surprise to him as she was to herself. Like he had reached out a hand and caught a golden sunbeam in his fist. Awed and terrified all at once.

"Eloise ..." Something flashed across his features, gone before she could decipher it. For a moment she thought it might have been regret, but he pulled her in and kissed her until it made her head spin and her heart flutter.

He held her as she shattered around him and dragged him over his own peak moments later, and if he was quieter and more serious than usual as she curled against his chest, she tried not to worry about it. Tried not to wonder about that look or what it could mean.

Whatever it had been, she was sure it was nothing that could hurt her. He had earned her trust and she was afraid her heart would not be far behind.

Fourteen

Ethan's favorite place was mostly empty at three o'clock on a weekday, which made it a decent enough place to have the meeting with Dylan that he'd been putting off. Public enough they'd both be forced to keep their voices down and their tempers in check but private enough that no one was likely to overhear anything they shouldn't.

Paula never looked less pleased to see him than when she realized he'd brought Dylan along. She still smiled at him when he brought Myles—and slipped the kid a desert on the house more often than not—but her entire demeanor shifted when she was forced to deal with Dylan. She was still highly efficient and ruthlessly polite, but with Dylan she made her dislike known through the tension at the corners of her mouth and the absence of her laughter.

Most of the community feared Dylan on his father's reputation alone—a suspicion that the apple didn't fall far from the tree no matter how hard he tried to hide his true nature—but it seemed that Paula was able to see right through to the heart of him. Whatever she found there had soured her on his existence faster than she could blink one heavily mascaraed eye.

After knowing Dylan more than half his life, with all of those years spent feeling like he owed the man a debt he'd never be able to repay, Ethan sat in the restaurant where he'd taken Eloise on their first date and began to wonder if maybe their hostess had a point.

Sometimes Dylan was an unbearable asshole.

Things had cooled off between them after Ethan's injury, mostly because he'd stopped pushing so hard for information from Eloise. But Dylan couldn't seem to resist the urge to make comments about Ethan's forced time off or how he was spending his time while he was away from the bar. It rankled, each petty jab giving Ethan a sour feeling in the pit of his stomach.

"You're spending too much time with that neighbor." Dylan reached for a slice of pizza before Paula had finished putting it on the table and missed the look she shot him from beneath her lashes before she walked away. "You still haven't been coming around the bar and we need you."

"Need me for what? I told you already I'll be back once I'm totally healed up. It wouldn't do you any good for me to come around and have people start asking questions about what happened. The news is still running stories about it. They say the cops are still looking for the suspects. That's us, remember?"

It was an excuse to avoid the bar, but it was mostly true. Staying away for a while after that last job had gone unexpectedly sideways had been Dylan's idea in the first place but they both knew he'd been pretty well-healed for over a week, and he still hadn't gone back. Ethan had spent more time in that bar than he had anywhere else in his life and the damn thing wouldn't fall apart if he spent some time with a beautiful woman before Dylan dragged him back in.

"Got a lead on a job," Dylan said cryptically. "Been cooking it up since the night you got shot. Ran into some good luck for a change."

Usually the idea of a new job was energizing, full of tantalizing possibilities, but this time it just caused a restless and uncomfortable itch beneath his skin. He was getting too old for this shit, he decided, and ruthlessly pushed the thought of Eloise out of his mind. He was having a good time with her, but he couldn't let it be more than that.

"Why didn't you say something sooner?"

"Like I said, you haven't been coming around. I was starting to think you'd lost interest, maybe started having fantasies about a wife and kids, golden retriever and all."

"I have the house for it now, don't I?" Ethan let the words roll off his tongue, testing not just Dylan's reaction to the thought of it, but his own. He'd never entertained such ideas before. His memories of family were not much more than loss and conflict—the kind of shit he thought would haunt him for the rest of his life—but Eloise had a way of making him forget. The house where he'd come to blows with his grandfather, where he'd been dragged out in handcuffs and tossed into juvie, hadn't been a place he'd really wanted to return to, but it was different when she was there.

Eloise was nothing like his mother, organized and prim where his mom had been wild and rebellious, but there was a kindness to her smile that made him remember what family was like when it was good, what home was like when it was safe, and it was more appealing than he'd expected.

"Is that what you want?" Dylan had gone still and dangerous, watching Ethan with a measuring gleam in his eye. "You want out now? After everything?"

"Of course not." If he did, what would Dylan do to him? To Eloise? If he did, that was something he would need to think about, to plan for. It wasn't something he could toss out over pizza and expect to walk away from unscathed. "You know better than anyone how much damage family can do to a man. Eloise is nothing more than a pretty distraction while I get back on my feet."

Dylan was still watching him, but his body relaxed. He flashed a smile that didn't quite reach his eyes as he nodded. "I didn't think so."

"I'll come by the bar as soon as I can."

"Of course, you will." Dylan returned his attention to his pizza, point apparently made. "The place just isn't the same without you."

Fifteen

"You don't really have to go back to the office on a Saturday night, do you?" Jackson pouted, his long body draped elegantly in the corner chair as he sipped lemonade and watched storm clouds roll in to cover the blue late afternoon sky.

"Don't go," David pleaded. He'd risen from his spot on the couch to wrap both of her hands in his larger ones. "You haven't been to dinner at our house in ages and you finally get a free evening when Ethan is busy, and you run off to work instead."

"I wish I didn't have to." She meant it. The last thing she wanted to do on a Saturday was go back into the office. "I'd put it off if I could, but I forgot to send a paper over to Sarah's department and she called a few minutes ago, just completely irate. Nearly took my head clean off over the phone."

"Short temper." Jackson clucked his tongue, face full of judgment. "Work is important, obviously, but is that any way to treat a friend?"

"I don't know what's been going on with her lately." Eloise

pressed her fingers to her eyes, trying to dull the headache that was building. She had been distracted lately because of Ethan, and she didn't blame Sarah for being frustrated, but surely it didn't warrant that level of vitriol. "With any of them, really."

"She wanted you to go in and fix it today?" David was at least looking a little bit more sympathetic than Jackson, though he was hardly swimming in it.

"No," Eloise admitted. "She didn't ask me to, but I feel terrible, and I know I messed up. I should have been spending extra time at the office, too, and I would have been, except—"

"Except you've been coming home on time because of Ethan," David finished, and she nodded miserably.

"I don't blame you." Jackson winked at her. "We've all seen the way that man looks at you. I'd be leaving on time, too."

"I guess I left them in more of a lurch at the office than I realized."

"I doubt you have, or your own boss would have said something." Jackson finished off his lemonade and stood up to walk his empty glass to the kitchen. "I think they might just be jealous."

"Jealous? Of what?"

"Either jealous because you've fallen into bed with your very hot neighbor and they wish they had one, or jealous about the time you're spending with him because it means you spend less time with them."

"That's silly," Eloise said, the defense rising to her lips automatically. Those women were closer to her than her blood family had ever been. Still, she wondered, deep inside in a part of her she wasn't proud of, if that might explain the strange way they'd been acting lately. It had started right after Ethan had been shot, when he'd come to her house and things had really started to change between them.

"Matters of the heart are often foolish," Jackson replied. He kissed her on the cheek, and she held the door for them as they left. "If you make it home at a decent hour, come on over. We'll have plenty of food if you're hungry or coffee if you've already eaten."

"We miss your face," David agreed. "Our door is always open."

"I know," she hugged him fiercely, a sticky guilt worrying its way into her heart. "I'll come around as soon as I can."

She hated that feeling, the idea that maybe her mother had been right and she couldn't balance work and friendships and all the other parts of her life that mattered to her if she let a man turn her head.

Or worse, a family.

She'd never spoken the desire for that out loud, certain she'd follow her mother's plan and keep her eyes on the promotions and not on the distractions. If she couldn't handle a boyfriend without hurting her friends' feelings and dropping the ball at work, it was clear she'd never be able to handle a husband or motherhood.

It occupied her mind as she drove, oblivious to the sinking sun slipping away behind dark clouds that began spitting rain onto the pavement as soon as she'd gotten in the car. She cursed her lack of an umbrella as she parked, the slow drizzle having already turned to a steady downpour that pooled on the pavement and splashed up to soak her shoes. Wind whipped through the trees, and she crossed her fingers that the power lines would stay up, just this once, long enough for her to do what she'd come for.

The rain was inconvenient, but the hot summer air at least made the cooler weather a relief and she wasn't freezing without her jacket. Lightning cracked across the sky, a rumble of thunder following almost immediately behind, and she scurried faster, eyes locked on the door and the safety of the building.

She didn't see the body until she nearly tripped over it in her haste.

Bare feet, dirty at the bottoms. Sweatpants, dark blue. A gray T-shirt. Red hair, tangled and floating in a puddle of muddy water. Green eyes and the familiar slope of a nose. Kim's face was gray and her eyes open and staring blankly at the sky. There were bruises on her throat, distorted blues and purples that would never heal.

Eloise turned her head and vomited in the grass before her mind had time to put together the pieces of what she was seeing. She clutched at her stomach, heaving until she could get control of herself enough to drop to her knees beside her friend. She pushed the wet hair back from Kim's face, checking the coolness of her cheeks and leaning down to feel for breath, though she already knew what she'd find. There was no sign of life, just blue lips and waxy skin that made her shudder as a new, terrifying thought occurred to her.

Someone had done this.

Someone had killed her, snuffed her life out, and they might still be watching. Eloise looked around, taking in the rain-soaked sidewalk and the wind-swept trees. Nothing looked out of place, but her skin tingled, alive with terror. She needed to call 911 but it wasn't safe for her to linger here. She had brought nothing but her phone with her. Nothing that could offer protection. She'd have to make a run for the safety of the building or the car, but doing so empty-handed was a terrifying thought.

Kim had dropped her purse, the contents scattered over the ground beside her, and Eloise lowered her eyes long enough to scan what was there. There was nothing useful, no hidden knives or pepper spray. Just some makeup, a tampon, and a pack of cigarettes with a matchbook tucked into the clear plastic lining.

An echo of Kim's voice flitted across Eloise's mind, "*God forbid my mom ever finds out,*" and she grabbed them on impulse as she stood, stuffing them into her pocket to protect her friend's memory from the disapproval of her family. They already had to lose her. They didn't need her memory tainted with habits that had embarrassed her.

She backed toward the building, hoping to take refuge behind a locked door, but found her fears about the electricity to the building going out had been well founded. This happened every time it rained, and the employees had been complaining about it since she'd been hired. She wondered, wildly, as the ID scanner remained lifeless and unresponsive to her panicked attempts to unlock the door, if this would be enough to get them to install some kind of backup system to work around the security door. Assuming she lived long enough to explain to management the way it had nearly killed her.

Left with no other choice, she ran back the way she'd come, each panicked step sending a spray of water flying. She kept her eyes moving as she ran, deliberately avoiding looking down at Kim's body as she passed and trying not to think about anything other than getting to safety. She'd figure out what to do about Kim, when she knew for certain she wasn't about to be next.

Her feet slapped against the pavement and echoed back to her, convincing her mind that there were others running behind her, that she might be grabbed at any moment, pulled off balance and thrown to the ground. She would take her last breath under a rainy summer sky, just like Kim.

It took precious seconds for her to fish the keys from her pocket once the car was in sight, then several more to hit the button needed to unlock the doors. She was shaking as she fumbled for the handle, even though there was still no one around when she looked over her shoulder.

It wasn't until she was in the front seat, wet and shivering with the doors locked, that she was able to take a breath and think about what she needed to do next. Kim was dead, and the only people that knew that were Eloise and whoever had killed her.

She needed to do something for Kim.

She needed to get help.

Her phone. She needed her phone. She had put it in her pocket when she'd gotten out of the car, and she found it there after a few more painful seconds of fumbling. She had to hang up twice, her adrenaline-fueled body unable to dial the numbers. It was supposed to be simple, so simple even a child could do it, but her irritation with herself grew as her shaking fingers couldn't handle the task.

It rang, finally, on the third time. Once. Twice. Again. How long was she supposed to wait before someone answered the damn phone? It was supposed to be for emergencies, and this was an emergency.

"Answer the phone, goddamn it!"

"911, what's your emergency?"

"It's—oh God." Eloise's voice broke, a choked sob coming out instead of an answer as she tried and failed to control her breathing. "She's dead."

"Can you tell me what happened and where you are? Do you need an ambulance?" The voice on the phone was calm but it felt like they were speaking to her from somewhere far away, the questions blurry and uncertain.

"She's—" Eloise fought down the urge to vomit again. She had to do this. Had to do it for Kim. Had to get help. "My friend. She's dead. I think ... I think she was strangled."

"Okay, take a deep breath for me. Can you tell me where you are?"

"Sun Valley Financial. The headquarters building. I found her. She's on the sidewalk leading up to the employee entrance. You can't see it from the parking lot or the road."

"Thank you. I'm pulling up the address now and I'm going to send help. The ambulance and police are on their way. Take some more deep breaths for me, okay? Can you start CPR?"

"What?" Eloise shook her head and then remembered the operator couldn't see her over the phone. "No, I— She was cold and blue. Just staring at me. And she'd been strangled, I could see ... I could see the bruises. I was scared and I ran back to my car. There was no one else around and I didn't know ... What if he's still out there?"

"Okay, honey. Are your doors locked?"

"Yes." Her teeth were chattering and her hands were still shaking but she double checked the door locks just to be sure.

"Can you listen for the sirens? You said they wouldn't be able to see her from the road and we want to get help to her as quickly as possible. Can you come out when the ambulance gets there and help them find her?"

"I can," Eloise agreed. "I just ... I'm afraid whoever hurt Kim ..."

"I understand, and I'll stay on the line with you until the first responders arrive."

"Thank you." There was nothing for several minutes, just the quiet inside the car and the sound of rain as it fell on the asphalt, and the rhythm of their breathing. "I hear the sirens," Eloise said, breaking the quiet and feeling some of the tension drain out of her. "Someone's here."

"Good," the voice on the line replied. "Can you help them? I'll stay on the line until they see you."

"Yes." Eloise opened the door and clutched the phone as she jogged back around toward the building, to where the ambulance could see her when she waved her arms. "They see me."

"That's excellent. Don't worry, honey, they'll take care of you now."

Eloise hoped that was true, but even that seemed like far too little when her friend lay dead and unmoving on the sidewalk and there was nothing anyone could do to take it back. "Over here," she yelled. She knew she must look like a wild animal, wet and muddy and panicked, but the cop that pulled in first didn't seem at all fazed by her disheveled appearance.

"Ma'am?" He glanced her way and she stopped where she was when his hand settled on the butt of his gun. "Did you call the police?"

"Yes," she was bouncing on the balls of her feet, restless and frustrated when the ambulance didn't immediately arrive. "I think she's dead and someone has to come and help her."

"I understand. We're just going to make sure the area is safe and then we'll let the ambulance in to help her, okay?"

Eloise nodded and followed their instructions to wait by the car. They stopped briefly at Kim's body, leaning over and checking for a pulse before moving on. It didn't take long for them to search the immediate area, and she watched the ambulance roll in only a few minutes later.

She watched and chewed anxiously on her thumbnail as the EMTs did their work. They leaned close to examine her but in the end they didn't do CPR or load her in the back of the ambulance. It confirmed what she already knew. Kim was well and truly gone before any of them had even known she was there. No miracle of medicine was coming to save her. It was already too late.

"Hey, what the hell is going on out here?"

Eloise looked up, surprised and confused, as Sarah and Chloe were both stopped by the police when they tried to leave the building. Sarah was being pushy, insisting they couldn't keep her inside against her will and Chloe was trying to peek around the officers and find out what was going on.

"Sarah?"

"Eloise?" Sarah stretched up on tiptoe and waved a hand at the officers. "Do you know what's happening?"

"I—" She choked on the words, not able to tell them that Kim was dead. She could barely see the body now, surrounded by uniformed officers as they waited for homicide investigators to arrive, but it wasn't just a body to her. It was her friend. *Their* friend. How could she tell them both that someone they all loved had been murdered? She couldn't and she turned away, moved a few steps closer to the parking lot as she tried to push down the guilt and the sick feeling of loss that threatened to choke her. If she'd come sooner, instead of lingering at the house with Jackson and David ...

She didn't look back until she heard voices coming closer and found Chloe and Sarah were both being led over to stand beside her next to the cop car. They stared curiously at the body as they walked by, but Eloise didn't see any recognition on their faces and she realized they must have covered her, probably to preserve evidence against the rain.

"Are you okay?" Sarah wrapped an arm around Eloise. "That cop told us someone had been murdered? I can't believe it." She looked around with wide eyes, taking in activity around them as she pressed a hand to her stomach. "I guess we're supposed to stick around until the homicide detective gets here, in case he wants to ask us any questions?"

"Not like we know anything," Chloe grumbled. "It was probably Dwayne. People are so sick of him, I bet half of Sarah's department have thought about doing him in." It was a dark joke to lighten the fear in the air, and she bumped Sarah with her shoulder and smiled thinly.

"It wasn't Dwayne." Eloise put a hand on Sarah's arm. "It was Kim."

"What?" The look of curiosity on Sarah's face faded, replaced by anger. "That's not funny. Why would you say that?"

"It's true," Eloise said, barely more than a whisper. "I found her."

"You're lying," Chloe said. She reached for her phone and started tapping the screen. "I'll call her, and she'll answer and then we'll see. You shouldn't play around about that kind of shit."

"I'm not," Eloise insisted. "I wouldn't do that. I found her and—"

They all fell silent when Kim's phone began to ring. The sound floated on the breeze, muffled by the light rain that was still falling, but clearly coming from the vicinity of the body. Chloe went green in the face when the truth of the situation hit her, and Sarah rushed over to the edge of the sidewalk to throw up in the bushes.

"She can't be dead, I just talked to her." Chloe reached for Eloise's hand, her fingers cold and wet where they gripped. "They said someone was murdered. Was she ...?"

"There were bruises." Eloise laid a hand against her own throat and Chloe's eyes followed, tears forming on her lashes. Were they both wondering what it had felt like? The fear Kim must have gone through in those last moments. "She was cold when I got here. So stiff and blue."

"We didn't know she was even coming." Sarah wiped her mouth with the back of her hand. "We didn't know either of you were coming."

"I wasn't." Eloise wished she'd agreed to stay and have dinner with Jackson and David. Someone else would have found the body. She wished she'd left her house sooner. Kim wouldn't have been alone and maybe she wouldn't be dead at all. "I just came up to deal with that paperwork you called me about earlier."

"This is so sick. I can't believe it. Do you think we're going to be suspects now?" Chloe was staring at Kim's body, her hands clutched in front of her as she spoke. There was a wild, terrified light in her eyes. "That's what all the true crime shows say, right? They always look first at the people that found the body? The people that were at the scene? We all knew her and we were all here."

"We don't know when she ..." Sarah shook her head and swallowed hard, "When it happened but we were here all afternoon. We didn't come down till the power cut back on because we knew we couldn't get out of the building."

Eloise leaned against the car; the breath knocked out of her again at the thought. "I was alone when I found her. I'm the one that called the police. The cameras were probably out just like the doors so there's no way to prove she was dead when I got here."

"This shit is supposed to have a backup power supply." Sarah ran a hand through her hair, leaving it tousled and untidy for the first time in Eloise's memory. "How long have we been complaining about the system not working right? It's bad enough that the power goes out when it rains. The least this fucking company could do is make sure the security systems still work."

"It's too late for that now." Chloe's face was still a little green and there was a thin line of vomit down the front of her shirt. "I can't ... This can't be happening. She can't be dead. Christ, what if we all go to jail because the power was out and there's no way for us to prove we were inside and ..."

"Hey, hey, hey." Eloise rubbed a hand over Chloe's arm to calm her. She was irritated at the selfishness of Chloe's concerns—their friend was dead, after all—but hadn't she run to her own car to hide instead of doing CPR? Kim was gone and there was nothing they could do about that. There would be time to grieve and she was sure they would each have to deal with that loss. It didn't stop them from wondering how it would change their own lives and the kinds of danger they might be in now.

"Just answer the questions honestly when the detectives show up and I'm sure everything will be fine," Sarah said, but the look on her face was worried and uncertain enough that Eloise knew she didn't fully believe it herself.

Sixteen

Eloise had never realized how busy a crime scene actually was. The front of the building had been so calm and quiet when she'd arrived but within a few short minutes it was overrun with indistinguishable beat cops in matching uniforms, EMTs packing up their equipment, medical examiners with apathetic faces, and homicide detectives in cheap suits holding clipboards and asking questions.

Everyone was busy doing a job, but Eloise's stomach revolted as she watched them move around with such apathetic efficiency. This was routine to them, crossing paths with death simply something they did between cups of shitty work coffee, but Eloise had never stared down at the shell a person left behind, especially not a person that she'd known personally in life.

Would they have examined her body with such curious indifference if they'd seen her while she was still alive? Seen those incredible eyes of hers bright and shining on a summer afternoon and not dull and glassy and staring endlessly up at a cloudy, rainswept sky?

"And you're sure you didn't see anyone else around when you arrived, Ms. Mason?" The detective, whose name Eloise had already forgotten, was watching her closely as she wrote down the answers to each of the questions she'd asked Eloise so far. She seemed young for a homicide detective, small and thin and with the faintest edge of a Chinese accent, but there was a calm look of determination in her eyes. She didn't look like the type to let off of a goal once she'd set her mind to it, which Eloise supposed was useful in her line of work.

"No one," Eloise confirmed. "It was raining, and I wasn't really looking around. I was watching the sky because there was some lightning and I was worried I wouldn't be able to get into the building."

"And the body was exactly as it is now when you found it?"

"I think so." Eloise glanced in the direction of the medical examiners, huddled around Kim as they collected evidence or whatever it was they did in these situations. "I tripped over her and then, when I realized ... I don't know. I checked, you know? To see if she was breathing?"

"But you didn't call 911 immediately?"

Eloise took a shuddering breath. It felt like a trap, but she'd already admitted as much to the dispatcher, so what else could she do now but tell the truth? "No, I didn't. Kim, she was ... It looked like she'd been hurt. She had bruising on her neck," Eloise stopped and placed a hand on her own throat to indicate, waited for the detective to nod her understanding, "and I thought, maybe whoever hurt her might still be around."

"You were frightened?"

"Yes, I was. It probably sounds pathetic but I was scared so I ran back to my car and called for help once the doors were locked."

"And you didn't see those two," the detective gestured to

Sarah and Chloe, each standing several feet away and talking to different detectives, "until after the arrival of the first police cars?"

"I didn't even know they were here," Eloise admitted, although she should have realized. The parking lot was virtually empty of cars on the weekend, even though they shared a lot with the office building on the other side of the street, but she hadn't noticed their cars. Maybe she would have, if it hadn't been for the storm and her own preoccupied thoughts, but she knew it looked strange that she hadn't. "I was distracted," she finished lamely.

"By the storm?"

"And some personal concerns. I was just trying to get into the office, grab some paperwork I'd forgotten about, and go home."

"And Ms. Campbell, she was a coworker in the building?"

"Kim was a friend," Eloise corrected. "We both worked for Sun Valley—different departments—but there aren't a lot of women working here so we tended to stick together."

"I understand that," the detective muttered and Eloise, her gaze taking in the number of men wearing badges around them, figured she did. "And them?" She gestured again to Sarah and Chloe.

"The same," Eloise said with a nod. "We were all close."

"And to your knowledge did Ms. Campbell have any enemies? Coworkers with a grudge? Ex-boyfriends?"

Eloise shook her head. "No, I don't think so. She dated occasionally but there was no one she'd had problems with. No recent breakups or unusual drama. Kim was sensible and careful about who she spent her time with."

"And the coworkers? Sometimes those boys' clubs don't like it when women start coming around, taking their promotions and such."

"I don't think so." Eloise paused, arms wrapped around

herself to hold in the sorrow and anxiety. "We've always got people making snide comments or saying something inappropriate, but I can't think of anyone that stands out. She hadn't gotten a recent promotion or had a bad interaction with anyone, unless she kept it to herself."

"Had she been acting like herself lately? No changes in routine or personality?" Eloise hesitated a little too long and the detective narrowed her eyes. "Ms. Mason?"

"She'd been stressed the past few weeks. Work hasn't been great on anyone and Kim worked in the auditing department so she wasn't exempt from that."

"Auditing, huh? So, her job was …?"

"To go over the accounts, make sure everything was normal and there were no discrepancies."

"What would happen if there were discrepancies?"

Eloise frowned. "She'd have to investigate it. Usually, it's an error of some kind, maybe someone gets reprimanded or even loses their job."

The detective tapped her pen against the clipboard. "And what if it's not an error? What then?"

"You mean, what if someone was purposefully putting in the numbers incorrectly?" Eloise wrestled with the idea of that, against the thought of someone in their company being that foolish. "That would be embezzlement and I suppose she'd have to report it, and the bank would notify the police."

"That's a powerful motive for murder."

"I suppose, but there are several people that work in the auditing department. Even if someone was attempting to steal money from the bank, they'd have no way of knowing that Kim was the one going over the accounts involved."

"Well, it's something to think about," the detective said, a tight smile telling Eloise she hadn't dismissed the idea as a possible motive. "I think I've got everything I need from you for now, but I need you to stay close over the next few days, just in case I have more questions."

"Am I a suspect?" Eloise cleared her throat when the detective lifted an eyebrow. "I mean, since I found her? That's how it works, right? So, I was just wondering if that makes me a suspect."

"Not officially." The detective tipped her head, gravity and the wind doing nothing to disturb the smooth black bun confining her hair as she stared at Eloise. "You're a person of interest because you found the body, but I doubt it will take long to move on to more likely candidates."

She'd known, but it was hard to hear it. Kim had been important to her, someone that she'd felt safe and happy with. To have others think she could have ended Kim's life, to believe even for an instant that she was capable of that level of violence, of betrayal, was enough to make her sick.

"Here's my card." The detective handed over a thin white business card with the police station logo and a name emblazoned on the front. *Detective Amanda Chen.* "Call me if you think of anything else that might be helpful."

"Thank you, Detective Chen."

"Once your friends are done giving their statements, you can all go home. We'll take care of notifying the family."

"They live here in New Orleans." And when Detective Chen merely lifted a brow, "Her parents." Eloise had never met them, but she knew from talking to Kim that they were close. The kind of parents that called often and expressed genuine interest in her life. What would a loss like this do to them? A dead child and no answers?

She was still pondering that, the depth of the tragedy and the inability to find closure, when Chloe and Sarah waved her over. They were alone and apparently done with giving their statements.

"We told them the truth, you know? That we hadn't seen

anything," Sarah said. Her hands were shaking, and she wrapped her arms around herself as she spoke. "Not until after we came down and found you."

"They asked if the two of you had any problems," Chloe added. "I told them you didn't, of course."

"Detective Chen admitted I'm a person of interest for now, but she seemed more interested in Kim's job. She seems to think it might be related to her position in the auditing department, but I told her that was extremely unlikely. How would anyone even know she was going over their accounts?"

"I'm sure she'll figure that out soon enough." Sarah reached out and wrapped one arm around Eloise. "I'm sorry they're even considering you as a suspect. It's ridiculous to think it could be any of us."

Chloe shrugged but she still looked uneasy. "I guess they really *have* to consider all of us, at least to some degree. It seems so strange, doesn't it? That it might be someone we know?"

"How are we supposed to look anyone in the eye anymore, not knowing if they did this?" Sarah shuddered, the force of it wracking her whole body. "There's plenty of people here I've never liked, but to do this? Who? I guess, I don't know if I'd quite put it beyond Dwayne, but I always thought of him more as just a sexist ass than a murderer."

"They'll look at everyone and I'm sure they'll still go over her accounts," Eloise mused. "Just to be sure."

Chloe watched as Detective Chen and her partner stood beside the body and talked to the medical examiner. "Do you really think they'll go that far? Will Sun Valley even let them?"

"I'm sure they'll have to if there are no other leads and that detective seemed like the kind of person to get a search warrant for every receipt that's passed through Kim's hands in the last five years. I feel better knowing she's taking it seriously enough to follow up on every possibility."

"Of course." Sarah squeezed her tighter, a quick look passing between her and Chloe as she did so. "Chloe's going to stay at my house tonight. Do you want to come over? I'd hate to think of you being alone."

"Thanks, but I think I'd feel better at home."

"Be careful," Chloe warned. "The roads are still wet, and you're upset."

"I will," Eloise promised. Maybe it would have been smarter to leave her car there and take an Uber, or ask Ethan to come and drive her home, but she needed the time and the quiet to start putting her thoughts together before she could explain to anyone else what had happened.

Sarah and Chloe seemed to understand, and they didn't argue when she let them walk her to her car. They all held on a little tighter when she hugged both of them before she drove away.

The storm had blown out as quickly as it had rushed in, leaving no trace behind except the smell of damp soil and a humidity level that made it feel hot even with the car's air conditioning turned up all the way. The sun had fully set by the time she exited the highway and pulled into her neighborhood, the stars a blanket of flickering lights on the milky dark blue of the sky.

She had mostly stopped shaking when she pulled into the driveway and the only sound that greeted her when she opened the door and stepped out into the night was the incessant chirp of the crickets and the odd, echoing screams of the cicadas in the trees.

If she could just get inside and close the door behind her, she could text Ethan, tell him what happened and explain that she didn't feel like having company tonight. Maybe she'd lock herself in the bathroom and draw a tub of hot water. Fill it with lavender bath soap and let the warmth and the smell calm her. Hope it carried away the ache in her chest and the stinging pressure of tears behind her eyes.

She was on the porch when a flash of headlights let her know she wasn't alone on the street anymore and the familiar rumble of a car's engine had her pausing with her key in the lock. There was no way Ethan hadn't seen her, and it would only cause more questions if she tried to run inside now. Better to stay here and face him, get the questions out of the way now instead of texting him.

"Hey, you're getting home late. Have you eaten ..." He stopped halfway up the stairs, the question unfinished as he caught sight of her face in the yellow porch light. "You okay?"

Her resolve dissolved under the steady weight of his gaze and the first fat tear slipped over her lashes onto her cheek. "I went ...I saw ..." She hiccupped, a sob pushing its way up past her defenses. "Kim was there, and she was dead. She was just there on the ground, and someone had hurt her, and I couldn't help her, and I was so ... so *scared*."

It wasn't clear how much of it he understood through the sobbing and the fingers she had pressed to her mouth, but he didn't ask for any further explanation before wrapping her in his arms and tucking her head under his chin. He let her cry until she was able to control it enough for him to fumble with the key and get them both inside, and he stayed, without having to be asked.

"Have you eaten?" His lips skimmed her ear as he guided her to the couch, tucked a blanket over her shoulders and brushed the hair back out of her eyes.

"There wasn't time." She closed her eyes and tried not to picture the scene on the sidewalk. The detectives and their questions. Kim and her staring, vacant eyes. "I've been with the police for hours."

"Why don't you go upstairs? Run a bath while I make you something for dinner." He was searching her face with worried eyes and she knew he was trying to figure out how to fix something unfixable. Feeding her was probably the thing he could think of to keep his hands busy and provide some comfort.

"I wasn't going to ask you to stay." She sniffed and rubbed her eyes. They were sore and she knew she must look terrible after crying so hard.

"I know." He pressed a soft kiss to her mouth, offering only warmth and comfort. "I wasn't going to wait for you to ask."

It washed over her. A balm to the hurts of her day. There had never been anyone who cared about her that much as a child. She'd come to expect a certain amount of love and consideration from her friends, still a miracle in her mind, but she'd never believed she'd find it in a lover. Ethan had changed so much about what she thought was possible and had asked her to really look at what she wanted for herself.

"Thank you." She cupped his face in her hands, her heart aching with loss and gratitude and something else she wasn't ready to face. "I'm glad you're here."

Seventeen

E loise didn't wait for him to get settled in the kitchen before she made her way to the bedroom upstairs. He wasn't a great cook, but he knew his way around and he'd manage a plate of scrambled eggs or a few pieces of toast if nothing else.

Her head was still pounding, eyes puffy and nose sore from wiping it too many times. Small irritations, minor discomforts. Symptoms of living that had been taken from Kim.

The sorrow hit her again and pieces of the afternoon's events, broken and out of order, began to flash through her mind.

Eloise took a slow breath.

In through the nose.

Out through the mouth.

Repeat.

She let the images behind her eyes run their course as she stood in the doorway. By the time she could hear Ethan rattling pans around and swearing viciously in the kitchen below, she had almost gotten control of her emotions.

Now that she could hear him and smell faint traces of what she thought was bacon starting to waft up the stairway, she realized how hungry she actually was. He'd be up to check on her soon and if she didn't want him wasting time fussing over her bath, she needed to get moving. Keep her mind busy, focus on the next steps and nothing else.

She kicked off her shoes, aiming for the general direction of the closet and wincing when she realized she'd been too preoccupied to take them off by the door as she normally did. Socks went in the hamper, still wet from the rain and her puddle-filled run to the car. Her jeans were just as wet, still cold and clinging to her legs, so she stripped them next, rubbing her hands over her calves and shivering at the sudden change in temperature against her skin.

She was sure she made an odd sight scrambling for the bathroom in her underwear and the oversized hoodie she had stolen from Ethan for her quick run to the office, but she was more comfortable without the wet clothes she'd been stuck in, and she wasn't ready to give up the comfort of Ethan's scent until she had no other choice.

Steam curled up off the top of the water when she ran it hot, fogging up the mirror as she added every scented bath product she could find. She owned at least four bottles, all purple and smelling strongly of lavender. It was supposed to help with relaxation and she certainly needed something to help her calm down now. Maybe she could soak away some of her fear before Ethan finished cooking. She emptied her pockets, tossing everything on the white countertop. Keys from her left hoodie pocket because she'd forgotten to hang them on the hook by the door. Something that crinkled in her right hoodie pocket, something damp and unfamiliar.

Her fingers trembled as she pulled out the pack of cigarettes she had taken from beside Kim's body. In the chaos that had followed, she'd forgotten about them.

It seemed foolish now, that she'd taken the time to hide them when her own life might have been in danger, but she wasn't sure she would have changed it if she could have. It was something Kim would have asked of her, a small shame that her memory wouldn't have to hold for her family, and there was no harm in it.

Eloise stood for a moment, torn as she considered what to do with it. There was no reason to keep it and she had never been particularly sentimental, but to throw it away so soon after the loss, when they still had no explanation for why it happened or who had taken her from them, felt disrespectful.

She ran her thumb over the logo on the matchbook inside and called herself a fool as she sniffled and tucked it away in a drawer so Ethan didn't throw it out by accident. She'd deal with it later when everything wasn't so new and so raw. Until then, she turned her back on the drawer and tried to put it out of her mind as she stripped down the rest of the way and settled into the hot, scented water.

She sank down and closed her eyes, letting the tub fill all the way before shutting the tap off and then sitting in silence as tears slid silently down her cheeks. The water had started to cool when she heard Ethan coming up the stairs.

"Hey."

She opened her eyes and found him standing just inside the door, cradling a plate in one hand and a glass of wine in the other.

"Toast?" she asked.

"Toast, bacon, and some scrambled eggs," he confirmed. "All only slightly burned."

"You're improving."

He grinned at that and set dinner on the counter to hand her the towel she'd forgotten to grab off the hook. "Smells good in here," he remarked. "But look how pink you are. Did you try to cook yourself for dinner?"

She snorted as she grabbed the towel and used it to do a quick rub down before wrapping it around herself and picking up the glass of wine. The first sip soothed the ache in her throat, an explosion of bubbles and sweetness that she knew would carry away her pain if she let it.

"You should eat," Ethan reminded her, plucking a piece of toast from the plate and holding it to her lips. "You look pale."

"Hmm," she took a bite, a sad smile playing at her lips as she chewed. "Is that your way of telling me I look awful?"

"It's my way of telling you that if you'll go crawl into bed, I'll bring you this plate and your wine and when you're finished with it, I'll stay beside you, so you don't have to be alone."

"Damn you, Ethan."

He lifted a brow, unfazed by her as always. "You're going to get used to me taking care of you, even if you're not happy about it, and someday you're going to explain to me exactly why it pisses you off so much."

She opened her mouth, only to snap it closed again when she had no easy answer. How was she supposed to express her reluctance to let herself depend on him emotionally when all she wanted to do was curl into him and let him make her feel safe and protected?

"Not tonight," he said, dropping a kiss to her cheek before giving her another bite of toast. "Tonight, you're going to let me take care of you."

"You make things tough, but I don't have the energy to fight you right now."

"Lucky me," he said, the corner of his lips twitching. "Into bed with you."

She went, tucking the blankets around her and fluffing the pillows even as she eyed the plate skeptically. "Eating in bed gets crumbs in the covers, you know?"

"I think we can handle it this once," he responded calmly.

"I'll bring Winston up tomorrow and let him rummage around between the sheets."

"You will not." She scowled at him with a mouthful of scrambled eggs. "We can wash them like normal people. Speaking of Winston—"

"I already brought him over," Ethan said, anticipating her worry and hurrying to soothe her. "He's asleep in the living room."

"You can bring him up." She shifted uncomfortably and pointed to the corner of the bedroom where she'd installed the new dog bed she'd bought that morning. "I just ...Well, I thought he's over here a lot so he should have someplace to sleep."

Ethan tipped his head and looked at the bed. "Eloise, are you asking my dog to move in with you?"

"Not permanently," she said quickly. "I'm not trying to *steal him* if that's what you're worried about."

"I'm not the least bit worried that you'll steal my dog." And then after a moment of hesitation. "Maybe I should be, though."

"I won't steal him, I just never got to have a dog as a kid and then I thought I was too busy to have one, but Winston is so cute ..." She shrugged helplessly and wasn't at all surprised when he chuckled under his breath.

"I'll get him while you finish eating."

He returned with Winston curled in his arms a few minutes later, the pup limp and relaxed as Ethan lowered him into his new bed. "I swear he could sleep through anything."

Eloise smiled as soft puppy snores filled the room. "I'm jealous. I haven't slept that well in years."

"Not even with me in bed next to you?" He looked slightly offended as he moved the empty plate to the bedside table and climbed into what she was rapidly learning to think of as his side of her bed.

"It helps to have you here, but I've never been a good sleeper."

"Well, let's hope tonight's the exception." He pulled her close and tucked her head against his chest, her ear pressed to the steady rhythm of his heartbeat. "You need to rest, and I need to know you're okay."

"I'm as good as I could possibly be." She could already feel her eyes starting to droop as his warmth spread through her. "Thank you for staying with me."

"I wouldn't leave you here alone." He hesitated and then said, "Do you want to talk about what happened? I think I caught the gist of it but I'm a little fuzzy on the details."

She ran through the story as quickly and succinctly as possible and he stayed silent until she was finished. It was a simple thing, but she was grateful. Once she started, she didn't want to stop until it was over.

When she'd gotten the whole thing out, he squeezed her tightly and kissed the top of her head, like he could press the comfort straight into her where she needed it most. "I'm sorry."

"I know."

They stayed that way, in sad silence, until her tears dried. She was already almost half asleep, eyes drifting closed as he caressed her hair and the curve of her neck. Even as tired as she was, as awful of the day had been, the touch of his fingers on her skin made her nerves hum and she stretched into the sensation, opening herself to further exploration.

He seemed to know what she needed; long, slow, lingering trails of warmth and comfort that began at the base of her neck and ran like water over her shoulders and her arms and her spine. Each inch of her was slowly invigorated and brought back from the edge of sleep to the full humming throb of wakefulness, from the edge of death to the bright blooming awareness of life.

She wasn't sure if it was him that slid under her skin to carve the ache in her chest or the beautiful miracle that she wasn't lying dead and sightless on a rainy sidewalk, but suddenly she was no longer tired. Her body was a great gasping void, a hungry and energetic thing that needed to feast and fill itself with the experiences of living.

"Ethan."

She turned to him in the dark, seeking sex but somehow so much more, and finding an affirmation of her humanity, her existence, her desirability despite what she'd seen and the scars she'd now carry.

He gave her everything. Mouth hot and roving over her flesh as though he, too, was driven to consume. His hands were brands on the soft skin of her thighs as she bucked against the onslaught of his tongue.

They rolled, tangled in the sheets and each other as each of them became lost and insensible to everything else. She was drowning in him. His teeth on her shoulder. His fingers tangled in her hair. His hips pressing into her, sharp and bruisingly hard when he drove into her again and again. She took the pleasure and the edge of tingling pain, affirmations that she was here, and no one had managed to take that away from her.

Not now.

Not today.

With that thought, she let him take her under.

She woke sometime later, floating near the surface of her mind with a vague sense that something was wrong, until memory snapped back into place and with it the knowledge that Kim was gone.

It still didn't seem real, like a nightmare that she should be able to break free from. When she opened her eyes, her life should be the same as it was before, but somehow the opposite was true. It was only in sleep that the horror of what had happened could disappear for a short while and waking brought the return of the terrible reality and the hole in her heart.

Ethan was asleep, wrapped around her protectively with one arm thrown over her hip to hold her in place, and she struggled for a moment against the weight of him before she was able to wriggle free. She hadn't had anything to drink besides wine since that afternoon and thirst drove her downstairs, padding down the steps in Ethan's shirt and bare feet with a puzzled Winston following closely at her heels.

He was a sound sleeper, but he had woken the moment her feet touched the floor and flopped down with a yawn on the rug in front of the couch as he watched her grab a glass from the cabinet and fill it with cold water from the door of the refrigerator.

"What's the matter, boy? Did I drag you downstairs in the middle of your best sleep?"

He blinked at her in the darkness, unimpressed with her questions and their midnight excursions.

"Come on, then, let's go back upstai—"

A low rumbling growl cut her off as Winston jumped to his feet, ears cocked and head tipped as though listening closely to something that she couldn't hear.

"Winston?"

He barked, by far the loudest sound Eloise had ever heard him make, and sprang from his spot on the rug to the window nearest the front door. The glass rattled in its frame as he whined and scratched, furiously trying everything in his power to get to whatever he saw on the other side.

"No," Eloise scolded, certain he had caught the sound of a cat sneaking across the porch or a raccoon on its nightly search for accessible trash cans. "You're going to pull down my curtains."

She reached for his collar, her fingers going stiff as she

looked out the window and caught the shape of a man scrambling down her front porch steps into the darkness. Her heart leapt into her throat, and she dropped Winston's collar and slapped blindly for the front porch light. Whoever had been out there, she wanted them to know that there was more awake in her house than just a yapping puppy.

"Ethan!" She backed away from the door, glancing at it quickly to confirm the deadbolt was still locked safely in place. Before she could call up the stairs for him again, she heard him coming, running at full speed down the hall until he crested the top of the stairs and found her frozen at the bottom. "Someone was trying to get in."

She yelped when he cleared the last few steps in one jump and sped past her to pull back the curtains on the window Winston was still stubbornly trying to escape from.

"Hush," he said, the single word causing the dog to lapse into nervous but silent pacing as he watched Ethan double check the lock on the door.

Eloise glared at the pup for obeying so quickly when he'd ignored her entirely only a minute before. Clearly, they needed to have a conversation about loyalties and which of the pair of them was willing to slip him the occasional slice of bacon under the table.

"Did you see someone, or do you just think there was someone out there because of Winston?"

"I saw him." She shrank back away from the door, out of the line of sight of the window. "I came down for a glass of water and Winston started barking. I went to the window to grab him so I could take him back upstairs before he woke the whole neighborhood and there was someone on the porch."

"Could it have been a neighbor or—"

"No," Eloise interrupted, already shaking her head as she tried to picture what she remembered from the quick glimpse she'd gotten of him. "I know my neighbors and—"

"Wait here and keep Winston with you," he said briskly, cutting her off and bounding back up the stairs. When he came back a moment later he was wearing a black T-shirt and tucking a small handgun into the waistband of his pajama pants.

"*Jesus*, Ethan, is that a gun? In my house?"

"Only a little one." She sputtered as he gave her a firm look and gripped her chin in his hand. "You can yell at me later but for now stay inside and lock the door behind me."

He gave her a quick, soft kiss and with that, he was gone, and she was alone in the dark with Winston curled at her feet.

Eighteen

He was gone just long enough to make her worry before unlocking the door with a helpless shake of his head. "I didn't see anyone, and I recognized all the cars parked nearby. Whoever it was, they took off."

"Probably just looking for whatever they could find to grab off the porch. We don't get a lot of crime around here so people tend to leave things out that they probably shouldn't."

"Maybe." He didn't sound convinced, and he double-checked the locks on the doors and windows again before turning his attention back to her. "I guess I'm pretty glad you've decided to steal my dog."

"Borrow."

"If you say so."

She rolled her eyes and picked up the pup before climbing the stairs and heading back to the bedroom.

"I mean it," he continued. "I think it's a good thing he was here and I want him to stay with you until we figure this whole thing out."

"That's sweet but I'm really not trying to take him from you, and I don't think whoever did that is coming back.

There's nothing outside for him to steal and it looked like Winston really scared him."

"You trust too easily."

She put Winston in his bed and turned to find Ethan staring at her with a serious frown. "Look at that grumpy face," she teased, amused when he refused to crack a smile even when she crossed the room to him and stretched up on tiptoe to kiss each corner of his downturned mouth. "I trusted *you* and look how well that worked out."

"Eloise ..." Something flashed across his face, a glimmer of uncertainty that was quickly gone. She thought for a moment that he'd speak but instead he brushed a thumb over her lips and kissed her softly. "Let's go back to bed, okay? You've had a very long day."

Guilt and pain rushed over her when she realized that she had, for the space of perhaps half an hour, forgotten about the events of earlier in the day. The fright she'd gotten had completely wiped her grief from her mind, and it came rushing back, a crushing weight that settled on her chest and squeezed her lungs until she couldn't breathe.

Her smile faded and with it her playful mood.

"I'm sorry." He wiped a tear from her cheek and pulled her into his arms. "I didn't mean—"

"It's not your fault. I just *forgot*, somehow. I got distracted and I completely forgot for a few minutes that she was gone."

"Come on." He picked her up, one arm behind her back and one beneath her knees as he carried her back to the bed. "That used to happen to me. The forgetting thing? When my dad left and then later when my mom died."

"You remember when he left you?"

Ethan nodded. "Yeah, he left when I was young but I remember enough. He wasn't cut out for marriage and kids."

"But he *left* you," she repeated. Her parents had never been particularly warm but at least her father had stuck around. Helped pay the bills and attended the dance recitals and school open houses. Not enthusiastically, but he'd been there.

Ethan lowered her to the mattress and then climbed into bed beside her. "He came around for a while, dropped off a couple of birthday cards, but by the time she died, the social workers didn't even know where to find him. That's why I ended up next door with my grandfather, even though she hadn't talked to him in almost twenty years."

"You weren't happy there." He'd never said as much, but he'd lived there for weeks, and the house was still barren of everything except furniture. There were still no photos, no personal touches, and he spent most of his nights at her house instead of asking her to come to his.

"We didn't get along and that's an understatement." He kissed the top of her head, holding her close as he spoke. "He wanted me to forget her, and I couldn't do it."

"I just can't seem to picture it." She paused and chewed lightly on her bottom lip. She'd only known his grandfather for a few short years but he'd been kind to her. "He seemed like such a nice old man when I talked to him. It makes me a bit sick to think he could be so cruel to you and I would never have suspected he was capable of such a thing."

Ethan laughed but there was no amusement in the hollow sound. "I guess he could be nice enough when it suited him and, hell, maybe I was the problem. Sixteen and angry at the world. He got sick of my shit and called the cops regardless of whose fault it was, and they shipped my ass off to juvie."

"I'm sorry." She wanted to hold him, to pull him and erase the haunted look in his eyes. "I don't understand how anyone would do that to a child."

"He was the one who called them but I was the one who threw a punch at a cop so I guess it took both of us."

"I thought my parents were bad, but I can't imagine

anything like that happening at my house." It made her uncomfortable to think of it and realize how simple her own family problems were. What was apathy in the face of what he'd had to endure?

"You had a different set of problems," he said, easily sensing the direction her thoughts had gone and brushing that aside, "but that doesn't mean it didn't hurt you. I've seen how upset you are when your mom calls and it's not pretty."

"We make quite the pair, don't we?"

He hummed an agreement. "A little ragged edge never hurt anyone." She didn't think that was true, but his eyes were already drifting closed and she let him slip into a still sleep with his heart beating softly beneath her hand as she contemplated his words. Sometimes ragged edges were soft and frayed, like a rope that was slowly coming unraveled. And sometimes it was a piece of shattered glass, sharp and dangerous to anyone foolish enough to handle it.

Eloise was pretty sure she was the soft and frayed kind. A little worn from too much rough handling, sure, but unlikely to hurt anyone. She wanted to believe Ethan was the same, but broken people were hard to judge, and she'd caught enough bitter anger in his story to know he'd been hurt—and badly.

Time would tell, or so her mother had always insisted.

As much as Eloise hated to take her mother's advice on anything, it seemed there was little choice in her life these days. Nothing but time would reveal Ethan's truest self to her and nothing but time would bring Kim's killer to justice.

The darkness in her bedroom deepened before it began to lighten with the dawn, and she slept fitfully until the first of the morning's birdsong finally lulled her into a deeper, dreamless sleep.

When she woke, the bed beside her was empty and the sheets were cold. Not all that surprising, considering one of them would have to have been awake at a decent hour to take the dog out, but several long minutes of careful listening didn't give any indications that Ethan or Winston were in the house. There was no music, and the TV downstairs was off. Nor could she smell any hint of breakfast being prepared in the kitchen.

"Ethan?"

She tugged on a robe and wandered downstairs, checking each room fruitlessly until she was convinced that he was indeed gone. It wasn't like him to leave and not say anything to her about when she could expect him to return.

When he didn't come back in the time it took her to pull on some clothes and eat a bowl of fruit and some yogurt, she gave in to her worry and picked up her phone.

Everything okay? You're usually here when I wake up.

She washed her dishes, dried them, and put them away before she let herself look.

I'm with Jackson and David. Could you come over here now that you're up? I didn't want to wake you.

It was a strange request, but she figured the best way to find out what was going on was to go over and ask them.

Be right there.

The front door was open when she got there and a quick peek through the screen showed Jackson waving her in before she even got to knock.

"There you are," David shot to his feet as soon as she stepped inside, his hug a little tighter than he usually gave her. "Ethan told us what happened yesterday, and we were so worried about you."

"I'm fine," she assured him. "Nothing to worry about."

"Mmm," Jackson hummed, somehow infusing the sound with the perfect mixture of doubt and concern. He was wearing a vibrantly pink button down this time, with a pattern of small yellow lemons. It was almost a comical combination with the serious look on his face. "That's not what Ethan told us this morning. You found a friend of yours killed at the place you work together and the same night there's a prowler outside your house?"

"Well, I highly doubt—" she began but David cut her off.

"You are not about to tell us that you don't think those things are related, are you?" The sleeves of his shirt were rolled up nearly to the elbow, like he had been working or thinking hard before she'd arrived. His dark eyes were direct and, though not unkind, more pointed than she was accustomed to.

"I *was* going to say exactly that actually." She looked over his shoulder to where Ethan was sitting on the couch, watching the whole event and trying to hide a smile. "A little help here? Since you started this?"

"No help from me." It wasn't exactly apologetic, and he met her eyes without any hint of remorse in his gaze. "I knew you wouldn't bring it up and even with Winston at your house, we still need a few more eyes on the place."

Eloise sighed and glared at Winston where he sat at Ethan's feet, watching them with curious eyes. "And you?" she asked. "Did you participate in this, too, you little traitor?"

"He can't be a traitor," David argued reasonably. "He's Ethan's dog."

"You were all supposed to be on my side," she grumbled.

"We are." Jackson passed a glass of orange juice into her hand and nudged her until she sat down on the couch. "We're looking out for your safety."

"What are you going to do?" She twirled the glass in her hands, suddenly uneasy that they all seemed to think she was in real, continuing danger. "I can call the cops just as well as you can."

"I'm sure you could," Jackson agreed. "And I can be at your house with a loaded gun long before they get here."

"You, too?" She looked to David for shock or surprise, but

his face was stern and unfazed. "Does everyone on this street own a gun except me?"

"This is Louisiana," David reminded her. "And we're an openly gay mixed-race couple *in* Louisiana. I'll be damned if some Bubba in a pickup truck is gonna roll up on us and he's gonna be the only one with a gun. We both served in the military before we met, and we know how to safely handle a weapon."

"I feel like I've stepped into the twilight zone." She set the glass of juice on the coffee table and pressed a hand to her queasy stomach. "Surely, it's not going to come to anyone running around here with guns."

"I don't think we can assume anything until we know for sure what's going on."

"Fine." She hated the waspish tone that reminded her of her mother, but she was already done with the three of them telling her what to do when they didn't know for sure that what happened the night before was even related to Kim's death. "But we're going to call the detective I met yesterday and let her know. Maybe there's something she can do."

"That's a better idea than just having random cops roaming around the neighborhood," Ethan agreed.

"No objections?" David and Jackson both shook their heads, and she pulled her phone out of her pocket. "I'm glad I kept her number yesterday."

The men sat in silence as she had a brief but unhelpful conversation with Detective Chen that left her feeling frustrated and embarrassed.

"No luck?" Ethan asked when she hung up.

"No, she said if I think there's someone trying to break in I should call 911 but they don't have any leads on Kim's death. Without some kind of theory as to why her murderer would have turned their attention to me, there's not much she can do except advise caution and ask me to call back if I have more information."

"There was no evidence of anyone snooping around outside, was there?" David looked back and forth from Ethan to Eloise and waited for them both to shake their heads. "Without some evidence that someone was outside, I doubt there's any way for us to even begin to figure out what they were after and there's nothing for the police to go on either."

"I don't think I'm at all prepared to do that kind of investigation, anyway," Eloise admitted. "I was terrified yesterday, and I don't want anything to do with whoever did this to Kim."

"We're not going to go looking for trouble," Ethan said. "I just want to make sure we're prepared if trouble comes looking for you. If what happened to Kim is related to someone showing up at your house last night, it might mean you know more than you think you do about her death."

"I don't know anything." She looked from Jackson to David, afraid she'd see suspicion on their faces. "I would never hurt her."

"That's not what I mean." Ethan reached across the space between them to grab her hand. "It could have been something as simple as a paper you signed or a conversation you overheard. Anything that would make them suspect you could figure out who they are, and you don't even have to remember it. As long as they believe you know it, you could be in danger."

"Oh, God." Eloise picked up her juice glass and drained the contents to wash the taste of terror out of her mouth. "What am I going to do?"

"Let Jackson and David keep an eye on the house," Ethan said patiently. "And while we wait to see what happens, you should check in with Chloe and Sarah. See if they've noticed anything strange or if it's just you."

"I should have called this morning to check on them and I didn't even think to." Eloise fumbled for her phone, worry for her friends overriding the worry she felt for herself. "I can't believe I'm that selfish."

"You're not selfish." David hugged her and got up to refill her glass. "You went through a lot yesterday. You're allowed to be a little shaken up."

"He's right," Ethan agreed. "Cut yourself some slack. None of what you've gone through is easy, especially not the idea that the next target might just be you."

Nineteen

"Wait." Sarah's voice on the phone was tired and thin, but there was her usual thread of steel winding through it. "Someone tried to break into your house?"

"Yeah." Eloise rubbed the bridge of her nose and shook her head when Ethan held up a bottle of wine and gave her a questioning look. She'd already agreed to order pizza for lunch, but she wasn't going to start drinking before noon, no matter how bad the last twenty-four hours had been. "I couldn't believe it after everything that happened yesterday."

"That's so scary. Did you get a good look at their face? Call the cops?" There was an edge of panic now that made Eloise almost wish she hadn't mentioned it.

"No, I didn't see anything well enough to recognize him if I saw him again but I'm okay and he didn't take anything."

"And the cops didn't find anything?"

"Ethan went out, but he didn't see anyone and there was no way to prove what I saw, so we didn't think it would do any good to call them."

"Well, I'm glad he didn't take anything and you're okay. I don't know what I'd do if something happened to you, too."

Sarah sounded so relieved, so fragile in her recent grief, that Eloise decided to not to worry her further by mentioning Ethan's theory that the attempted break-in might be related to Kim's murder.

"I'll be careful, and I want you and Chloe to do the same. Maybe we'll find out soon what Sun Valley plans on doing about the security issues at the building. If you find anything out, let me know."

"I will." She hesitated a moment, then cleared her throat. "Do you think we'll hear something about her funeral soon?"

Eloise closed her eyes and took a deep breath as a wave of grief washed over her and settled in her chest. It felt like her heart would collapse under the weight of it. "Probably."

"I thought so." Sarah sniffed and her voice was suddenly wet with tears. "I guess I'll see you at the office tomorrow."

"Yeah."

It seemed impossible that the world would simply go on as it had been. Monday morning would come, and her coworkers would return to the office, all of them walking past the place where Kim had taken her last breath as they scurried toward the elevators and the day's second cup of coffee.

"Everything okay?" Ethan asked when she hung up and wandered back into the kitchen. The pizza had arrived, and he was already setting slices out on plates for both of them.

"They're okay. Nothing strange happened to them last night, so for now I guess we can assume that either the two things are unconnected or whoever it was is only after me."

She bit into a slice of pizza and frowned. It was her usual from the pizza chain with a location closest to her house, but disappointing after their trip to Paula's. Green olives. Who knew?

"He might be after them next," Ethan said. "Just because he came for you first, doesn't mean they're safe."

"I know but we don't have any proof that this had anything to do with Kim and I couldn't bring myself to make them worry any more than they already are."

"I hate this. I'm not the kind of guy to sit around and wait for someone to make the next move, especially when something as important as your life might be on the line."

"Oh." Eloise set her pizza down, her stomach revolting at the sudden memory of Kim's eyes, looking back at her unseeing. "I didn't realize ... Somehow I guess I thought maybe he could have been looking for something or trying to scare me. You think he actually might have wanted to ..."

She couldn't say it. The words died on her lips, fading away into nothing as the fear of it hung in the air so thick, she wondered if Ethan could feel it.

"It's possible." Ethan crossed the kitchen and put his arms around her. "We know he's capable of killing and if he thinks you might be able to figure out who he is, he might be willing to do it again to protect himself."

"And there's nothing the police can do about it, because we have absolutely nothing to go on and no suspects."

"Well, whoever it was, has to be close enough to her to know you were friends with her. They'd either have to already know where you live or have been around yesterday to follow you home."

"That would narrow it down to people we work with," Eloise said, quietly puzzling out the implications. "Or that he actually was waiting around there yesterday when I found her. I honestly don't know which idea is more upsetting."

"There's not much we can do about it if it was someone that only knew Kim and followed you home, so let's focus on the coworker idea and see if there's anyone that might stand out. At the very least, it could be information to pass along to that detective."

"I can try but it's like I told the detective yesterday—I really have no idea who it could be. She didn't have any enemies or rivals and she wasn't the kind to get into any kind of trouble."

"You'd be surprised what people hide," Ethan said simply. He didn't elaborate but it didn't take much for her to read between the lines.

Everyone had secrets.

Even Kim.

And, Eloise realized, everyone was willing to cover for others under the right circumstances. She thought sadly of the pack of cigarettes she'd shoved in the drawer upstairs and the night Ethan had come to her, bleeding and desperate for her not to call the police.

She'd covered for both of them, taken their secrets and their explanations and tucked that information aside to protect them.

"Okay," she agreed. "So, we assume she had secrets and she was covering up something for herself or someone else?"

"It could be that or it could be that she had stumbled onto someone else's secret, and she'd decided not to keep quiet about it. What department did she work in?"

Eloise sighed, having already covered this ground with the detective and her friends. "Auditing but there's no way for anyone to know she was the one going over their accounts."

"Unless she went to them and told them what she'd found. If she thought she could convince them to come clean about whatever they'd done."

"That does sound like something she might do." Eloise considered it as she chewed, aware of Ethan's eyes on her face as the seconds ticked by in silence. It was as though he was waiting for her to elaborate and she finished lamely, "Kim always believed the best in everyone. She wasn't the kind to cause conflict but she would have wanted to give them the chance to do better."

"So, maybe she found out someone was up to something and instead of taking the chance she was giving them, they killed her for it. If you had to guess, who would you think was capable of something like that?"

"I wouldn't like to think anyone I know is capable of that."

He rummaged around in a kitchen drawer until he came out with a pen and pad of paper, then leaned on the counter and waved an encouraging hand. "Come on, start with the biggest assholes you work with, and we'll go from there."

"You're making a list?"

"Do you have a better idea?"

"No, but I don't think there's enough potentially murderous assholes to warrant a whole list."

"Eloise."

"Fine," she huffed. "I guess the first person that comes to mind is Sarah's boss. His name is Dwayne and he's an asshole."

Ethan nodded and wrote the name down on his list. "What kind of an asshole? Strict about deadlines kind of asshole or—"

"The sexist kind of asshole," she clarified. "The kind that is always saying something inappropriate and touching you in ways that make you uncomfortable."

Ethan wasn't writing anymore and the look on his face was hard and cold. "He did this to you?"

"He's done it to everyone."

"Well, let's mark that down here." There was a forced note of lightness in his tone that made her shiver. "Even if he's not a murderer, it sounds like he needs an explanation on how to treat people."

"We're only worried about the possible murder part."

"*You're* only worried about that part," he argued. "*I'm* worried about you. So, does this guy have the ability to get into trouble with the auditing department?"

"Yeah, he does. He handles a lot of accounts and is responsible for moving a significant amount of money around."

"Sounds like an ideal suspect to me but we should keep going and see if there's anyone else that comes to mind. The more thorough our list is, the more help it'll be to the detective."

"I know you're probably not too thrilled about the idea of working with the police. Not after what happened when you were a kid and, well, to be honest, I'm pretty convinced you get up to some shady things when you're with Dylan—"

"Hey, I'm—"

She held up a hand to ward off his denial. "Don't lie to me. I think we're a little beyond that now. I just wanted to say thank you, for what you're doing to help me."

"I'm going to keep you safe." He kept his eyes steady on hers and he looked calmer and more determined than she'd ever seen him. "You know that, right?"

She covered his hand with hers, linking their fingers and holding on tight. "I know. I don't think there's anyone else I'd trust more to get me through this."

He kissed her softly, mouth tender and full of what might have been promises he wasn't ready to make out loud, and then leaned his forehead against hers. They stayed that way, taking solace in a brief moment of connection, until he cleared his throat and reached for the pen again.

"Okay, let's finish this up and see what we've got to work with."

She spent more than an hour going over every person she worked with, or at least all the ones she could think of, rating them on proximity to Kim and how likely they were to have access to something that might have raised a red flag for her. There were many possibilities, but even after an exhaustive listing, none seemed as promising as Dwayne.

"I can call Detective Chen back and let her know," Eloise told him as she picked up the list and scanned the list of names. "It might at least give her a place to start, though she'd still have to go over all of Kim's files and see if she can match it to any kind of suspicious activity."

"Do you think the bank is going to cooperate?"

"Knowing what I do about the company?" She paused for a moment and shot him a disgusted look. "Absolutely not. They *should*, obviously, but I don't trust the higher ups to do the right thing. There's a lot of restructuring right now and downsizing rumors have been going around for a while. We weren't given an official explanation but people are getting suspicious that the company isn't doing so well. I think whoever makes those decisions is going to be more concerned about someone coming in and revealing possible discrepancies than they will be with helping to solve Kim's murder. If something illegal was going on right under their noses, that can't look good to our shareholders, right?"

"That's pretty heartless." He looked surprised, his brow furrowing as he considered her explanation, and something inside her twisted uncomfortably. Ethan didn't exactly run with the most empathetic crowd and it was eye opening to see him respond critically to her prediction.

They all knew how little an individual employee meant in the grand scheme of company profit and it was odd to see that questioned when for how long it had been simply a fact. Just another unpleasant reality in the midst of so many others. Had she grown numb to being treated as though she were disposable? She didn't know how to respond to his observation so she nodded silently and looked away.

"She'll need a warrant, then," Ethan continued. He looked like he had wanted to say more about the company but had decided against it. "Which will take time because they'd have to have enough evidence to convince a judge the murder is likely connected to her job. They need more to do that than just suspicion or our gut instincts so it's assuming a lot that she can get one at all."

"A woman was murdered." Eloise forced the word through stiff lips. It was true, but it was no easier to say now than it had been the day before. Not just gone, taken from them. Stripped from the world and people who loved her years before her time and there was only one person who could possibly know why. Surely a judge would do anything necessary to see that her killer was brought to justice.

"Yeah, but there's no hard evidence that it had anything to do with her job, just our suspicions. A judge isn't going to hand out a warrant based on speculation." His tone was patient enough to rub her just the wrong way, like he was talking to a child with too much optimism and not enough experience to temper it.

The warm feelings she'd had toward him a moment before vanished on a thin twist of resentment. "How would you know what a judge does?" she asked, though she knew the answer already. She knew how important it was for those who broke the law to understand everything they could about how to avoid getting caught in it, and the momentary meanness that surged in her wanted him to admit it. It wasn't fair to blame him for telling her the truth but there was no one else to blame. Lashing out at him wasn't going to improve their situation, of course it wasn't, but it made her feel better in the moment to see his eyes narrow at the bitter edge in her question.

"Sometimes it pays to know how the system works." He threw it down between them, a deliberate challenge that she recognized even as his voice stayed level. He'd sensed the change in her, the anger shifting aimlessly below the surface, and had given her the opening he knew she was looking for.

"I know you feel like you owe Dylan, but he's going to end up ruining your life," she said, layering sweetness into her voice as she returned his bitter truth with one of her own.

He absorbed it with nothing more than a flicker of his gaze. "Let's worry about saving your life first, then we can worry about who's ruining mine."

Eloise hissed a breath between her teeth, the anger she couldn't unleash writhing inside her. "I hate this."

"Me, too." He ran a tired hand over his face and some of her anger abated as she noticed the dark circles under his eyes and the small tremor in his fingers. "I don't want anything to happen to you and I feel like we're running in circles today with no clear way to keep you safe. "

"We've done everything we can." It was a weak attempt at providing solace, but there was nothing else she could think of that might help. "We'll give the list to Detective Chen and let her do her job."

"I'm on board with giving her the list but I don't like the idea of relying on her entirely. No offense to her, I'm sure she's as good of a cop as the next one—" his voice was strained as he said it "—but I don't have a lot of faith in them as a whole." He glanced out the window, toward the house he'd lived in with his grandfather and she wondered what memories he was reliving. "What I'd really like is to get into Kim's office and see what kind of dirt we could dig up."

Eloise laughed softly and held up a hand to stop him before he could get too carried away with that line of thought. "There's no way you're getting into that office. You're not even getting into the building. And even if you somehow did manage to get in there, your face would be all over the security footage."

"Maybe you could—"

"I couldn't. I wouldn't."

Ethan was determined but even the thought of trying something like that made her nauseous and lightheaded. "If I got caught, I'd lose my job."

"Okay." He wasn't happy about it, and the little tick in his cheek told her he was working his jaw as he thought it over. Ethan wasn't the kind to let things go without a fight, but she was relieved when he seemed to decide not to push it for the moment. "We'll do it your way for now."

Twenty

Eloise and her grief were afloat on an endless sea of black. She had been dreading Kim's funeral since the details had been announced but after a week of dragging herself into the office and being forced to behave like nothing had changed, it was a welcome relief to find herself surrounded by other people with tear-stained faces and broken hearts.

She'd come alone, not wanting to drag Ethan to a place of mourning for someone he barely knew, but Sarah and Chloe had waved her over to a seat beside them as soon as she'd finished giving her condolences to Kim's family.

Eloise sat beside her friends and watched Kim's inconsolable parents as they cried through the service. She had never met them before today, but it was immediately apparent that apart from the slope of her nose, which she had gotten from her father, Kim had been the spitting image of her mother. The same green eyes. The same red hair. The same gentle smile.

It had been disconcerting, looking at Kim's mother and seeing the ghost of her friend looking back at her. Laugh lines

Kim would never have. Gray hairs she would never get the chance to complain about.

It was a stark contrast to the pictures they showed of her as a smiling little girl with a gap-toothed grin and her hair in pigtails. Her parents had held her as a baby, eyes tired and hearts full of hope. They had seen her off to her first day of school and prom and then to her first apartment. Each step on the road to a full and happy life. Had they worried about her? Feared that she might never get the chance to chase the dreams she'd told them about?

The coffin at the front of the church must have been the culmination of every nightmare they'd ever had as parents and Eloise shuddered as she looked at it. It was shut and draped in white and pink flowers, but she knew what was enclosed within it.

She saw Kim's blank stare every time she closed her eyes.

The last speaker finished talking and people began to mill about as they prepared to move from the church to the burial site.

"Are you okay?" Sarah whispered and Eloise nodded, wiping the tears from her cheeks with a little more force than was necessary.

She was tired of crying. Tired of aching and feeling broken, split open and vulnerable with every breath. The fear had only grown as the days passed, even though there had been no more attempts to break into her house, because there had also not been any steps taken closer to finding Kim's killer.

Her phone call to Detective Chen had been met with polite gratitude but nothing more—there was physical evidence at the scene but it would take months to process—and as far as she and Ethan could tell, no search warrants had been executed on Kim's office at work.

"Do you want to ride with us?" Chloe was hesitant as she

stood at the end of the church pew. "We can bring you back here afterward to pick up your car."

"I'll be okay." Eloise sniffed and tried to smile. "I could use a few minutes of quiet."

"We'll see you there, then, if you're sure you don't want to go together." Sarah was less hesitant and Eloise thought she heard a note of relief in her voice. It had been this way since the day Kim was killed. The two of them together, standing just outside her own circle of loss and shock.

They had all loved their friend, but Eloise was the only one that had been forced to see the way death had stolen the color from her cheeks. The only one who knew that the sight of those bruises on her neck could put a fear into your heart that made it impossible to move.

The small crack she'd sensed between them in the days leading up to Kim's murder had grown into a chasm, and she didn't know how to reach them now.

"I'm sure," she assured them.

Sarah's eyes were hidden behind the black veil she wore with her tiny, fashionable hat but she sniffled and dabbed at her wet cheeks with a white handkerchief as they walked away, and Eloise felt her heart tremble. She hated leaving them alone in their grief, but she already felt like her own was deep enough to drown in.

The short drive to the cemetery gave her time to clear her thoughts, to push the intrusive images out of her head and try to pull together what she should say to them, but the words vanished as she stepped out of her car and saw them huddled together beside Kim's grave. A fresh wave of pain washed over her and with it a surprising spark of anger.

They had each other and somehow, by losing Kim, it seemed she was losing them, too. She greeted them quietly and they responded with polite smiles, but the connection between them was strained and thin.

There were birds chirping in the trees when they lowered Kim's casket into the ground and afterward, that was all Eloise could remember. Her friends and Kim's family had drifted away into the background, and she'd cried, silently and more alone than she'd ever felt before, while butterflies flitted from flower to flower, and the breeze danced among the branches.

She jumped when the first shovelful of dirt hit the top of the casket, body taut and emotions drawn painfully tight. There was a limit to what she could endure for the sake of saying goodbye and she moved as quickly as she could once the first mourners turned toward their cars.

"Eloise, wait!"

Chloe and Sarah were hurrying toward her, and she paused as she reached the line of cars parked beside the narrow lane that wound through the rows of tombstones. It was a beautiful place, quiet and peaceful, but she felt an itch under her skin, the urge to flee making her fingers twitch. Kim would be here forever, and whatever Chloe and Sarah wanted to talk about, it could wait until Eloise was somewhere as far from here as possible.

"Maybe we could talk about this later?" She tried her best to give them a tight smile as she reached for the car door. "I'm not feeling well."

"We just wanted to make sure you were okay," Chloe said quickly, stepping in beside Eloise to block the door from opening. There was a crease of worry between her brows that did little to soothe Eloise's fracturing nerves. "You seem really upset."

"Not that we blame you," Sarah added. "After Kim and then that thing at your house the other night. It would be enough to make anyone unsettled."

"I'm not unsettled," Eloise corrected. "I'm terrified that the next time the two of you go to someone's funeral, it's going to be mine. I don't want you or my family to have to go through this."

"Nothing else has happened since then." Sarah reached for Eloise's hand and her fingers were cold despite the warm day. "I'm sure it's going to be fine."

"Yeah," Chloe agreed. "It was probably just a coincidence. I mean, there's no reason for anyone to be after you, right? You didn't see anything and there's nothing connecting you to whatever happened to Kim?"

Eloise didn't miss the questioning note in Chloe's voice and it grated on her already brittle patience. It wasn't the first time since Kim's death that one or the other of them had hinted that she might know more than she was letting on and though it would explain some of the strange distance between them, it reignited her anger.

"I told you I don't know anything," she said stiffly. It came out less kindly than she'd intended, and she wasn't shocked to see the look on Chloe's face change from guardedly friendly to frigid.

"Then I'm sure you have nothing to worry about." Chloe flashed a quick smile and moved away from the door. "We'll see you at work."

"Yeah." Eloise tugged the door open and slid behind the wheel. "I'm sure you will."

It had always been the two of them that were closest, so it shouldn't have surprised her when they walked away together, neither of them looking back as they went. Sarah had been Eloise's best friend, but she couldn't say that the same had been true for Sarah. They obviously thought she had something to do with Kim's death. Why else would they keep asking her about it?

They didn't trust her.

If it had been one of them that had found her, would she have trusted them? Eloise wanted to think she would have, that the bonds of their friendship went deeply enough that she would never have suspected them of something so heinous.

But she knew she'd never really be sure.

She drove home in a daze then sat in the driveway, trembling with sorrow and impotent rage until Ethan found her. The soft rap on her window startled her and she jumped, heart leaping in terror, until she recognized the exact shade of his hair and the puzzled frown on his familiar, plush mouth.

The tears that had been frozen inside her rushed out as relief chased the fear from her mind and she sagged against the seat, sobbing openly. Such a raw display of vulnerability in front of him would have shamed her only a few short weeks ago. Was it Ethan that had changed her? Or the shock of her loss and the subsequent fear?

He opened the door and unbuckled her seatbelt, welcoming her into a soothing embrace as she turned into him, seeking comfort in his strength and his warmth, the solid and steady beat of his heart and the faint smell of cologne.

"I knew I shouldn't have let you go to the funeral alone." There was a frightened catch in his voice, and he was running his hands over her subtly, checking for injuries as well as he could without letting her go. "Did something happen? Are you hurt?"

She could only shake her head, unable to catch her breath enough to explain the horrible mix of loss and anger that had overtaken her. It seemed like such a foolish thing to lose her composure over so completely, but she knew if she'd been able to get the words out, he wouldn't have judged her for it.

"Shh," he soothed. He pressed his lips to her temple then buried his face in her hair, tightening his grip when she only cried harder into his shoulder. "I'm here and I'm not going to let anything happen to you."

He let her go until she'd cried herself out of tears and her breathing evened out apart from a few small hiccups. She wiped her cheeks and subtly dabbed at her nose before pulling back enough to see him watching her in patient, albeit bewildered, concern.

"It was just the funeral in general," she explained with an embarrassed smile. "Seeing Kim's family so heartbroken and then Sarah and Chloe were there and somehow I seem to have become the outsider. I don't know what happened to us and I was so sad and then so angry ..." She didn't finish, unsure what to say or what the implications of it all might be. She'd crafted a perfect life and it had fractured, one blunt blow sending cracks running wild in unpredictable directions.

It was becoming apparent that the damage was worse than she'd thought and there was a growing worry nagging at her mind, one she refused to examine too closely, that she might not be able to fix it. That by trying she'd only cut herself on the pieces.

"Come on." He reached across the car and grabbed her purse before standing and holding out a hand for her to take. "Let's get you inside. You can change into something comfortable, and I'll put on a movie or something."

She let him lead her toward the front door but the thought of being inside, trapped and frightened of everything that moved or made noise outside, made her restless. "Could we do something else instead? We could go out to see a movie? Or just grab dinner? I don't want to be here."

He waited for her to cross the threshold before closing the door and locking it behind her. "I was actually on my way out." He met her gaze, but only briefly. "I've been putting it off, but I need to run by the bar and talk to Dylan."

"Oh." She knew he'd been home more lately, keeping an eye on her and the house, and she'd let it convince her that maybe he was pulling away from Dylan and whatever trouble the two of them got up to when they were together. Realizing it hadn't left her hollowed out inside like it had ripped out something important, though she wasn't sure exactly what it might be.

"Does it have to be today?"

He ran a hand through his hair, tugging a bit on the ends and puffing out a breath. "I don't want to leave you alone right now but—"

"I don't want to be alone."

"I tried to put it off but he's been pissed that I haven't been around lately and I need to deal with it. Maybe you could take a nap, get some rest, and I'll be back by the time you wake up."

The idea of being alone in the house, in their bed, with nothing but cold sheets and her own thoughts made her stomach turn sour. If he couldn't stay then she'd rather be anywhere but here. "I could go with you?"

"What?" He froze, hand on the doorknob and the familiar crease deepening between his eyebrows. "You want to go to the bar?"

She heard the doubt in the question, the slight tint of suspicion in his tone, and scrambled to come up with an excuse. Surely anything would be better than the truth—that she didn't want him around Dylan where she couldn't keep an eye on him because Dylan made her skin crawl.

"I just want to get out of the house," she said with a placating smile. "It's a bar, right? I could have a drink, play some darts or something?" That, at least, was true. She would welcome a drink and the distraction. "I mean, you said Dylan cleaned the place up after his dad died, so it should be safe?"

A muscle in his jaw ticked as he contemplated that, and she knew she had him pinned. He either had to take her or admit that Dylan's bar wasn't as safe and wholesome as he pretended it was. He'd never claimed to live a squeaky-clean life, but he'd deflected enough for her to know that he was up to more than he'd told her.

"Okay." He shrugged but wasn't able to hide the tension in his shoulders. "You can go if you want to, but you've met him, so you know how much of an ass he can be. I wouldn't expect him to be more respectful just because you're with me. The opposite, if anything, because he's always had a thing about relationships. His mom took off when he was a kid and he's been determined not to get seriously involved with anyone because of it."

"His parents got divorced so he makes a game of trying to drive off your girlfriends?"

"It's a little bit more complicated than that but I usually don't bring anyone around anyway. I don't typically get seriously involved, remember?"

She wanted to ask if he considered himself seriously involved with her, but the courage to ask was just out of her reach. Maybe another time, one when she wasn't already worn so thin that it felt like his response could shatter her like glass. She wasn't sure anymore which answer she preferred but she was absolutely certain she wasn't in any condition to be on the receiving end of the wrong one.

She knew she needed to keep her mind on her financial future, that her mother would be upset about her having a relationship, especially before she was higher up the ladder in her career, but somehow, he'd managed to work his way closer to her heart than she'd intended to let him get. He was kind and sincere despite his rough edges and his smile made butterflies flit in her stomach even now, after she'd given into temptation and let him do unspeakable things to her body.

She'd believed it was possible for her to keep her feelings out of it, but he'd worked his way into her bed and then made himself a part of life, part of her daily routine. He was there for her when she cried, when she was irritable or frightened. He was rapidly on his way to having seen the worst of her and, surprisingly, he'd never turned away.

"I can ignore Dylan easily enough."

He lifted a skeptical eyebrow at that, and she gave him an annoyed huff. "I really can, so just wait here and let me change. I'll be back down in a few minutes, so you won't be late."

"I'm already late."

She sped up, taking the stairs two at a time and unbuttoning the front of her dress as she went. "Then you won't be much later," she called, twisting to shout it over her shoulder and catching a glimpse of his amused grin. He might have been worried about Dylan saying something offensive to her, but if that smile was anything to go by, he didn't seem terribly upset at the idea of taking her with him.

That bolstered her mood and she felt much better as she sat in the passenger seat of his car and watched the world rush by outside her window. The trees were dappled and green beneath a cloudless blue sky and she was still alive. It washed over her, a rising swell of triumph and gratitude after the dreariness of the morning that left her with a weightless euphoria.

"If I'd known this was all it took to see you smiling again, I would have taken you out driving sooner."

"It's a nice day," she said, turning her attention from the view outside to his profile as he navigated traffic with practiced efficiency. She refused to look at the speedometer, knowing they were probably driving faster than the limit allowed, and let herself focus on the handsome lines of his face instead. "And I have good company."

He flicked a glance at her, one corner of his mouth turning up, and patted her knee affectionately. "I'm glad you're with me. I wasn't looking forward to dealing with this today and having to leave you at home alone."

"You worry too much."

"I don't think so." His expression hardened, something violent and protective flashing across it. "I know it's quieted down but you're still afraid—I can see it in your eyes—and I think your instincts are telling you the same thing mine are."

"It's not over."

"Exactly."

She mulled that over, now blind to the view that passed by, until the car slowed, and he turned off the road and into a gravel parking lot. Dylan's bar was set back on the property, nearly concealed behind a line of thick trees. Neon signs, pale and unlit in the daylight, filled the windows, advertising beer and liquors of various kinds. Above the entrance, a sign with chipped paint that had been dulled by years in the sun proclaimed it the Tough Break Bar and Grill.

Beside the name was an 8 ball with a crack down the center, an odd logo that was still familiar to her somehow, though she couldn't seem to recall where she'd seen it. She puzzled over it while Ethan parked the car before finally deciding she must have seen it on one of his T-shirts or something. As much time as he'd spent here, surely he had some kind of merchandise or promotional material. It made sense, but it didn't quell the unease that settled like a stone in the pit of her stomach.

Ethan parked the car and reached over to grab her hand, rubbing a thumb over her knuckles. She wasn't sure if he was trying to soothe her or himself, but she thought they both probably needed it. "Ready?"

She wasn't—Ethan had secrets and this was the place where most of them seemed to be buried—but she was here now so there was no turning back. Her pasted-on smile barely trembled as she reached for the door handle. "Ready."

Twenty-One

than figured he'd made a lot of mistakes in his life but bringing Eloise with him to the bar was probably in the top five.

It wasn't just that she stuck out like a sore thumb with her expensive shoes and perfectly manicured nails—though that was absolutely part of it—it was the sinking realization that she could never really be part of the life he had made for himself. It was watching her tiptoe her way to the bathroom with her nose scrunched in distaste. It was the way Dylan's eyes moved to follow her as she went and the too sharp edges on Sunny's smile.

Bringing Eloise around not just Dylan but also a woman he'd slept with—one that was still clearly holding a grudge—was unfair to her. She wasn't cut out for handling these situations and watching her try made a cold knot of dread tighten in his gut. He might as well have thrown her to the wolves, and it was too late to do one single thing about it.

"I can't believe you would do something this stupid." Myles turned to him as soon as she disappeared into the bathrooms at the back. His expression was skeptical and he whistled low under his breath. "She doesn't seem too happy to be here and Sunny hasn't even gotten her claws into her yet."

"I wasn't thinking," Ethan said, struggling not to sound ashamed of himself. He could admit that now, with Eloise out of the room and Dylan grabbing drinks from Sunny at the bar. It was only him and Myles at the table in the corner and the first time he'd been able to relax since he'd walked in the door with her behind him. "She wanted to come and there's been some shit happening at her house … It doesn't matter. I shouldn't have brought her."

Myles leaned in, casting a quick glance toward Dylan at the bar before speaking quickly in hushed tones. "I see the way you look at her and if you love her as much as I think you do, you'll get her the hell out of here as soon as you can. Not just the bar, but away from Dylan and the house and the whole mess he's made of our lives. You know how he is, Ethan. You know exactly the kind of bullshit he keeps us mixed up in and you want her around? Involved in that?"

"I'm not in love with her." It was reflexive, an automatic response that sounded flat to his ears and had no effect at all on Myles. "Besides, I know Sunny's not thrilled to see me bringing someone else around but she's not a serious threat. She's barely even a serious bartender."

"This isn't about Sunny …" There was no time to say more. Myles smiled blandly and let the warning hang as Dylan came back from the bar with several beers in his hand.

"If you wanted to set Sunny off, you've done a great job." He put the beers down, then patted Ethan on the back and grinned. "I haven't seen her this pissed since you broke things off with her."

"That's not why Eloise is with me." He honestly couldn't say why the hell he'd brought her. Had he really thought it could go any differently? That somehow he might be able to keep her as part of his life if he could figure out how to integrate her into the world he lived in? It seemed foolish and he was embarrassed now that he had ever let the idea cross his mind, however briefly. "She wanted to see the bar."

"And you let her." Dylan's grin became less friendly. "I've warned you about getting too involved with this girl, but I think living in that house again after all these years has fucked with your head. Maybe you should sell it and get out from under the house *and* the bitch next door."

"Maybe I like being under her." Ethan said it quietly as she came back into view, still tiptoeing but he could see the determined set to her jaw even in the dim light of the bar. Sunny said something to her as she passed, and he was half out of his seat before he could think better of it. He was too far away to hear the exchange between them, but Eloise tossed her hair over shoulder as she walked, and Sunny didn't follow. "She's something special."

"There's no such thing," Dylan said with a bitter laugh. "And even if there was, is this the life you want to drag her into? Does she know how you really got that gunshot wound? Maybe I should have a talk with her and find out—"

"Leave her alone." Ethan sat forward, his beer rocking in its bottle as it hit the tabletop.

"I didn't think so." Dylan didn't move, his confidence never wavering even in the face of Ethan's cold anger. "Take her home, do what you have to do to get rid of her, and come back on Saturday ready to start thinking about the next job. You're healed up and enough time's gone by that the heat should be off anyway."

Ethan pinned Dylan with a cold look as Eloise returned to the table. She gave him a quizzical glance, obviously picking up on some of the tension in the air, but he couldn't do anything more than squeeze her leg under the table and hope she took the hint to be quiet.

He'd been prepared to give his loyalty to Dylan for the rest of his life—if his grandfather's mistakes had taught him anything, it was the importance of unshakable loyalty—but he'd never actually expected Dylan to threaten him that way. If Eloise knew the truth, she'd leave him, and despite what he'd said to Myles about not loving her, he wasn't sure he was ready to see her walk out of his life.

He needed time and space to think, to plan his next moves and make sure that whatever he decided to do would keep her safe. She'd never said anything about her feelings for him, but he could see the way her face softened when she looked his way. If she wasn't in love with him yet, it was only a matter of time. The thought should have made him nervous, but he was starting to suspect he felt the same way about her.

He wanted her safe. Happy. And he was willing to do whatever it took to make sure that became the reality.

Twenty-Two

The next handful of days passed slowly, each one long and uneventful. The air hung hot and sticky as the summer dragged on. The sun rose early and stayed in the sky until well after Eloise had returned from work, baking the ground until the heat rose in waves and leaving all the hours in between as a time for sweat and short tempers.

She wanted to believe that the quiet meant her instincts had been wrong. That Kim's death had been a random, terrible act and her killer was no threat to any of them. But there was a tension growing in her mind, a weight centered in her chest and digging a trench between her shoulder blades, that told her something was coming. Detective Chen had no leads no matter how often she called to check and every day that nothing happened seemed to push them all closer to the day that something would.

Eloise went into the office early and left late, managing to avoid Sarah and Chloe entirely by eating lunch at her desk. They sent her a few texts to ask where she was when she didn't show up for their usual cafe lunch plans, but she brushed them aside, making excuses about needing to do more paperwork or not feeling well. The truth was, she just couldn't face another conversation with them like the last one. She might have understood why they looked at her with that glint of suspicion in their eyes, but it didn't make it any easier for her to accept it.

Besides, she had enough on her mind without them adding to it.

Ethan had been withdrawn since their trip to the bar and she'd let him pull away. She'd been irritated by the insulting comments Dylan had managed to interject into the conversation at every turn but the bartender had upset her the most. It didn't take any kind of sixth sense to know jealousy when it hit you in the face and the woman might as well have done exactly that during their brief interaction.

Eloise hadn't caught her name—Ethan had been painfully obvious in not introducing them—but she was young and pretty. More than that, she was blatantly sexy in a way that made Eloise feel bland in comparison. She had looked at them sourly when they'd come in together and had taken the first opportunity she saw to lean over the bar, eyes full of malice, and tell Eloise that she was nothing more than a replacement. A poor substitute for what she'd had with Ethan only a few months before. She'd broken up with him, she'd explained, and Eloise was simply a convenient rebound.

It had hit her right in every insecurity she had, knocking the breath out of her and leaving her numb and reeling for several long seconds. She'd glanced at Ethan—wishing perhaps to find the truth of his feelings for her spelled out in the air above him —and found him already rising to his feet with the expression of an avenging angel. It had steadied her and given her strength enough in the moment to simply smile and walk away.

It seemed likely that Ethan had been in some sort of

relationship with her and now that it was over she had a chip on her shoulder and had decided to direct all of her anger at Eloise, even though only the bartender had even known the two of them were in some sort of competition. That was irritating but, in Eloise's opinion, the woman's own problem to deal with.

What bothered her more was Ethan's lack of warning. She didn't expect him to have been a saint before she met him, but if he was going to take her around a former lover, it would have been nice if he had let her know in advance. He could have given her a chance to prepare herself instead of springing it on her in the form of venomous glances shot her way across a bar that was definitely *not* neutral ground.

The bar was *her* space, not Eloise's. She looked comfortable and at home in her tight-fitting red top and snug jeans, where Eloise had felt out of place as soon as they'd walked inside. She'd made an effort to be casual with jeans and flat, black shoes but she'd still been instantly at odds with the worn bar top and scuffed floors. The sweet scent of her floral perfume had curdled when it met the stale smell of cigarette smoke and spilled beer.

Ethan had slid right in, impossibly far beyond her grasp even as he sat beside her with his hand on her thigh. She'd thought she could pull him away from Dylan, make him see that whatever the two of them were up to, it wasn't worth the risk. She'd been a fool and learning that lesson had been humiliating.

It had hit her then, sitting in a corner booth of a mostly empty bar she never would have been in without him, that perhaps she had been nothing more than a distraction for him while he was healing. Maybe he'd never intended to let it be anything more than that. He'd warned her, hadn't he? That he didn't do long term commitments? She'd been grateful for that, worried about her own feelings getting too strong, but now the thought left her bereft.

She'd felt herself start to slip but that had confirmed it in a way that made it bigger and more frightening. When he'd pulled back, started creating space between them, she hadn't asked for an explanation or tried to hold him closer. He should have been relieved by that, but more than once she'd caught him ending a conversation with something that seemed like disappointment in his voice.

Well, that was just *fine* with her. Let him be disappointed. She had better things to do and more important things to worry about. No sense in letting him tie her up in knots when he could wake up and decide tomorrow that he'd rather be spending time with a pretty bartender. In fact, it would be best for everyone involved if he did exactly that.

That's what she told herself, anyway, as she watched him get on his bike and drive away. He hadn't said as much but she knew he was headed to the bar, back to Dylan and whatever the two of them were cooking up. Not that she *cared*.

She *didn't*.

Really.

Winston nudged her leg and she looked down to find him staring up at her with a look that could only be described as judgmental. It was like he could hear what she was thinking and knew it was a lie she was trying to tell herself.

"Nobody asked you," she mumbled, bending to give him a soft pat as her phone began to ring. "I know exactly what I'm doing."

He huffed, unimpressed, and flopped down at her feet as she looked at her phone screen and saw Chloe's name displayed. Her finger hovered and paused over the screen. It was tempting not to answer, but loyalty won out over the tension of the past few weeks.

"Hello?" She was met with the sound of muffled sobs, breathless and panicked in her ear.

"Hello? Chloe? Are you okay? Can you hear me?"

"Eloise?"

"I'm here." Eloise pressed the phone to her ear and tried to hear the words mingled amongst the crying. "What's wrong? Are you hurt?"

"Someone was here," Chloe managed to say. "They broke into my apartment. I think they're gone but ..."

"I'm coming," Eloise promised. She was already stuffing her feet into her shoes, scrambling around the living room looking for her keys. "Hang up and call the cops, okay? Get inside and close the doors until someone gets there."

"I tried to close the front door, but they kicked it in, and the lock doesn't work. I can't believe this is happening." She hiccupped hard and sucked in a new sob. "This wasn't supposed to ...Why would they come here?"

"Can you go to the neighbor's? Lock yourself in your car?"

"The car ..."

"Go to the car and call the police."

"Please don't hang up." The fear in Chloe's voice was palpable and Eloise wondered if this was how she had sounded to the 911 operator. Wild and panicked, searching for anyone who could save her?

"Just hold on." Eloise chanted it like a prayer, her vision blurred with tears and images of Kim's staring eyes playing across her mind. "I'm coming."

<hr>

Ethan didn't come back until well after dark and she was waiting for him when he did, barefoot and drinking wine straight from the bottle while sitting on her living room rug.

"Are you okay?" He looked around quizzically, taking in the disheveled state of her hair and the dog nestled close at her side.

"No." She took another drink and saluted him with the bottle. "Someone broke into Chloe's apartment today."

"Is she alright?" He hurried forward, brows scrunched with worry, until he towered over her. "Was she hurt?"

"She's fine." Eloise handed him the bottle and shook her head. "Terrified and she can't go back right now because they destroyed her front door so she's staying at her mom's right now."

"So, it wasn't just you they were after."

"Looks that way." He sank down beside her on the rug, and she leaned against his shoulder. She was still shaking from the wild drive to Chloe's and pissed off that she'd been summarily dismissed as soon as Sarah had arrived. She hadn't answered Chloe's calls but had come running as soon as she checked her messages. Once she'd arrived on the scene, Eloise might as well not have existed as the two of them stood around whispering and waiting for the cops.

She'd left as soon as the police arrived, feeling more like an intruder than a friend. There was nothing these cops could do, anyway. They were beat cops, there to take a report on a petty break-in and nothing more.

Eloise had called Detective Chen as soon as she got home, waiting impatiently for her to answer until she'd gotten her voicemail instead. She'd left a message, but it wasn't likely she would hear back anytime soon, and even if she did, they still had almost nothing to go on. It was looking more and more probable that the murder was connected to something happening at Sun Valley, but the pool of potential suspects was large, and the motives were in painfully short supply.

"What were you doing at the bar today?"

He hesitated, fingers flexing on the bottle before handing

it back to her. "Just needed to run some stuff by Dylan. He's planning to make some changes to the bar."

"Yeah?" She nodded and thumped the bottle down on the coffee table in front of them. The wine hummed in her veins alongside the anger that had been simmering there. Maybe it wasn't all his fault, but she was willing to pin it on him anyway. "That's bullshit," she said flatly, sniffing and running a frustrated hand over her face.

"Yeah." He didn't add anything else, no excuse to soften the blow. They both knew he was lying and he looked defeated, like he couldn't find the energy to pretend anymore.

"You're not even going to bother denying it?"

"Not much point." He pushed a stand of hair back out of her face and didn't flinch when she slapped his hand. "You're a smart woman, Eloise. I know we'll have to deal with Dylan and the rest, but for now ..."

"What?" She lifted her arms, opening them wide to invite an answer. "What else do you think we should be doing? There's nothing we can do about Chloe's apartment or what happened to Kim."

"We can stop waiting for this son of a bitch to come to one of us and make the whole situation his problem instead."

"How do you propose we do that?"

"We need to find out what it was that he's trying to cover up." He picked up the bottle and took another long drink. The look he gave her spoke volumes about how well he thought she'd receive what he was going to say next. "We need to get into her office."

"You wouldn't even make it into the building." Never mind that he was demonstrating a woeful lack of respect for the law and her place of employment, what he was suggesting was impossible from a practical standpoint. She refused to sugarcoat that, even if she did wince internally at the condescension in her voice.

"Fair point." He tipped his head, conceding that the likelihood of him getting upstairs and past security was small enough to be functionally nonexistent. "But I'm not really the one who *needs* to get in. I wouldn't know where to even begin locating anything useful. You, on the other hand ..."

"You think I'm going to do it?" She blamed the alcohol for the volume of the snort that followed her incredulous question. "You want me to break into someone else's office at the place where I work? Are you trying to get me fired and ruin my life?"

He shook his head and bumped her lightly with his shoulder. "No, I'm trying to keep you safe and figure out who's after you and your friends."

She relaxed back into him, her annoyance of the last several days fading somewhat. He was full of bad ideas—and bad friends, bad habits, bad ex-girlfriends, etc.—but he was doing his best to keep anything from happening to her and she couldn't stay angry with him for long. "Why can't we just let Detective Chen do her job instead of committing a crime?"

He picked up one of her hands and pressed a kiss to the palm, eyes intense on hers. "Let's just say, I'd rather not take that kind of chance with your life. The sooner we figure it out, the less chance there is of him coming after you again."

"You make it hard for me to argue when you look at me like that."

"That's the idea."

She laughed and some of the tension she'd been feeling all day was carried away by the sound. He was good at that, keeping her grounded and feeling lighter than she ever had. A remarkable feat, given the current circumstances.

"I shouldn't let you get away with that when we're trying to talk about something so important." She was already curling into him, and he lifted a brow, all mock innocence.

"Me? I think it's you that's the problem here." He kissed

one side of her mouth and then the other. "You laugh too much. I think you do it on purpose to distract me from important subjects with this pretty mouth I can't stop staring at."

She wondered idly how it was possible for a man to look at her with that much heat and not cause her body to go up in flames. "You could do more than stare, if you want to be really distracted."

"Do I want to be distracted?" He looked around at the pristine room and the bright sunlight pouring through the windows and her sheer curtains. "Here? In the middle of the day?"

She was already hooking her fingers under the hem of his shirt. They could form a line outside the window for all she cared. "I don't think the neighbors will mind."

He chuckled but helped her pull the shirt off. "I think I've awoken something in you. Not so prim and proper anymore."

"If you don't shut up and kiss me, Ethan, I swear—"

But the rest of it was lost as he slotted his mouth over hers and set her nerves ablaze. His mouth was always so hot on hers, so demanding. He kissed like he wanted to meld them together and she had long since decided that she didn't mind that thought at all.

Buttons popped when he tugged open her blouse, but she hardly noticed. That was a problem for Future Eloise to deal with. Current Eloise was busy having her mind thoroughly blown by a pair of rough hands that had pushed their way inside her ruined top to tug her bra aside and focus an indecent amount of attention on her breasts. She'd never been particularly fond of having her nipples touched, but something about the way Ethan did it made her toes curl.

Clearly, he knew what her body needed better than she ever had, and all she had to do was let herself be carried away. She could float, mindless on a sea of sensation as he fumbled with the fasteners on her skirt before giving up and shoving it up around her waist. A few extra seconds to tug her panties down her legs and unbutton his jeans and she was going to be getting thoroughly fucked on her living room rug.

She might even end up with rug burn. God, what would her mother think? A horrified sound escaped her; part laugh, part wine-induced hiccup.

Ethan stopped with her panties around her knees and frowned at her. "Are you okay?"

"I am perfectly fine," she lied. "I was just thinking how very unlike me this whole thing is and how horrified my mother would be."

"Oh." He pulled a face and she laughed again, a full belly laugh that shook her whole body and made her exposed breasts bounce enough that she had to clap her hands over them to still the jiggle. That got his attention back on her body, but he still mumbled, "Maybe we could not talk about that?" under his breath.

"That's an excellent idea." Her cheeks were painfully hot —why did she have to always say the worst possible thing when they were having sex—but he was already moving past it, hands once again roaming to all her sensitive places, so she let it go without further comment.

Her body was humming, eager and ready, and she tried to pull him in the moment the condom was on but he had other ideas. She let him guide her until she was kneeling over the coffee table with her face pressed against the warm wood surface and his hard body curved over her while he nudged his knees between hers and pushed into her from behind.

It was absolutely ridiculous and still somehow achingly erotic that he could be so tender and possessive of her when she was splayed out across a table like a sacrificial offering. He knew just the right way to touch her, just the right things to whisper in her ear, to make her shake and tremble as much from that as she did from the orgasm that rocked through her.

Afterward, she lay on the rug. Boneless. Shameless. Utterly satisfied and sure of one thing. She was going to have to wear pants to work to hide the rug burn on her knees.

Twenty-Three

Getting into Kim's office wasn't as difficult as Eloise had feared it would be. She wasn't about to get fired over this whole situation, no matter how insistent Ethan was that she needed to be stealthy, so she did this the way she did everything else—as honestly and by the book as possible.

Sun Valley had already started to pack up Kim's belongings and it had been as simple as batting her lashes at Kim's immediate supervisor. He was quite possibly the oldest man Eloise had ever seen and Kim had never liked him much, though she'd had less intense feelings than Sarah had for Dwayne. It made Eloise a little nauseous to pretend to flirt with him—his skin was so thin and wrinkly that it looked like crumpled crepe paper—but it was the only way to convince him to let her slip inside for a moment under the pretense of retrieving some sentimental items.

The man was gruff, and he mumbled under his breath about not letting people poke around out of idle curiosity, but Eloise saw him waver when the first tear had fallen, and she was alone in the office less than five minutes later.

Sure, he was going to know she'd been in here, but she wasn't after anything except for information. Nothing that would be noticed if she left the room with it, so it couldn't arouse suspicion or interest from the police or the company. All she had to do was find something useful, a task that seemed simple enough right up until the moment she opened the door to Kim's office.

She took a deep bracing breath and looked over her shoulder at Kim's boss. "It may take me a few minutes to find what I'm looking for."

They both peered into the space, taking in the desk with its scattered papers and colorful decorations. There were odds and ends spread haphazardly throughout the room, crowded next to each other on the desktop and shelves on the walls. Kim had been thrilled when she'd gotten this little private space of her own, Eloise remembered now, because she'd always been too messy to share cubicle space peacefully with her coworkers.

Kim's workload had already been passed along to someone else but her stuff didn't look like it had been disturbed and Eloise wondered if Detective Chen had been able to do something to prevent it. It seemed from the outside like the cops weren't making much progress, but then, it was unlikely that the detective had told Eloise everything that had happened behind the scenes of their investigation. She only took the information Eloise gave her and promised to look into it. The exchange of information didn't go both ways.

Kim's boss grunted as he stepped back. "Good luck, little lady."

Eloise smiled tightly, surprised he hadn't tried to pat her butt before walking away. He seemed like the old school type that genuinely believed that kind of thing was a compliment, but she wasn't in the mood to deal with that today. Maybe she'd been spending too much time with Ethan, and he was starting to rub off on her, but she couldn't imagine cheerfully tolerating that kind of thing again.

Her patience had thinned, and it no longer seemed like something she had to put up with. A dangerous thought, with her career depending on how well she went with the flow in a business like this. Another thing she'd have to deal with when all this was over, and the list seemed to grow longer by the day.

As soon as she had the office to herself, she set to work. Rifling through loose papers and checking the names on files, snapping pictures of Kim's date book pages with her phone. Most people had switched to digital a long time ago, but Kim insisted she preferred pen and paper for scheduling. There were several entries in the weeks leading up to the murder, but nothing that jumped out to Eloise as an immediate red flag.

She moved on to the computer and drummed her fingers on the desktop as she encountered the screen that asked for Kim's login credentials. Every computer in the company required this kind of protection and if Kim had been more of an organized person, Eloise knew she'd have no chance of getting in. As it was, Eloise knew how impossible it had been for Kim to remember her passwords, even the ones she used daily. They weren't supposed to write them down but ...

"If I was Kim, where would I hide something like that?" Eloise sat down in Kim's chair, poking around the desktop for a good hiding place that was easily accessible when Kim had been logging in. She found it written on an old yellow sticky note under the keyboard. "Ah, there you are."

Logging in was easy but she was frustrated to find the computer just as disorganized as Kim's physical space. There wasn't time to go through everything and she had no idea what might be important. There was no choice but to go with her gut, so she started copying the files that seemed to be most accessible, sending up a quick prayer that these were the ones Kim used most often, starting with the ones that looked like they dealt with recent audits. There wouldn't be more than a few she could get to before Kim's boss came back, but she was counting on luck to be on her side for once.

The only other choice would be trying to take the whole computer out with her and that was guaranteed to draw more attention to her than she wanted.

"Find what you were looking for?"

To her credit, Eloise didn't jump as she turned to face Kim's boss with a grateful smile. She pocketed the USB stick with one hand and reached for a random stuffed animal on the desk with the other. It was pink and hideous, and she'd never seen it before in her life.

"I gave this to her for her last birthday," she lied, giving it a little wave to draw his attention away from the disturbed paperwork. "She always loved pink, you know?"

"Did she?"

Eloise nodded even though it wasn't true. She would have bet her house that the man had barely known Kim's name and certainly nothing else about her, anyway. "Thanks for letting me come in and get it. I promise I'll keep it our little secret."

She slipped past him and down the hall before he could say anything else, grip tight on the plushie just to give her something tangible to hold onto. It was possible she'd missed anything helpful amid the mess, but it was also possible she'd gotten the answers to the mystery of Kim's murder and was now carrying them around in her pocket.

There was only one way to find out.

* * *

"Do you know what to look for?"

Eloise frowned down at the phone and memory stick she'd dropped victoriously on the kitchen table at Ethan's house as soon as he'd returned home. She'd waited by the window watching for his car, drumming her fingers on the windowsill, and seething with impatience because she'd been sure he would be able to tell her what to do next.

His question had knocked the wind out of her. "Umm ... no? Don't you?"

"No."

"No," she repeated slowly. "You sent me into the office to try and steal information and now *you don't know* what we're looking for?"

"I thought *you'd* know what we were looking for." He was gaping at her like she'd just told him she couldn't tie her own shoelaces. "This is your job. And besides, you didn't ask what to look for when you went into the office, so I assumed you knew."

"You've got to be kidding me." She rolled her eyes to the ceiling and silently counted to ten. "I didn't have time to be picky about what I grabbed. I don't even know if there's anything useful in there."

He opened his mouth, a determined glint in his eye that told her he was about to start arguing with her again, but she held up a hand to silence him when her phone started ringing. "You just hold that thought and we'll figure this out in a minute."

"Still not gonna be my fault," he muttered, but she was already turning away, her attention on the incoming call.

Sarah.

She'd run into her on her way out of the building after leaving Kim's office, and the two of them had exchanged awkward small talk until Sarah had begun to tearfully confess how much she'd missed seeing Eloise.

"I've been such a mess," she'd said, pointing to a dark bruise on her arm. "I can't seem to do anything these days without hurting myself. Head in the clouds and just not paying attention at all. I ran smack into my car door this morning on the way into work."

"I'm sorry." Eloise had felt like she should have said more, but the strain that had been lingering between them had robbed her of her confidence.

"I know it hasn't been easy on you," Sarah had continued. "You were the one who found her and everything. It's just ... I guess I haven't been handling things well and seeing you? Seeing how upset you've been? It just made it seem too real."

"I guess I can understand that."

"I miss you."

Eloise had never been good at holding grudges and her heart softened. "I miss you, too. If you want to get a cup of coffee or something soon ..." She left the sentence open, not quite a question but a hopeful vacancy.

"Yeah." Sarah had brightened at the suggestion. "That sounds like a great idea. We can talk about what happened that day. You know, if you want to. I don't want you to think I'm not here for you after what you went through."

"Maybe." Eloise hadn't been able to think of anything she'd rather do less than talk about finding Kim's dead body, but Sarah was making an effort and she didn't want to shut down the fragile truce between them. "I was just on my way out, but you can call or send a text when you want to meet up."

"Oh?" Sarah had seemed to realize for the first time that she'd found Eloise on the wrong floor of the building. "Dropping something off?"

"Picking something up," Eloise had said with a guilty lurch in her stomach. She hated lying to anyone, especially the people she cared about, and she wanted to keep as close to the truth as possible.

"Oh." Something curious passed over Sarah's face, quickly repressed and Eloise wondered again if her friends really suspected her of being involved in Kim's death. "Well, I won't keep you but I'm glad we had the chance to talk."

After that, it shouldn't have surprised Eloise for Sarah to get in touch with her, but she hadn't expected it to be later the same day. There was a moment of panic when she remembered the last time one of them had reached out to her. Maybe something had happened to Sarah.

"Hello?"

"You're not going to believe this," Sarah said, breathless and without preamble.

"What? Did something happen? Are you okay?" Eloise's heart squeezed hard in her chest, this long moment of painful fear stacking onto so many others. So many times now one of them had been in danger, how long would it be before someone else was ripped away from her?

"I'm fine." Eloise could imagine her waving the question away as she spoke. "Someone broke into Kim's office."

Eloise nearly dropped the phone. "What?"

"No one knows who did it, but her office was trashed when security did their evening rounds."

"Was anyone hurt?" Eloise was still trying to process the fact that someone else had broken into Kim's office the same day she had. Okay, her little adventure hadn't *technically* been a break in, but the sentiment was the same.

"No, but they *destroyed* her office. Took off with her computer and everything. Chloe started seeing one of the security guards and he told her that apparently they called the cops but there was some kind of glitch with the security footage in that part of the building. It didn't record anything all day."

"When did Chloe start dating ... You know what, nevermind, that's not the important thing right now ..." Eloise's head was spinning. No footage meant no chance of catching the person that had taken Kim's computer but it also meant there was no record of *her* going into Kim's office, either. "Does everybody know about this? Or just you and Chloe?"

"You know how fast office gossip spreads." Eloise couldn't argue with that, and Sarah didn't give her time to anyway. "Do you think it's related to her murder?"

"Yeah." It was right there on her tongue to tell Sarah everything, but she didn't want to get them any more involved in this than they already were. "I don't know how exactly but it sure seems like something weird was going on."

"That's exactly what I was thinking."

"Listen, Sarah, do you have somewhere you can go for now? Someplace safe? I think Chloe's been staying with her mom since the incident at her place ..."

"I mean, I have family I could stay with, but you don't think that's necessary, do you?" Sarah sounded skeptical and Eloise could see Ethan watching her with a worried expression that told her he'd heard enough to know something else had happened.

No sense in trying to hide it from him.

"I think it might be." She hated to worry Sarah, but scared was better than dead. "Just until we know more and can be sure you're safe."

"If you knew something, you'd tell me, right?"

"Of course." She was a liar and a thief now, but she wouldn't risk Sarah's life by telling her the truth. "You know I would."

"Who are you staying with? Are you going to be safe?"

"Ethan's with me," Eloise assured her. "He'll keep me safe."

"Lucky you."

There was an awkward pause and Eloise shifted uncomfortably, the conversation she'd had with Jackson about

Sarah being jealous of her relationship screaming through her mind.

"I'm sorry. I didn't mean that the way it sounded. Just a little worked up right now."

"I think we all are." She'd been snappish herself lately, so she understood the urge to lash out even when it didn't make sense. "Just stay safe."

"You too, okay?"

Ethan barely waited for her to hang up before launching his own line of questioning. "Something happened?"

She explained it quickly, filling in as many of the details as she knew while he sat pensively and shook his head.

"This guy is one step behind us." He looked more frustrated than she'd ever seen him. "It has to be someone from work. How else would they know the power goes out like that when it rains? No one else would be able to get into the building."

"It was a weekend when Kim died. I got locked out because there was no one there to push the door open from the inside. On a weekday, near closing time? Completely different. You would just have to wait for someone to leave and slip in behind them before the door closed."

"Then it could be someone who knows an employee." He acknowledged defeat but didn't look happy about losing the potential clue. "A friend or a spouse or something."

"Or a boyfriend."

He frowned when he caught her eye and realized she was looking at him speculatively. "Very funny."

"If it was an employee or someone close to an employee, then they would know exactly what they were trying to hide and how to get rid of any evidence. They weren't stumbling around in there looking for clues like you were."

"So now they're one step ahead of us and not behind."

"Unless we can find some answers here." She tossed her

phone back down onto the table beside the USB stick. "That's all we've got to go on now."

He sighed as he got to his feet and opened a kitchen cupboard. "Looks like we're gonna spend most of tonight going over all this. You want some coffee?"

"Yeah." She was already pulling out her laptop and plugging in the USB stick. "Detective Chen still hasn't called me back. Maybe if I call her tomorrow and I've got some real evidence, it'll get her attention."

"Then we'll get to work."

Twenty-Four

Eloise woke the next morning with her face stuck to Ethan's dining room table. He was asleep beside her, head pillowed on his arms and face relaxed after a fruitless night. They hadn't made it through half of the pictures and files from Kim's office before she'd laid her head down to rest and slipped off to sleep. He must not have been far behind her and if he'd found anything, he would have woken her, so she was sure he hadn't had any luck, either.

The sun was just starting to creep through the windows, and she was exhausted and sore from spending the last few hours asleep sitting up, but she was going to be late for work if she didn't get up now. Ethan spent far more time at her house than she did at his, so she hadn't built up a stash of clothes or personal items here like he had at her place.

He was the only man that had ever had a toothbrush in her bathroom or a drawer with underwear and T-shirts in her dresser. It had happened so quickly that she hadn't noticed how intertwined their lives had gotten until now. If he'd woken up with *his* face pressed to *her* dining room table, he would have had everything he needed upstairs to go about his day without ever having to go back to his own house.

Neither of them had questioned it and Eloise wondered if he even realized that he had made a second home with her. Had he simply drifted into her house because he was drawn to her? Or had it been more intentional on his part, a calculated way to escape the painful memories of his grandfather's house?

Once they figured out the motive behind Kim's murder, there was a lot that they were going to have to talk about. Her own resolve to keep emotions out of their relationship was being eaten away and she wasn't going to fall in love with someone that didn't have the same feelings about her. Clearly, she was going to have to sit him down and discuss what the future might look like for them. It was simply the logical thing to do before she got in too deep and allowed herself to get hurt.

"Ethan." She rubbed his shoulder, still marveling slightly at how firm the muscle was beneath her hand even when he was fully relaxed. "I've got to go."

"Hmm?" He sat up and rubbed his face. "Is it morning already?"

"Yeah." She pressed a kiss to his cheek and smoothed the hair that was sticking up at odd angles from where he'd slept on it. "I've got to get ready for work and I didn't want to leave without saying goodbye."

"I'm sorry I fell asleep."

"We both did." She stretched and tried to ease the ache in her knotted muscles. "There was a lot to look over and we got started late. Should we plan on doing the rest tonight?"

He grimaced—not that she blamed him for not being excited about the prospect of another night of fruitless searching—but nodded. "I'll pick up something for dinner and come over after you get home."

"Pizza?"

"I've created a monster." He chuckled when she swatted softly at his arm. "Yeah, I'll swing by Paula's place."

"Thanks." She leaned down to give him a quick kiss, her mind already pivoting to the office and the long day ahead of her on precious little sleep, but he caught her chin between his fingers. Warmth skimmed along the surface of her skin, pushing away the aches and fatigue and replacing it with a pleasant buzz. "I need to go."

She mumbled it against his mouth and felt his lips curl in response as his hand slid up to cup her breast.

"You can be a little late this once."

There were countless reasons she really shouldn't be—not the least of which was the career she'd put so much work into and was no longer sure she wanted—but all of them faded into nothingness when he set his other hand on her thigh.

"Maybe a little bit late."

There was no time to linger, and he didn't try. Within seconds she found herself tossed onto the tabletop with his hands under her shirt and his lips on her neck. She was working the button on his jeans, and he was already hard and ready for her.

"Don't you ever get tired of this?" She lifted her hips so he could slide her pants off and toss aside her underwear. "I swear you're hard all the time."

"Do you?" He pressed a hand between her legs and came up with two shining fingers. "You're always wet."

She grinned at him, shameless in her greed. "I guess not."

"You're incredible." He went back to kissing her neck, whispering praise between each press of his lips. "Beautiful. I can't keep my fucking hands off you. You're the first thing I think about in the morning ... and the last thing I think about at night."

"Hurry." She was amazed at her ability to catch fire from a

single look or caress, but everywhere his body was touching hers was immediately electrified with want. "Now, please, now."

He pushed into her with a grunt of satisfaction. "Perfect," he said, breathing the word out between clenched teeth. "You're fucking perfect."

His dishes shook and his table rattled, but she was beyond worrying about it. If they broke it, she would buy him a new one. As many as they needed. She couldn't imagine a better thing to do than fuck their way through a furniture store full of tables.

They were wrapped around each other, as close as they could get with their mouths and their tongues and their bodies. Pleasure set every nerve ending alight, but she was thrumming with warmth and something that felt like joy.

She'd never known intimacy that reached all the way into her heart, but she suspected that was what she was experiencing now. It was more than just the general pleasure of having an attentive lover. She felt safe, protected, cared for.

And if the way he was looking at her was any indication, he was having the same conflicting thoughts.

It was too much for her—too soon and too overwhelming and too far into a place she'd promised herself she would not go—and it rocked her to her core because she realized she enjoyed those feelings, and she didn't necessarily want to go back to living without them.

She buried her face in his neck and let her body override her thoughts. She couldn't think about that now, so she did the safe thing and shoved it to the back of her mind.

A long day at the office, four more hours of searching, and an entire pizza later, Eloise was convinced that whatever the killer was trying to hide wasn't in the files she'd managed to download from Kim's office. Her table was littered with scraps of paper and crumbs from the cake Ethan had brought in with the pizza, but they were no closer to answers than they had been the day before.

There were no suspicious entries in Kim's appointment book, no signs of a secret boyfriend or unusual meetings with her coworkers. All of the files Eloise had smuggled out of the office seemed to be in perfect order. The accounts showed regular activity and the only errors they had found were small ones with notes from Kim about the source and the company's follow-up.

There was nothing that could possibly justify a murder.

"We spent all this time for nothing, didn't we?" She buried her face in her arms and sniffed against the urge to cry in frustration. "I can't believe I risked my job for this and we're no closer than where we started."

"Maybe we were wrong, and it was something about her personal life that she was trying to hide. You were her friend outside the office and so were Sarah and Chloe. Maybe whatever has all of you as a target is something that has nothing to do with work."

"Maybe she was hiding a secret life as some senator's dominatrix, and he was afraid she'd spill the news to the press."

It took him a moment, staring at her wide eyed, before the deadpan tone of her comment registered. "Hmm, that seems a bit tame for a senator."

She laughed softly and closed her eyes, the ridiculousness of it all just a little too much for her handle.

"Why don't you go up and take a shower?" Ethan ran a hand over her back and pressed a soothing kiss to her temple. "We've been working on this for hours and I know you're tired after sleeping on a table all night last night."

It was hard for her to admit defeat on anything, but nothing sounded quite as good as cleaning the day off her skin and getting some decent rest. "Maybe that's a good idea. I always have my best ideas in the shower. Maybe the answer will come to me while I'm washing my hair or something."

It didn't, but her mind was blissfully empty by the time she was clean and wrapped in a warm towel. After days of worry and grief, it was a relief to have even a few stolen moments when exhaustion and lavender body wash stripped them away and left her with nothing but the desire to close her eyes and slide into dreamless sleep.

The pleasant emptiness was ripped away when she opened her bathroom drawer and her searching fingers brushed against the cigarette pack she had shoved at the back instead of the hairbrush she was trying to find. It had been foolishly sentimental of her to keep it, she'd known that when she'd done it, but she hadn't expected it to serve as such a potent reminder of her pain. She caressed the pack with her thumb, tracing the edge of the black matchbook inside the clear plastic packaging for a moment before she tossed it into the trashcan beneath the sink.

She'd done her best by Kim and would continue to do so until her killer was found, but she didn't want hidden reminders waiting to pop up and rip her heart out again.

"Feeling better?" Ethan was leaning against the door frame, watching her with a puzzled expression on his face.

"Much more relaxed." She found her brush and went to work detangling her hair. It would have been faster to simply fall into bed but she knew she'd regret that in the morning when she woke up looking like birds had made a nest in her long tresses.

He reached for the brush, one brow lifted in question, and took over when she handed it over in relief. "You looked like you were thinking hard."

"I suppose." She fiddled with the ends of a stray strand and tried to ignore how domestic the scene was. It was intimate, almost painfully so, but he stepped into it without a thought, like caring for her was instinctive. "I'm always thinking hard."

"That seemed harder than usual."

It was almost a question, but she pretended not to notice. She was tired of talking about it for today. They'd done enough for now and all she wanted was some peace and quiet.

He let it go, allowing them to slip into a comfortable silence as he finished brushing her hair. They both knew he was staying and when she left the bathroom to crawl into her bed with its pink sheets and floral bedspread, he followed without prompting. He had his own side, his own pillow, his own dent that was beginning to form in the mattress.

They turned to each other in the dark, familiar now with how they fit together for sex or for sleep. She was too tired to want anything besides his warmth, but once he was settled against her with his chest pressed to her back and his arms around her, the ability to sleep became elusive.

He murmured something unintelligible and pulled her closer when she began to trace the lines of his tattoos with her fingers. It was a habit she'd gotten into on the nights when grief or anxiety made it difficult to sleep. After a moment he stilled again. It never seemed to bother him for long and she had memorized the images that covered his arms.

Sometimes, when her mind started to drift on the familiar patterns, she'd been able to figure out a problem at work or plan the next day's activities, but her mind remained stubbornly blank. There was a feeling in her chest, something restless and impatient, but the source of it remained just beyond her reach and sleep overtook her before she could decipher what it was trying to tell her.

Twenty-Five

Admitting they weren't going to find answers in the stuff she'd stolen from Kim's office meant officially going back to square one. It was disappointing, even more so when Detective Chen finally called her back and confirmed that she had no new leads, either. She finally agreed that the series of break-ins were probably connected to the murder and that it was highly likely that the murderer was trying to cover up some secret, but neither of them had a solid idea of who that could be.

Eloise promised to contact her if anything else happened, but she turned down the offer to have uniformed officers keep an eye on her house. There hadn't been any disturbances at her house since the night of the murder and it made her nervous to think about people staying outside all day and night. Detective Chen had agreed not to do that but insisted on having a few extra passes each shift if Eloise still insisted on staying in her own house instead of going to a hotel.

"So, they're just going to drive by and make sure there's no one peeking in your windows?" Chloe looked skeptical as she sipped her lemonade over lunch. Eloise had waited to bring it up until after they had placed their orders, unwilling to ruin the first lunch they'd all had together after Kim's death until she had no choice.

"I think it's to make me feel safe more than anything else." Eloise stirred her tea and tried to focus on the ice as it swirled in the glass and not the way Sarah and Chloe were looking at her.

"I doubt it would keep someone from breaking in, but I guess the illusion of safety is better than nothing." Sarah had hardly spoken at all before now and she barely glanced up from the tabletop as they waited for their food. There was a new bruise forming on her cheek and she had dark circles under her eyes that matched the ones Eloise and Chloe both had.

It seemed none of them were sleeping well and the stress of everything that had happened was getting to each of them in different ways. Sarah was clumsy, Chloe was paranoid, and Eloise had become withdrawn.

"I suppose it is," Eloise agreed. This was the closest they'd come to bridging the gap that had formed between them and she felt the necessity of coming up with something to say to fill the awkward silence that followed. Nothing that came to mind seemed appropriate and then the waiter arrived, and the moment had passed.

They ate quickly, passing stilted small talk between them to lessen the tension. Eloise was dreading the walk back to the office and was relieved to hear her phone ring from inside her purse as they were paying the check.

"You two go ahead without me." She was already reaching for her bag with an apologetic smile. "I'll be right behind you."

The sense of respite was replaced with dread as she answered without looking and was met with the sound of her mother's voice.

"It always takes you so long to answer the phone, Eloise."

"It's lovely to speak with you, too, Mother."

"Oh, hush. You know I'm pleased to talk with you." Eloise did not know any such thing, but she was not in the mood for another argument. Her silence was her answer and stretched long enough for her mother to cough gently and press on with the conversation herself. "I'm sure you're wondering why I called."

"In the middle of a workday," Eloise rebuked. It didn't matter to her one way or the other, but she knew her mother's strict work ethic would let the barb land as she intended. "How can I help you?"

"I was merely going to inform you that I intend to be out of town for a few days. Your father will still be home, of course, but I've been invited on a very exclusive trip at work and—"

"Why did you need to tell me this?" Eloise could feel the headache coming, the tension forming in her muscles with every word. Deborah had complained for years about how much her career had suffered because of her parental obligations and it wasn't that Eloise didn't believe her, it was just that she was tired of being blamed for it.

"It's rude to interrupt, Eloise. You know I raised you with better manners than that. I simply thought it best if you knew I was going to be unavailable."

"You've never been available." It slipped out before she could stop it, a product of a lifetime of strain on their relationship and her own recent stress. Eloise had given all she had to give lately of her patience and understanding. There was none left for the woman who had never given her any.

"Excuse me?" Deborah sputtered, shocked, for several seconds before Eloise realized she wasn't going to say anything else. Waiting for an apology, as she had always had whenever Eloise or her father said something she didn't approve of.

"I'm sorry, Mother, I have to go." Eloise hung up before

her mother could say anything else. Her stomach was rolling, and her palms were sweaty, but she felt like she could run ten miles without being out of breath. She couldn't remember the last time she'd dared to speak to her mother that way and there was as much exhilaration pumping through her veins as there was guilt.

If nothing else came from this tragedy, maybe she could finally be brave enough to shake off the shackles of her mother's opinion and live her own life. It occurred to her now to wonder if Kim had had any regrets, things she wished she might have done differently. Surely, she had. Everyone did. But Eloise had the chance to change things. To make different choices for herself before it was too late. She wanted to grab that chance and she thought she owed it to Kim's memory to live her life as fully as possible.

Eloise lingered on the walk back to the office, her mind full of possibilities. She wanted to forge a future separate from her mother's expectations, mend her relationship with Sarah and Chloe, find out what part Ethan wanted to play in the rest of her life.

As Sun Valley loomed into view with its glass front and neatly manicured landscaping, she realized she also wanted a different job. Something that didn't fill her with dread and lay like a dark cloud over every other aspect of her days. She had devoted so much time to this path that she wasn't sure what else she'd be qualified to do, but she had a lifetime to figure it out.

Until then, she'd keep the secret close to her heart, an impossible fantasy that she was certain she could move into the realm of possibility if she just put her mind to it.

One day she wouldn't have to walk up this sidewalk and imagine Kim's body the way it had been when she'd found it. No more sexist coworkers. No more numbers to tally or papers to file. No more silent elevator rides or high heeled shoes.

She'd start looking at options and putting together a plan.

———

"You told off your mom?"

Ethan sounded impressed but Eloise couldn't see his face as he stood behind her in the shower and rubbed shampoo into her scalp so she couldn't be sure. "Not exactly, but I did make a few very pointed comments."

"Little rebel." He was laughing at her, but she didn't mind. "What did she say?"

"She did a lot of indignant sputtering and then I hung up." Even hours later, it still felt like a dream. She had never hung up on her mother before and she'd also refused to answer the series of increasingly outraged calls and texts Deborah had sent throughout the afternoon. "It felt great."

"I'm sure it did." He had finished with the shampoo and moved on to nibbling at her neck, leaving her hair piled high in a sudsy mess on top of her head.

"You have to let me rinse. I taste all soapy."

"You taste amazing."

"Clean bodies first, dirty thoughts later." She'd developed a sort of mantra for their showers, a reminder that often went unheeded as he pinned her to the shower wall with his head between her thighs.

"You like my dirty thoughts."

"I never said I didn't, but I'd like a clean smelling man in my bed tonight."

He grinned and handed her the soap, a clear challenge in his lifted brow. "I'll let you make me as clean as you want me."

"We'll see."

She washed him slowly, rubbing suds into the skin of his

shoulders and his neck before working down across his chest and stomach. The muscles flexed under her touch and his cock was already hard and jutting toward her, but she ignored it. She cleaned his legs and feet one at a time, crouching low and peering up into his eyes with her best sexy smirk.

"Turn around."

He turned toward the back wall of the shower and let her rub soap over the backs of his legs and each firm ass cheek. He was ticklish at the sides, just above the hips, and she took extra time there to torment him before moving on. There would be a price for that later, and she knew he was probably already thinking up ways to torment her in return, but she felt powerful watching him jump and struggle to remain still under her caress.

She turned her attention to the broad expanse of his back, up his spine and toward his shoulder blades, where the unmarked skin met the tattoos from his arms. She'd spent hours learning the lines and colors from the shoulder down, but far less than that on the ones this far back.

There was a skull just behind his right arm with a snake curled around the bottom and across from that, behind his left, a cracked 8 ball ...

The bar logo, she remembered. That must have been why it had seemed so familiar to her the day they'd visited Dylan at the bar.

"I never looked at this one so closely. This is from the bar, right?."

"Hmm?" She tapped the tattoo when he glanced back at her curiously. "Oh, yeah. I designed the logo when Dylan took over. He wanted to rename it, so it had less association with his dad."

"Right." That made sense and some little sliver of tension she'd been holding slipped away now that she'd placed the familiarity of the image from that day. "It's clever."

"I'm very clever." He turned around and caught her in a soapy hug, pulling her beneath the spray as she squealed and cursed and tried futilely not to get shampoo in her eyes.

"Ethan!"

"You said we had to be clean and now we're clean." There was a little bit of the devil in the wicked smile he gave her. "Let me touch you."

She was helpless to resist him, and he lifted her easily, one hand at her waist and the other cupping one cheek of her behind when she wrapped her legs around him. She thought he might pin her against the shower wall—he'd done that before and she'd had no complaints—but he stepped out and carried her dripping across the floor until he could follow her down onto the bed.

They were still soaked, and she knew they were going to regret this when it was time to sleep and all their blankets were wet, but it was hard to focus on some nebulous and far away consequence when he was kissing his way down her body, and she could already feel the heat building between her thighs.

Tonight, he was ruthless, his mouth and hands moving over with one purpose. He knew every place on her body that made her tremble with pleasure and he exploited them without mercy. She was a quivering mess of need before he ever parted her legs to use his tongue on her most sensitive parts.

He drove her to one peak with only his mouth, and then another when he started to slowly pump his fingers inside her. She was wet enough that the room was quickly filled with obscene noises, but he didn't seem to mind that any more than he cared about the cries he managed to pull from her. Before him, she'd always been shy and ashamed.

He seemed determined to drive that shame out of her.

She was beyond ready for him when he finally relented and settled himself over her. The taste of her arousal still lingered on his tongue, and he kissed her deeply as he slid into her slightly before pulling back out. No amount of pleading seemed to affect him, and each thrust was only marginally deeper than the last. By the time he was fully inside her, she was desperate and halfway to another orgasm.

He decided to take pity on her then and the bed frame shook beneath the force of his thrusts. It was exactly what she needed, and she clung to him, her fingers clutching his back and her legs locked around his hips. A pair of wild horses couldn't have pried him from her grasp and her third peak had white sparks going off behind her eyelids and fireworks shooting through her veins.

She was nearly certain she had resorted to insensible babbling, but she shut her lips tight against the most traitorous thought that crossed her mind. It was fine to tell him she wanted him, that she needed him, that she'd do anything he wanted if only he never stopped touching her.

But she wasn't going to tell him *that*.

Some four-letter words were better kept to oneself.

He was asleep almost as soon as he'd rolled over and wrapped an arm around her and she was grateful that he couldn't see her face. She'd been so close to saying something she couldn't take back. They needed to talk about what was happening between them, but blurting out her feelings during sex, before she'd had a chance to fully decide what she wanted to do about it, was not the way she wanted to start that conversation.

She thanked God and all her lucky stars that she'd come to her senses just in the nick of time.

Adrenaline was still pumping, keeping her up and restless, so she wiggled out from under his arm and, remembering the last time she'd tried to sneak into the kitchen in the middle of the night, quietly indicated to a curious Winston that he should stay put. He glared at her reproachfully, but the puppy classes she'd insisted Ethan enroll him in had taught him manners and he stayed in his bed.

A cold glass of water calmed her nerves and soothed her anxious stomach but by the time she crept back up the stairs and tried to squeeze her way back into bed, Ethan had sprawled fully across the mattress. He was face down in the center of the bed, arms spread wide from side to side.

"You can't be serious," she grumbled. He was a heavy sleeper, and it was difficult to move him once he'd settled in. She'd have better luck grabbing a blanket from the closet and sleeping on the couch, but her pride didn't like the idea of letting a giant golden retriever of a man push her out of her own bed.

"Move *over*." She gave him a good shove, grunting with the effort, but he refused to budge. There was clearly not enough room for her to get comfortable, even if she was able to wedge herself in on one side of him, and she was standing beside him, unfocused gaze idly taking in his tattoos as she pondered her predicament, when it hit her.

The Tough Break logo wasn't only familiar to her because of its permanent position on his back. She had seen it somewhere else. And thought she knew exactly where that had been.

Winston rolled over to huff at her when she backed away from the bed and tiptoed to the bathroom. She closed the door with a soft click, wincing at how loud it sounded in the silent house. The last five minutes had proved how difficult it was to wake Ethan, but that didn't stop her heart from pounding as she locked the door and started rummaging in the little bathroom trash can.

Pushing aside used tissues and empty toilet paper rolls, she found what she was looking for near the bottom. The pack of cigarettes she had taken from beside Kim's body, with a black matchbook tucked into the front.

A black matchbook with a familiar logo.

There was no name on it, but the design was identical to the one she'd just been looking at. It was unique, Ethan had designed the image himself. There was no mistaking it, no way to convince herself that it must be a mistake or a coincidence.

Kim had been at Dylan's bar before she died.

And Ethan had never mentioned it.

It was possible he hadn't known, since he'd been away from the bar for so long, but what were the odds that Kim had ended up in that exact bar? It was all the way across town and Eloise's relationship with Ethan was the only connection between her friends and his.

She carried it back downstairs and tucked it into her purse before spending the rest of the night trying to sleep on the couch as a thousand questions ran in a loop through her mind. None of the explanations she came up with made sense as an answer to all of them and a horrible suspicion began to grow inside her.

Dawn was just beginning to lighten the sky when she got dressed and left Ethan a note about him being a horrible bed hog before slipping out the door. She couldn't face him without some space to think, afraid that she might accuse him of something that she couldn't take back.

There were other people she needed to talk to, questions she needed to ask before she could form an opinion about anything, so she sat in her car and waited for Sarah to pull into the parking lot at work.

"Hey! Sarah! Do you have a minute?"

"Eloise!" Sarah's hand flew up to cover her heart, the coffee she had clutched in the other sloshing in its cup. "You scared me."

"I'm sorry." Eloise held her hands up and gave Sarah a nonthreatening smile. "I just needed to ask you a quick question before we head into the office."

"Sure, you can always ask me anything. You don't have to ambush me in the parking lot."

"I know, it's just ... Is that another bruise?"

Sarah pressed her fingers to the purple and blue splotch beneath her eye. There was a layer of foundation over it, but the color was too dark to be concealed properly. "I've become such a klutz lately."

"You were never this clumsy before." Eloise laid a hand on Sarah's arm, inspecting the black eye and the yellowing bruise on her cheek from a few days prior. "Are you sure you're okay? You can talk to me if something's been going on since you started staying with your mom—"

"I stopped staying with my mom a few days after I went over there." Sarah brushed her off and started walking toward the front doors of the building. "I'm fine. What did you need to ask me?"

"Oh, right." Eloise had been so caught up in her worries about Sarah that she'd forgotten for a moment. "I just wanted to know if Kim ever mentioned a place called the Tough Break bar?"

"What?" Sarah stopped and took a deep breath before she turned back around to Eloise, her face blank and her voice slightly irritated. It was a seemingly random thing to ask and Eloise didn't want to have to fully explain it to get an answer.

"I know it sounds like a silly question, it's just that there was ... well, I just thought maybe she'd been there with you or something?" Eloise gripped her fingers together and tried not to fidget. She didn't want Sarah to see her nervousness and start having questions of her own.

"Never heard of it."

"You're sure? It might be important—"

"I didn't really hang out with Kim outside of work unless it was with you, okay? Neither did Chloe." She shook her head and smiled tightly. "I know it makes us shitty friends, and I feel bad about it every day, but we didn't include her as much as we should have."

"Oh." The small hope Eloise had carried that one of them might be able to put her fears to rest faded. "I don't think you were a bad friend. It's normal to have regrets when something terrible happens."

"Yeah." Sarah started walking again. "We all have regrets."

Twenty-Six

Ethan woke to an empty bed and an empty house. There were blankets folded on the end of the couch downstairs and a note next to the coffee pot.

Ethan,

You stole the whole bed last night. Didn't anyone ever teach you to share?

Eloise

He supposed they had, but what a man did in his sleep was another story. He figured this meant he owed her flowers or some shit as an apology for having kicked her out of her own bed with his selfish, sleep-ruining habits. He could handle that. Flowers were a little outside of his comfort zone, you didn't tend to need them when you avoided emotional entanglements, but she seemed like the kind of woman that would go for some good, old fashioned red roses. Or maybe some of those big white ones with the fancy petals, whatever they were called.

There was a florist not far from the bar and he could make a stop there after he finished up his work for the day. He'd been going by Tough Break as little as possible, but Dylan had reacted with exactly the ugly threats that Ethan had expected when he'd tried to convince him that it was time to stop with the other bullshit and start focusing on the legit business at the bar. It had the potential to be a steady source of legal income and Ethan had been thinking about trying to improve it for a while, but Dylan only put enough effort into it to keep the doors open.

Once it had become clear that Dylan didn't intend to let him out of their shadier practices without a fight, Ethan had considered ending his relationship with Eloise to keep her safe. He hated that his presence in her life made her vulnerable, but she'd done nothing to stop him when he started pulling away, and he'd been hit full on with the realization that she was more important to him than he'd been willing to acknowledge.

He hadn't said anything to her when he realized he was in love with her. Partly because he needed to figure out an exit strategy that would involve him still having an income while keeping Dylan from losing his shit, and partly because he didn't want to spook her.

Eloise was an anxious woman despite her ballbusting bluster, and he knew she tended to approach things from a more logical angle. Simple sentiment wouldn't be enough to break her down and convince her to let him into her life on a more permanent basis, so he was going to have to work on making himself indispensable.

Kicking her out of her bed wasn't exactly an item on his checklist, but he could fix that with the flowers and then move on to mowing her grass and packing her lunches. He'd never set out to make a woman fall in love with him, but it couldn't be *that* hard, could it?

Getting out of his predicament with Dylan and finding a real job after so long making money through exclusively questionable means seemed like the harder part of the plan.

He was still working out the details when he arrived at the bar and started helping Myles with inventory.

"You okay?" Ethan tried to ask the question as casually as possible but he wasn't sure he was able to mask the concern in his voice.

He'd known Myles since the day he had gotten out of juvie and he'd never known him to be an unhappy kid. Quiet and timid, but always optimistic. It was no small feat to keep a smile on your face when you had a family as messed up as his was, but Myles had always managed it. Something had shifted in the last few weeks and his excuse that he'd just not been feeling well was starting to wear thin. His skin was sallow and there were circles under his eyes like he hadn't been sleeping.

"I'm fine." Myles's tone was sour and his expression could have curdled milk.

"Are you really?"

"I don't need a babysitter, Ethan." He slammed a glass down on the bar top hard enough to crack it and then tossed it carelessly in the direction of the trash can. "I can handle myself."

"I know."

"Then worry about your own problems." Myles swung around, face hard as he confronted Ethan. He looked like he'd aged five years in the last month. "Did you do what I told you to do and get that girlfriend of yours the hell out of town?"

"Eloise does a pretty good job of taking care of herself." Ethan spread his hands out, palms up to show he didn't intend to fight. Myles was riled up, fists bunched, and he cared too much about the kid to break his nose in the state he was in. He had no idea why Myles was suddenly so obsessed with Eloise and his love life, but he was sure that wouldn't help. "I don't know what's going on with you, but you don't need to worry about her. I'm going to make sure she's happy."

"Happy?" Myles laughed, short and bitter, like glass

sliding over gravel. "I don't give a shit if she's happy. You can't just bring women around Dylan like that."

"I know he's an asshole," Ethan assured him, hoping reason would talk Myles down enough that he could figure out what was happening in his head, "and I don't plan on bringing her around him again."

"You are so far up his ass that you can't see how fucking dangerous he is, can you?" Myles didn't wait for Ethan to try and figure out his meaning. "He helped you out once when you were kids, probably because there was something in it for him. You don't owe him the rest of your life."

"He was always there for—"

"He was there for himself," Myles cut in. "And he expected both of us to be there for him, too. You can get out, Ethan. You're lucky, you don't share blood with him. You can get out."

"I'm working on it," Ethan admitted. It seemed like the kid needed to hear it, and Ethan needed to say it out loud to make it real, anyway. "I just need to make sure I can do it without Eloise getting hurt."

Myles sagged in relief. "Good. She doesn't deserve to be caught up in this. No one deserves that."

"Are you going to tell me what's going on with you? What's got you all wound up like this?"

For a moment it looked like Myles was thinking about telling him, but then the door opened, and Sunny came in to start setting up for her shift behind the bar and he closed up again. "Just don't say anything about this to anyone else," he warned and then he went back to polishing glasses in stony silence.

"Still got a stick up your ass, Myles?" Sunny asked cheerfully as she slid in behind the bar. "You've been a real jerk lately."

"Mind your own business, Sunny."

"Oh? Look who's decided to show up just in time to take care of Dylan's little baby brother." She leaned in to close the distance between herself and Ethan, her breasts tipping dangerously toward the top of the little black T-shirt she was wearing. "We've missed you around here. Did you finally get rid of that stuck up bitch you brought in the other day?"

"Nope."

"You know where to find me when you do."

"Don't hold your breath on that one."

She tossed her hair over her shoulder, revealing an expanse of bare skin at the neck and wafting vanilla perfume his way. "Dylan doesn't like you running around with someone that doesn't understand how things work around here," she reminded him. "All you're doing is setting the poor girl up for a broken heart."

"Maybe." He shrugged and went back to his paperwork. He couldn't afford to let her get under his skin. If he tipped his hand early or admitted how much he cared about Eloise, it would get back to Dylan and cause him nothing but problems. "Guess you'll have to wait and see."

Twenty-Seven

Ethan wasn't home when Eloise arrived back at her house after work, and she sat in the car for several minutes trying to sort through her jumbled thoughts. There was so much to try and navigate that it made her slightly nauseous. All the terrible feelings around Kim's death were now intertwined with her mixed emotions around Ethan. The future she'd begun to look toward was slipping through her fingers faster than she could hold onto it.

She had to decide what to say to him. It was impossible for her to imagine he might have had something to do with murdering anyone, but she wouldn't be able to live with herself if she let her feelings for him blind her to the evidence in front of her face.

He was connected to the bar, the bar was connected to Kim, and Kim was dead.

She had to find out if he knew more than he was telling her, but her mind was tumbling over itself trying to connect the pieces of the puzzle. Was it her fault her friend was dead because she'd gotten involved with someone like Ethan? The insidious guilt, wrapped in the sound of her mother's voice admonishing her about involving herself in relationships, made it hard to think of anything else.

It was clearly not a good idea trying to confront Ethan until she had herself under control and after a moment spent thinking through her options, she opened the door and darted across the street to knock on Jackson and David's front door.

"Hey." David looked surprised to see her, but his smile was welcoming as he opened the door wide. "Come on in."

They had always been there for her, ever since they'd seen her struggling to adjust to the new neighborhood and taken her under their wing. She'd cried at their table over career frustrations more times than she could count and they had never complained once about how often she turned to them for support.

If anyone could help her sort through the mess her life had become, it was them.

"We were just about to open a bottle of wine." Jackson popped his head out of the kitchen to lift a glass questioningly. "Want some?"

"Please." Eloise sank down on the couch and waited, arms wrapped tight around her torso as she stared at the view out their front window. Her house and Ethan's, side by side. A pretty picture—but then pictures never showed you what lurked beneath the surface.

"This looks like a serious visit." David took his glass from Jackson and handed the next one to her before settling back in his chair. "Spill."

"It's about Ethan."

"What else?" Jackson sat on the arm of David's chair and watched her knowingly. "You two were bound to have a fight eventually and the first one's always rough."

"It's not exactly a fight." Now that she was here, the whole thing seemed so hard to explain. "It's just ... I think he might have done something terrible. No, that's not quite right ... Unless it is? Maybe it is."

"You're not making any sense."

"It's about Kim."

"Your friend? The one that ..." Jackson looked at David and gave a gentle cough. "You know?"

"Yes." She wiped away a tear as it escaped. "I think he might have been involved somehow."

"Oh." Jackson tipped his glass and swallowed the contents in one gulp. "Drink up and I'll get the rest of the bottle. I think we're all going to need it."

They sat quietly as she explained what she'd found and how it connected Ethan to Kim in the days before her murder. No one could come up with a reason why she might have been at a shady bar halfway across town unless she knew someone that worked there. It wasn't the kind of place she was known to frequent in her spare time and the odds of it being a coincidence seemed slim to none.

"It does seem strange," David mused. "I think you need to talk to him but I've got to tell you, I just don't think he had anything to do with her death. Maybe he mentioned the bar to her at some point and she decided to check it out."

"Why would she do that? When?"

"I don't know about when but maybe he convinced her they sell the world's best cheeseburger or have a fantastic karaoke night." Jackson lifted a brow when they both turned to him with skeptical expressions. "Hey, you never know! The point is there could be any number of reasons and they don't all have to mean he's involved in this whole thing."

"But what if he is?"

"If that man has done a single thing that would hurt you, I'll eat my hat."

"But—"

"Sorry," David cut in. "He's right. Ethan is so clearly in

love with you, I don't think he could do something that would hurt you. I don't think he's a murderer, either, he just doesn't seem like the kind of guy that could do that to a woman, and he definitely isn't going to hurt you."

"He's not in love with me," Eloise said quickly. "He's never said that."

"I've never said I'm not a velociraptor," David shot back. "Doesn't mean it isn't true."

"That's ... That's not the same—"

"It's exactly the same. You don't have to say a thing for it to be true."

"Can't you tell from the way he looks at you?" Jackson was staring at her with something that might have been pity. "It's written all over his face."

"I don't know ..." She'd made it a point to avoid talking about her family with anyone and they didn't know how cold her mother had always been, not just toward her daughter but her husband, too. Her father was hardly any better, he'd been distant and uninvolved for as long as she could remember. There had been plenty of obligations in the house she'd grown up in, but very little love.

"Well, I know, and I say he's in love with you." Jackson nodded once, like his decision had settled the matter for everyone involved. "I know love when I see it."

Eloise didn't doubt that last bit. He was completely devoted to his husband and the two of them were always a united front against any problem. Even now, sharing a single chair and an identical judgmental look, they were a perfect example of domestic tranquility.

"Talk to him and find out what he has to say about all of this," David advised. "I think he deserves the chance to offer up an explanation."

"And, regardless of what he says, just because she was at the bar, doesn't necessarily mean that had anything to do with her death. The odds of it being a coincidence may seem small but it's not an impossibility."

"Right." Eloise fiddled with her wine glass. "I guess I was just letting all of this get to me."

"It's been a lot." David patted her arm and offered her an encouraging smile. "I don't blame you for feeling overwhelmed."

"I guess I should go home and wait for him. We have a lot to talk about."

"Why don't you stay and let us feed you dinner? You can take some time to sort through what you want to say."

"Are you sure?" An hour or two of wine and good company sounded like exactly what she needed, but she had shown up entirely unannounced. "I don't want to derail your plans for the evening."

"We always have time for you."

"It's true." Jackson poured her another glass and lifted his own in toast. "We're never too busy for our girl."

She came home a few hours later with a full stomach and a slightly tipsy head. Not the best circumstances for a serious conversation, so she decided to send Ethan a text and ask him to stay at his own house that night. A little sleep would help clear her head of the alcohol and give her some more time to get control of her runaway emotions.

It was easy to let herself believe in Ethan when she was tucked safely away in her friends' living room. They had faith in his feelings, and she was able to lean into that as a crutch. It was a lot harder to keep that belief in her own empty kitchen, when there was no one around to bolster her and all she had to go on were her own suspicious thoughts.

She was in a bad mood already when she heard the front

door open and his voice calling out softly in the dark for Winston.

"Come on, boy. Let's take you outside before we head up to bed. I bet Eloise is already upstairs."

His back was turned when she walked out of the kitchen and found him crouched down with the dog's leash in his hand. Winston had always been at ease with him and there was no tension in his broad shoulders as he patted the pup. Everything seemed so normal, so much of what she had come to expect from him, and it was hard to imagine that he could be anything other than the man she'd come to trust, maybe even love.

"I asked you to stay at your place tonight." She sounded gruff and cranky, not a great start to avoiding a confrontation.

"What?" He glanced back at her, surprise turning to confusion as he registered what she'd said. "When did you say that? Is everything okay?"

"I texted you an hour ago."

He pulled his phone out of pocket and read the message. "Shit. I'm sorry, I didn't even notice. I can take Winston and head home if you're not in the mood for company. Are you not feeling well?"

"Yes. No." She sighed and crossed her arms protectively across her middle. "I don't know."

"You know I don't mind taking care of you when you're sick." He stood up, lifting a wiggling Winston in his arms. "I can stay if you need me."

"It's not that." All her doubts and insecurities were bubbling inside her, Jackson and David's good advice almost forgotten. "I'm not sick, I mean."

"Did I do something?"

"I don't know." The wine was swimming in her head, and he was in the worst place at the worst time. It burst out of her;

a bomb dropped at the center of their relationship. "Did you kill her?"

"What?" The color drained from his face. "Kill who? What are you talking about, Eloise?"

"Kim." In her slightly intoxicated state, that seemed like a sufficient explanation. She waved a hand at him, brushed aside his dumbfounded expression. "I need to know if you hurt her."

"Why the hell would I have killed her? I didn't even know her. How could you think that?"

"I don't know!" His anger was a spark to her own. "Why didn't you tell me she'd been at the bar?"

"Sweetheart, I don't know what you're talking about. Can you start from the beginning and explain what the fuck is going on here?"

"I think you know exactly what's going on here." She sniffed and wobbled, pointed an accusatory finger at him. "I saw the matches she was carrying when she died, and they had the bar's logo on the front. Where did she get that, Ethan?"

"I have no idea."

"It's a coincidence, then? I meet you and you show up at my house with a bullet hole in you because you and your friends were up to only God knows what, and then my friend ends up dead?"

"Listen, I—"

"No." She held up a hand to stop him when he tried to get closer. "*You* listen. I don't know what's going on here, but I want an explanation. Where were you the night she was killed? Hmm?"

"Sweetheart, I know you're upset, and I think you're a little bit drunk—"

"That's true but very much beside the point. Where were you, Ethan?"

"You can't actually think I had something to do with this

just because she was at a bar that I happen to go to? That's insane."

She tipped her chin up stubbornly. "Oh, yeah? Well, you don't '*just happen*' to go there. Your friend '*just happens*' to own it. You '*just happen*' to spend a lot of time there. You '*just happened*' to not mention to me that she was there."

He pushed a frustrated hand through his hair, voice rising as he lost his temper. "I didn't know she'd been there!"

"Don't. You. Yell. At. Me." She enunciated each word clearly and with increasing volume. "Just tell me where you were. Give me an explanation I can believe about how my friend ended up at Dylan's bar and then ended up dead."

"I don't know, but I promise I had nothing to do with it."

"Where were you, Ethan?" Her mind was stuck on that point. If he could give her something, anything to cling to. "Where were you when she died? You weren't home and you weren't going to the bar. So, where were you?"

"I don't remember where I was."

"That's a lie." She knew it, could feel it in her bones, see it in the slightly panicked look in his eyes. "You're lying to me."

"Not about Kim. I swear to you, I would not hurt her." He said each word slowly, emphasizing it clearly as though it would help make his point through the alcohol clouding her thoughts.

"And what about Dylan? Would he? Did you set her up?"

"No! Damn it, Eloise—"

"You need to go." She shoved past him and threw the front door open. "I can't look at you right now."

"I would never hurt you." He stopped at the doorway, eyes pleading as he reached for her cheek with his free hand. "Don't you know that?"

"I thought I did." She leaned into his hand for a moment, closed her eyes and let his warmth soothe her before the doubts crowded in again. "I wanted tonight to try and think, to figure it out, but then you were here, and I didn't know what to say. I can't think straight, and I don't know what to believe."

"Eloise, I—"

She pulled her face away, heart breaking with the loss of his touch. "Please just go." He went without another word and she sank down in front of the door and sobbed.

Twenty-Eight

Losing Eloise was not something that Ethan had expected to happen when he'd walked into her house that evening. He stood outside her door, hand on the doorknob and heart in his throat as he listened to her cry. She'd made it clear she didn't want him with her, but there was nowhere else he wanted to be.

He knew she was upset and that at least some of the reason she'd lit into him so strongly was because the wine had loosened her usually tight grip on her feelings, but he wasn't blameless in what she was going through. He hadn't been honest with her, and because he'd tried to hide the parts of himself that he thought she wouldn't accept, she'd been unable to fall back on her trust when his character had been called into question.

He'd wanted her to see him as a good man, but he'd tried to fulfill that goal by pretending to be something he wasn't instead of trying to become the person he wanted her to see in him.

And all of that was beside the very obvious point that she had clearly found the missing piece of their puzzle. From what he'd understood of Eloise's drunken accusations, it sounded like at some point her friends had been at the bar—at least Kim had—and that was a red flag that set off all his instincts. He remembered now that conversation he'd had with Dylan at Paula's, about how he had a job for them when Ethan came back. It had been pushed to the back burner, with Dylan making up some lame excuse about the contact falling through.

But if Dylan had somehow gotten in with Eloise's friends and talked them into his plans to try to get his hands on the bank's money with their knowledge ... Then it wouldn't be outside the realm of possibility that he could be behind what had happened to Kim.

Ethan didn't want to admit that, even to himself, but now that Eloise's life was on the line, he was forced to look at his friend without the blinders of his own loyalty. Dylan was a scary man. Selfish, cruel, and dangerous.

Myles was right. He should never have brought Eloise around him and as much as he wanted to open that door and try to convince her that he was the man she needed and he would never hurt her ... The simple fact was that he wasn't that man.

Not yet.

But he was going to be.

First, he needed to untangle his life and his finances from Dylan as much as he could and that would mean transferring a whole lot of money and cutting his losses on some of their shadier investments.

It wasn't something he'd be able to tackle tonight, but he was going to get started first thing in the morning. By the time Eloise had calmed down enough that she might be willing to talk to him, he'd be ready.

He was going to make his life a clean slate and then lay his sins at her feet and beg for forgiveness. If he could do that, then he could explain to her where he was the night Kim was killed. She wasn't going to be happy about him spending his nights in some back alley on the other side of town, pretending to do a little personal drug deal while he scoped out the back entrance of a check cashing place.

But it was a hell of a lot better than murder.

Maybe that would be enough to convince her that he hadn't been a part of whatever might have happened at the bar. That gave him hope and he led Winston down the steps and across the lawn from Eloise's front door to his own.

It never got any easier, walking into the house he'd shared with his grandfather. Eloise had described him as a nice old man, but that wasn't the way Ethan remembered him at all. These walls held nothing but memories of hurt and disappointment. The night his own flesh and blood had laid hands on him in violence and told him he'd never amount to a damn thing in this life.

He'd carried that with him for too long, let it color his choices and set him on a path that he was no longer proud of as he jumped from one abuser to another, something he hadn't even realized he'd done until Eloise came along. Looking back now, he knew he'd been seeing Dylan the way she'd seen his grandfather. The surface of acceptability that they presented to people other than their victims was hard to see through.

She'd taught him to view his life through different eyes, to value different things, and he was going to have to face what involvement in his life had done to her because he'd been too blind to protect her.

That meant doing more than just untangling himself from Dylan. He was going to have to make sure that Kim's death wasn't left unsolved. If Eloise had evidence and reason to believe that Dylan was involved, then they had to take that evidence to Detective Chen.

Doing that went against everything he'd believed for more than half his life, but he wasn't going to let Eloise down. He wasn't going to let Kim down. He'd protected Dylan and his secrets for a long time, but as often as they'd broken the law, they had never done anything like that. They lied and they stole, and sometimes they threatened people, but they didn't commit murders. It was clear what he had to do and there was no room in his mind for the possibility of failure.

Twenty-Nine

She woke the next morning with a headache and regret. Nothing about the night before had gone according to plan. After talking to Jackson and David, she'd envisioned a conversation where everything remained calm and rational as she'd asked for explanations that he had seamlessly provided.

What actually happened had been closer to a train wreck than a controlled conversation. She'd lost her composure and blasted him with accusations when he didn't understand at all what she was talking about. It wasn't fair and she should have approached the whole situation differently.

Not that she didn't still think she deserved answers, but it would have been nice if she'd given him a fair chance to provide them. If he was involved in any of this, she'd have to know, but coming at him presuming his guilt hadn't been the best move.

Her house, which had felt like a place of solace before he'd barged into her life, now felt empty without him and she wandered from room to room cataloging the changes he'd made to her space. Winston's beds and toys cluttered her floors and most of the rooms had a gift he'd given her on some surface or other. There were his books on the bookshelf, sci-fi next to her cookbooks. His toothbrush in the bathroom. His favorite salty snacks in the pantry and sweet tea in the fridge.

Had she started making a life with a monster? She didn't think so, but could she have been so blinded by his charm that she'd turned a blind eye to the warning signs? He wasn't exactly a rule follower, and she knew he was up to something with Dylan that he was determined to hide, but a *murderer*? Or someone that could help cover it up?

It made her sick to her stomach to think that he might have known all along what happened to Kim. He could have been keeping that from her while she slept with him, and she really didn't have any way of knowing for sure.

Jackson and David were convinced he was in love with her, that he wouldn't do anything to hurt her, but he was definitely hiding things and until she knew what they were, well, maybe it was best if they ended things.

She clearly couldn't trust him.

Even if he wasn't a murderer, he was certainly a liar. His charm had made it hard for her to hold onto her senses, but hadn't she known from the beginning that something about him wasn't quite right? She'd thought then that he was going to be the death of her, but now it seemed the death sentence had fallen on Kim instead.

That thought made her even more nauseous and she sat down at the table with a cup of peppermint tea and plain toast. She still had to go to work today, and she needed to get a hold of herself.

She rattled the teacup in its saucer when her phone rang and clenched her teeth when she realized it was her mother on the phone. Deborah seemed to have a sixth sense that informed her when her interruptions would be the most inconvenient and this time was no exception. Eloise still hadn't responded to any of the many calls and texts since she'd hung up on her and for a while it seemed Deborah had given up.

If she was calling this early in the morning after all that, it *might* be an actual emergency. It probably *wasn't*, it was probably an attempt to get Eloise to panic and answer the phone, but it *might* be. The idea of it was enough for Eloise to panic and answer the phone.

"Hel—"

"Finally." Deborah started talking over her before Eloise could even begin speaking. "Do you know how long I've been trying to get in touch with you?"

"I do, actually."

"You know better than to treat your mother this way. What has gotten into you lately? You owe me—"

"I owe you? What? An apology?"

"At the very least an apology for treating me so disrespectfully."

"Mother ..." Eloise bit it back, swallowed a mouthful of words that would have taught her the true meaning of disrespect. "I think I need to go."

"Don't hang up on me," Deborah snapped. "Honestly, what has brought on this terrible behavior? It's a man, isn't it? I told you—"

"Ahhhh!" Eloise held the phone in her hand, fingers clenched as the short, enraged scream echoed around the kitchen "We are *not* going to talk about this again. If I want someone to rail me into next week, that's my business. I'm twenty-seven years old, Mother. If I want to get married or have children or quit my job to become a *fucking* pumpkin farmer, there's nothing you can do about it."

"You wouldn't." Deborah had gone cold and quiet, nearly whispering, Eloise wasn't sure if it was the mention of children or pumpkin farming that had pushed her over the edge. "You wouldn't give up your career to be someone's ..."

"Someone's what? Someone's spouse? Someone's mother? Just because you never wanted me and you resented Father for it every day, doesn't mean I feel the same way."

"You always wanted that career."

"*You* always wanted me to have it," Eloise corrected. "That's not the same thing."

"I know this attitude." Deborah wasn't one to give in and Eloise could almost picture her tightening her lips in disappointment. "It is a man, isn't it? You've fallen in love with someone and think that can take the place of an accomplishment of your own."

"I think that it was never meant to be a choice between one and the other, but if you really must know, then, yes, I have met someone. Someone I love and I think ... I think he loves me, too."

"You *think* he loves you?" She had obviously spotted an opening and was piling on the condescension. "He hasn't told you? You've been wasting time when you could have been doing something of value."

"Jesus, Mother, is this what you called me for? My friend is *dead*"—Deborah sucked in a harsh breath but Eloise plowed on—"and you think I should waste more of my life in an office making money for someone else? What about *my* life? What about *my* happiness?"

"Nobody is going to care about your happiness as much as you do. Do you think a husband cares about your goals? Your ambitions? That a child will? You'll spend years without a moment to yourself and no one will ever care about your dreams again."

"I'm sorry my father made your life miserable and that you had a child you didn't want, but it's not the same for me. I want a family, Mother."

"And if this man you think loves you turns out to be like your father? If you derail your life for him, give him children, and then all you're left with is shattered hopes?"

Something in Eloise's gut lurched. Hadn't she just been thinking how little she could trust him now after everything? He'd lied to her, at the very least, and who knew what else he'd done? Falling in love with him had been an accident and the foundation they'd built had been unintentional, but if they were going to keep creating a life on that foundation, it would have to be a choice.

She couldn't do that if she didn't trust him.

Deborah spoke into the silence, seemingly picking up on Eloise's hesitation even if she didn't know the exact reasons behind it. "Don't put yourself in that position. I know I haven't always done the right thing by you, but I didn't want to see you make my mistakes."

She didn't want to make Deborah's mistakes, but she couldn't live in the shadow of her regrets anymore, either. It was time for her to make a choice about what her life was going to be, and she was the only person who could decide what was right for her future.

"I'm not going to make your mistakes, Mother, but I'm not going to let your fear keep me from making my own. I know you're trying in your own way, but you have to let me be in charge of my own life. That's what you really wanted for yourself. The ability to make your own choices. Don't try to take that away from me."

Deborah was quiet for a long moment and then she sighed heavily. "I was only trying to keep you from making choices you can't undo but if you're determined then I can't stop you from doing what you want."

"I love you, but I have to go." She needed to find Ethan and try to work out the mess she'd made.

Love was a lot of things, but it was mostly a leap of faith.

The feeling had been inside her almost since the day she'd stopped actively trying to hate him and let him convince her to make him spaghetti in his kitchen.

But she'd been scared to make the jump.

"I love you, too." Deborah rarely said it and Eloise knew that it was a complicated feeling for her, but, for once, it rang true. "Be safe."

"I will."

That promise might prove difficult to keep, but that was a worry for later. For now, she was focused on finding her shoes and then the man she'd almost let walk out of her life. She didn't know why Kim had been at Dylan's bar or what the connection was, but she did know that it wasn't because Ethan was in on it. He wouldn't do anything like that, and he loved her too much to try to hide it if he had any idea who had done it. He was a loyal friend, and he was willing to keep most of Dylan's secrets, but he wouldn't protect him if he had been responsible for something that had stolen someone's life. Someone that had made Eloise cry and frightened her by trying to break into her house. He'd been furious when that happened, nearly unhinged with rage and concern.

He was protective of her because he loved her, and she had been a fool to think he might have tried to hurt the people she cared about.

She found her slippers by the door and ran out across the yard still wearing her pajamas. It meant she'd be late but somehow that didn't matter as much anymore.

Sun Valley could live without her today and all the other days. The world would not come crashing down because she didn't show up. It was a liberating thought and when she got done apologizing to Ethan about her behavior, she wanted to tell him about it.

She made it up his front porch stairs in a single jump and slid to a stop in front of his door. He had a key to her house because he was always there, but she'd never bothered to get a key for his, so she raised her fist and pounded on the heavy wood. It echoed inside but the house remained still, and the lights didn't come on.

She pounded again but as she swiveled to try and peek in his window, she realized the obvious. His car wasn't in the driveway, so he wasn't home.

"Damn it." If he'd left the house already, she'd have to try and reach him some other way. It was important that she didn't let him think she believed he was a killer any longer than he already had.

She'd left her phone on her kitchen table, so she ran back across the yard, waving at a stunned Jackson as he walked out his front door on the way to work, and back up her own porch steps. Her call went straight to voicemail, and she shot off several impatient texts before standing at the table for fifteen minutes nibbling on her thumbnail.

He didn't answer her immediately and she flopped down in a chair, chewing on her leftover toast and racking her brain for a plan before deciding it would be best if she just got dressed and went to work. It would be a long day, but he was bound to answer her eventually and since she had no idea where he'd gone, there was nothing she could do to speed up the process.

When he hadn't answered her by lunch, she got angry. When he hadn't answered her when she got off work, she got worried. Maybe he didn't intend to answer her at all. That seemed reasonable after what she'd said to him. She'd told him in the messages that she was sorry but maybe that wasn't enough.

He still wasn't home when she pulled her car into her driveway, but after a full day of thinking she had a pretty good idea of where he might be. He was pissed off at her, so he'd probably gone to the bar. That was basically what she would have done after a fight, if she hadn't been the one to start it. She would have run to her friends for a little solidarity and support.

The longer she thought about it, the more sense it made, and even if she wasn't all that thrilled about seeing Dylan or that one flirty bartender again, she had to find him. *Especially* now that she'd remembered the bartender. Did he think she'd broken up with him and gone to her that night? Was twenty-seven too late in life to get into her first fight over a man?

Probably, but the thought sounded appealing when she pictured Ethan with someone else and it was an idea that she was willing to entertain, if only in her fantasies. She'd never thrown a punch before, but that didn't keep her from winning in her imaginary bar brawl.

His car wasn't outside when she pulled into the parking lot, but it looked like there was employee parking around back so that didn't mean he wasn't there. There weren't any other cars in the front and the neon 'Open' sign wasn't on, but it was late enough in the evening that the bartenders would be setting up even if they hadn't opened for customers yet.

She gave the front door a tug, prepared to stand outside knocking if she had to, but it opened smoothly to reveal the dimly lit interior. There were people inside, she could see them moving around toward the back, but they were too far away for her to make out their faces. Almost certainly Dylan and Myles. Ethan if she was lucky. The angry bartender if she wasn't.

"Hello?" She stepped in and closed the door behind her. Without the open door to let in the last of the day's sunlight, her vision went dark, and she couldn't see anything but the low lights that were on over the bar.

"We're closed." The voice was low and gruff, not Ethan but still vaguely familiar.

"Yeah, I know." Eloise came closer, feeling her way forward

toward the bar with her feet so she didn't trip. "It's just that I'm looking for Ethan. Have you seen him?"

"Eloise?" *That* voice she definitely recognized and after a few confused blinks her eyes confirmed what her ears were telling her.

"Sarah?"

Thirty

"Eloise, what the hell are you doing here?"

"I was looking for ..." Eloise fell silent as she took in the scene before her. Dylan was there as she'd predicted but Sarah was sitting on his knee. Chloe sat across the table from them beside Myles and the two of them looked by turn miserable and terrified. "What do you mean what am *I* doing here? What are the two of *you* doing here?"

"Eloise!" Dylan smiled, that awful creepy smile that she hated, and patted Sarah's hip. "What a surprise. I think you've met my girlfriend?"

"I don't ... What?"

Eloise was looking at Sarah, but Sarah was looking at the table. So was Chloe. Both of them refused to look at her, even when Dylan grabbed Sarah's chin in his hand and pressed a kiss to her lips.

A noise of distress escaped from somewhere in Eloise's chest. It was the closest she'd ever come to hearing a heart breaking.

"It was you." That much Eloise thought was certain. She didn't understand why or how her friends had come to be involved in it, but she knew the blame rested on Dylan. "You killed her."

"Guilty." He had the audacity to wink at her and Eloise was afraid she might vomit. "She was a lot like you. Too noble and nosy for her own good. She paid for it and now ... so will you."

"You knew about this?" Eloise ignored Dylan, her attention focused on Sarah and Chloe. "You knew he killed her?"

"Not at first." Sarah still wasn't looking at her, but Eloise could hear the tears in her voice. "Dylan invited me to the bar, that morning I met him at your house. He slipped me his number on a business card, and I didn't want to come alone so I brought Chloe and Kim with me. I knew you didn't like him, so I didn't say anything to you. It was just supposed to be the money, that's what we decided that night, but then—"

"What night? When did you ..." Eloise couldn't picture it and her brow furrowed as she tried to trace it back and put the pieces together. Sarah's bruises. Kim's death. Their strange attitudes in the days before the murder ... It all led back to the night Ethan had shown up bleeding at her door. She'd thought they were jealous after that—mad that she'd started spending more time with Ethan and less time with them—but that hadn't been it at all. They'd been hiding something from her. A plan Ethan hadn't known about because he'd been away from the bar, nursing a gunshot wound. "Why would you do this to Kim?"

That was the part that still didn't make sense. Kim was no threat to them. She wasn't a threat to *anyone*.

"She got cold feet and threatened to back out." Sarah's eyes were puffy from crying and there was a fresh bruise forming on her cheek. "She said she was going to go to the cops if we didn't call the whole thing off, but I still didn't think he'd actually hurt her. It was just supposed to be about the money."

"You were embezzling from the bank." Eloise's voice sounded far away, distant and thin like it was someone else that was speaking instead of her.

"That's enough." The hand on Sarah's chin turned from gentle to punishing. "My lovely little lady here wanted all the fun of being bad and none of the tough decisions. But that's not how it works, is it, honey?"

Sarah whimpered and shook her head. Eloise could hardly look at her—it made her feel sick—but looking at Chloe was no better. She was further from Dylan, but her shoulders were trembling with small, pitiful sobs.

"You could have come to me or gone to the police." Eloise wanted to reach out and shake them both till their teeth rattled.

"That would have been a very bad idea, wouldn't it?" Dylan shook his head. "I never do business with anyone unless I know their weaknesses. A little research goes a long way and it's never a good idea to piss off a man when he's capable of murder and knows where your family lives."

"I can't believe this." Eloise's head was spinning. It felt like a nightmare, but she couldn't seem to wake herself up. "If they won't do something about this, then I will."

She started to back up, but Dylan was laughing as he turned to ask Sarah, "Is she always this stupid?" He pulled a gun from under the table and pointed at Eloise's chest. "I'd prefer not to use this here, but I can't have you running your mouth. Remember when I said Kim paid for being nosy? That *you* were going to pay?"

Eloise swallowed but her mouth had gone dry, and her head was fuzzy. She was sure there had to be a way out of this —she couldn't let the son of a bitch win—but trying to grab hold of any single thought was like trying to catch smoke in her hands. As soon as she started to pull something together, it vanished.

"You're going to regret this." Eloise tried to make it sound like a promise, but her voice wobbled. He wouldn't regret it. She wasn't sure he was capable of remorse, but it was the only thing she could think of saying. If she could stall him, get a little more time, maybe she could clear her head enough to figure out a plan. She didn't want to die and be buried in some hole beneath the singing summer birds like Kim.

"You're wrong about that but I have to say I admire your talent for being able to show up at exactly the worst time for yourself. First, practically tripping over Kim's body and now this." He paused, lingering like he wanted to savor the moment. "You saved me a lot of trouble. Now I can get rid of you and my other little *problem* at the same. We can't just leave witnesses running around but trying to find the right time and place has been more of a headache than either of you are worth."

Sarah looked at him, dawning horror replacing the defeated misery on her face. "What? What do you mean, your *other* problem?"

Dylan ignored her, turning his attention and the gun from Eloise to the other side of the table. "Isn't that right, Chloe?"

Chloe blanched, the color leaching from her face as she looked around wildly. Her gaze landed on Myles and her expression was pleading but he looked away, a muscle ticking rhythmically in his jaw.

"Oh, come *on*." Dylan laughed, darkly amused in a way that reminded Eloise of a cat she'd seen tormenting a mouse, carrying around only to drop it so it could catch it again. It was sick. Sadistic. "You had to know it would come to this, right?"

"You ... You said—" Chloe tripped over her words, eyes swinging from Dylan to Sarah and back again. "You both promised me that the break-in at my apartment was a coincidence. You said you didn't know anything about it!"

"I didn't!" Sarah was reeling, tears spilling over her lashes to run down her cheeks. For a moment, it seemed like she might try to get up, to go to Chloe and offer some comfort, but Dylan tightened his grip on her waist, pinning her in place. "I didn't know he was planning *any* of this! I just wanted the money and to get out from under Dwayne and Sun Valley. You know we're going to be the first ones gone when they start downsizing and we've given everything to that company. I just ... I just wanted what they owed us. That was all. I didn't sign up for any of this!"

Dylan yanked her arm until she fell silent except for her sobs and Eloise flinched as she recalled all of Sarah's bruises. There was no doubt about where they had all really been coming from. All the tension and the tired eyes and all the rest had come from whatever was going on between the two of them. He'd lured her in and chewed her up, reduced her to a shell of her former self and Eloise had been attributing all of it to the wrong sources. Sarah had been in trouble, they all had, and she'd been blind to it.

"Leave her alone." She meant for it to sound intimidating, but it came out as barely a whisper, inaudible above Sarah's tears and Chloe's mumbled begging.

"Now," Dylan turned his attention back to Chloe and ignored both women's pleas. "I know I asked you here so we could have an honest discussion about the future of our little business venture, but as you can see, I think it's time we terminated your involvement in the project."

"Dylan, please." Sarah sat up straighter, wiped her cheeks and forced a trembling smile. "Please don't do this. We don't need to kill anyone else. We have the money already so we can just ...We can just go. Leave the country and buy an island somewhere. They'll never find us."

"We'd be in handcuffs before the year was out. That's what happens when you leave loose ends. If we want a clean getaway, then we can't have the threat of a prison sentence hanging over our heads. Your friends here know too much."

He waved the gun at them and, though he was speaking to Sarah, his eyes never left Chloe's terrified face. It was as though he wanted her to fully understand the danger she was in, to accept the inevitability of her death before it happened so he could watch the fear claim her.

Sarah changed tactics, kissing him deeply and pressing her body against him. "You know I love you, Dylan. If you love me, if you care about me at all, you won't do this. Let them go, please."

For a moment, Eloise thought it had worked. He cupped Sarah's face in his hand and pressed a small kiss to the end of her nose before leaning close to her ear to say, "If you don't shut up, I'll put you in the hole right next to them." She froze on his lap, an animal in a trap, and he nodded. "See? That's not so hard, is it? You're mine and you'll do as I tell you. Do you understand?"

Sarah nodded jerkily but her eyes were wide and terrified when her gaze met Eloise's. She had done all she could to help them without sacrificing her own life and despite the frightening circumstances, Eloise felt sorry for her and for Chloe.

She was angry about what they'd done and hurt about the lies they'd told, but they hadn't meant to hurt anyone. They'd been foolish and greedy, but somehow she found it hard to blame them for getting involved in this mess. How could she, when she'd fallen in love with Ethan just as hard and just as recklessly as Sarah had apparently fallen for Dylan.

They'd made mistakes but hadn't she made her own questionable choices? She'd bandaged up a gunshot wound in her kitchen without calling the police and put her trust in

Ethan when all the evidence had pointed to him as a possible killer. She'd chosen to love and to trust against the odds. Sarah simply hadn't been as lucky as she had.

Her friends hadn't been responsible for what happened to Kim—blame for that landed squarely on Dylan—and they must have been terrified of what Dylan might do to them if they resisted. They'd gone along out of fear and look where that had gotten them.

Eloise didn't want to die but she didn't want them to suffer anymore, either. It had been impossible enough to try and get herself out of this situation, but she needed to try and save Chloe, to free Sarah from Dylan. He was outnumbered, but the only one with a weapon. As far as she knew, Sarah and Chloe had no more self-defense skills than she did herself. Getting them out of this seemed about as likely as having time run backwards.

There was nothing the three of them could do but her panicked gaze landed on Myles, sitting silent and sullen the whole time beside Chloe. She'd barely spoken to him, but she remembered how flustered he'd been when he'd destroyed her hydrangea, just a kid with a big heart and a bad family.

"And you?" she asked. "You're just going to sit there and let this happen?"

Dylan laughed when Myles refused to look at her and took another long drink of his beer. "Didn't you know? My baby brother was in love with that little friend of yours. He couldn't save her, and he isn't going to save you."

Eloise got a glimpse of Myles' expression as he lowered the bottle and the look that he gave Dylan was one of pure hatred. Whatever he'd felt for his brother before Kim's murder had been replaced by only that and nothing else. A tragedy that Dylan seemed to miss or perhaps to revel in. There was certainly no remorse in him for what he'd done.

"Please help us." Eloise wasn't going to waste her time

pleading with a monster, but maybe there was enough fight in Myles for him to do the right thing. "We loved her, too, please don't let him get away with this."

"Hey." Dylan waved the gun and then pointed it back at her chest. "Shut up."

Eloise stopped talking but she was still begging Myles to help them with her eyes. She knew Dylan had allowed this to go on so long because being in control fanned his ego, but they had to be running out of time.

That suspicion was confirmed when he stood up, practically dumping Sarah on the floor in the process, and started giving orders. "Now, what we're all gonna do is take a little walk out back and get into that SUV in the parking lot. Then we'll take a drive outside of town and when we get to a place where no one can hear you scream, two of you are gonna end up gator bait."

Chloe started crying again as he herded them all toward the back door, but Eloise was searching frantically for a weapon or a distraction, anything she could use to keep him from putting them into a vehicle and driving away.

It was getting dark outside and if she could get her hands on anything at all, she might be able to use his momentary lack of attention to make a run for it. He couldn't chase after her and keep the others in line, so he'd have to choose. Either way, there was a good chance at least one person would make it to safety and from there, they could call for help. She had no idea how much space there was between the back door and whatever car he intended to shove them into, but surely it was enough for her to make a break for it.

The problem with her plan was that he didn't give her time or room to find any kind of weapon as they crossed the bar. Anytime one of them slowed down or tried to resist, he stuck the barrel of the gun threateningly between their ribs and insisted they keep walking.

By the time they were nearly to the door, she'd resigned herself to the inevitable truth. She'd just have to do it without the weapon and hope that simply knocking him off balance would be enough for her to run without getting shot. It lowered her chances of success but there was no way she was going to meekly climb into that waiting vehicle and wait to be driven to the scene of her own murder.

Myles reached the back door first and held it open as Chloe and Sarah passed through. When it was her turn, he caught her eye and gave a nearly imperceptible nod in Dylan's direction. His face was pale but determined and his eyes on hers were full of focused intent. Relief washed over her. He was going to help them.

As soon as she stepped out into the dark parking lot, he tried to swing the door closed behind her, to block Dylan from being able to get through. There was a dull thud and a loud, pained grunt and for a moment she thought Myles had managed to get the door closed but her hopes were dashed as it began to swing open again a second before it latched. Myles tried to lean against it, throwing his whole weight onto the steel frame, but Dylan had already gotten a shoulder through. The door swung back and forth as both men cursed and shouted, and Sarah and Chloe watched wide-eyed and frozen with uncertainty.

"Help him or run!" Eloise screamed. It seemed to break the spell that fear and surprise had cast over them and she threw her own weight against the door at the same time that Sarah did. They both pushed as hard as they could as Chloe turned and began to sprint along the back of the building toward the small alleyway that would lead her around to the front and the road beyond.

Eloise hoped she'd have enough of her wits about her to remember to call for help when she got here, but it turned out that she didn't need to. As soon as Chloe turned the corner and became visible to the front parking lot the air filled with shouted commands.

"This is the police!"

"Stop where you are!"

"Get down! Down on the ground now!"

Chloe slid to stop and threw her hands in the air. "Back here!" she screamed. "He's trying to kill my friends. Please help us!"

The darkness was driven back by the crisscrossing beams of many flashlights and then there were people everywhere. Myles, Sarah, and Eloise all stepped away from the back door of the building with their hands in the air and Dylan charged through, gun raised, into a crowd of SWAT officers with their own guns pointed at his chest.

There was a momentary standoff as they screamed at him to lower his weapon and Eloise was sure for a second that he wasn't going to comply, but the gun slipped from his hand and into the dirt a moment later.

"Eloise?"

Her head snapped up at the sound of her name and she saw Ethan pushing and shoving his way through the crowd with Detective Chen right behind him. She was speaking, "Mr. Callaghan, you have to wait until the scene has been cleared," but he was ignoring her as he searched each face he passed.

"Ethan!" She knew the instant he'd spotted her, his body language changed from desperate to relieved from one breath to the next, and then he was there, and his arms were around her and she was finally, finally safe. "You found me."

"You scared the hell out of me," he returned. "We've been outside for ten minutes trying to figure out a way to get you out without getting anyone hurt. I thought I was going to lose you. Don't *ever* do anything like that to me again, do you hear me?"

"I won't." She buried her face in his neck and cried, all the tears she'd been holding onto for the last hour suddenly trying to escape all at once. "I promise I won't and I'm so sorry and I never should have said those things to you. I love you ..." She stopped babbling when the strength of her sobbing made the words incoherent.

"Shhh," he soothed. He was running his hands over her back and hair, trying to comfort her and check her for injuries at the same time. "It's all right. I'm here and you're gonna be fine now. I love you so much. You have no idea how scared I was."

"I'm so sorry."

"No, don't apologize. It's my fault. If I had been honest with you from the beginning, this would never have happened."

"Callaghan!" Dylan was yelling and struggling against his cuffs as they tried to drag him away. "You traitorous piece of shit! You think I'm going down by myself? You don't betray your family!"

"She's my family." Ethan turned his back on Dylan and drew Eloise closer into his arms, as though he could shield her with his body.

"Somebody shut him up!" Detective Chen shook her head and waved over a handful of officers, instructing them to collect evidence from the scene. "The rest of you, stay where you are. We're going to need to collect statements from everyone."

Ethan pulled Eloise into his arms and dropped his mouth close to her ear so no one else could hear him. "He's going to take me and Myles down with him. Probably Chloe and Sarah, too, if they were doing what I think they were. There's nothing I can do to stop him, but I couldn't let him kill you. When I got your voicemails and realized you were coming here ..."

"Where were you?" She pulled back, brow furrowing and she slapped his arm. "I called you. I texted you all day."

"I know." He held his out, a gesture of surrender and a plea for forgiveness. "I was handling some business, cleaning up some loose ends so I could prove to you I would never hurt you. I cut all my financial ties with Dylan and then I went to the police station to try and convince them he was probably involved in Kim's death."

"So you couldn't answer your phone?" She was touched by what he'd done, but still not quite over how a simple returned text message might have kept her from ending up almost dead.

"I was trying to give you some space. Figured it would be better to talk things out in person. Then I spent all afternoon at the police station waiting to talk to a detective. Phone service there is basically nonexistent. I didn't get any of the messages about the bar until you were already here. I raised hell and we came as quickly as I could get them here."

"So, you talked to Detective Chen? She knows about Dylan and Kim?" Eloise felt like her brain was running slow, trying to absorb too much information at once and unable to grasp the important bits. "You said ... You said he was going to try to take you all down ... But then, you talked to her, too? What did you tell her?"

Eloise was shaking as his meaning ripped into her brain. Dylan would go down for the murder, but he would take the rest of them down for embezzlement and who knew what else. She had no idea what sort of crimes Ethan had been involved in, but the heartbreak in his voice told her he was looking at serious time. He'd told Detective Chen that Dylan was dangerous, and she'd believed him, so he must have admitted to something. He'd done that for her, to save her life.

"Nobody says a word to the cops," she said, pinning Ethan, Myles, Chloe, and Sarah with stern looks by turn. She wasn't going to let Dylan take them from her. "Not one word until everyone has a decent lawyer."

"Where are we going to get a decent lawyer?" Sarah was holding Chloe as she sobbed against her shoulder, and her gaze was weary. "If we end up depending on some public defender, we're screwed and we can't afford anything better without the money that we ..." She looked quickly over her shoulder at all the officers milling around. "You know?"

"Let me handle that." Eloise was already reaching for her phone and it only rang twice before Deborah picked up.

"Hello? Eloise?" She was clearly surprised by the unscheduled call but her tone was concerned instead of irritated.

"Hello, Mother." Eloise smiled tightly at Ethan when his eyebrows rose. "Sorry to bother you at this hour but ... I need your help. It's a lot to explain and I promise I will, but I need to borrow some money. A lot of money, actually."

"What, are your parents loaded?" Ethan was clearly baffled at how he hadn't known, but she could only nod helplessly. They had never really discussed her parents beyond her tense relationship with them.

"Very loaded," she mouthed, half listening to the reaction of Ethan and her friends and half trying to answer Deborah's barrage of questions. "Everything is going to be okay."

Epilogue

ight Months Later

"I can't believe I let you talk me into this."

"What?" Ethan sighed dramatically. "Did you want to keep working in finance?"

"There are other options," Eloise reminded him. "But no, that's not what I meant."

Eloise had her hands on her hips as she stood in the middle of the parking lot with Ethan and Myles, evaluating the new sign above the bar entrance. The old 'Tough Break' name and logo had been taken down and, in its place, 'Second Chance Bar and Grill' was spelled out in fresh, white letters. The new logo, a red phoenix rising on a black background, had also been designed by Ethan but this time, it wasn't for someone else.

He'd sold his grandfather's house—and all the bad memories with it— to invest in the bar with Myles. He already had the experience and the sale of the house gave him enough money for the two of them to finally turn the place into a legitimate business.

Dylan had been furious about signing over his portion of

his inheritance, but after Eloise's mom had found them all lawyers and then flown in from Chicago to start pulling strings with every friend and acquaintance she had in the entire state—a large number that was surprising even for Eloise— he'd realized he was going to prison, *alone*, and he'd become open to bargaining. Myles had agreed to provide him a payment each month to spend at the commissary and in exchange he'd handed over his rights to the bar.

Myles and Ethan had taken his arrest as well as Eloise thought possible. They were angry at what he'd done, but also hurt by the loss of him. Myles had gone alone at first to visit him—to handle the necessary conversations about the future of the bar and the legalities—but he'd come back so shaken that Ethan had started going along for emotional support. Now, they both went to visit him once a month as Myles tried to work out his conflicted feelings toward the brother that had done him so much harm.

Eloise hated that Ethan went, but she wouldn't ask him not to. As difficult as it was, she understood the complex loyalty of family. He had chosen her to be his new family when he'd betrayed Dylan and gone to the police, but she knew how he felt about Myles. As long as he needed to go, Ethan would go with him.

Ethan said he considered himself lucky as he looked back on all they'd been through and how the system had failed them. Dylan had caught the worst of the abuse, the neglect, and the pain. He had become a dangerous man because of it but all Ethan saw was a path he could easily have gone down himself. He was facing a death sentence if he was found guilty, but Eloise knew Ethan was hoping he'd get life in prison instead. That maybe, somehow, he'd find peace and purpose at the end of all the mess he'd created.

Eloise didn't harbor much hope, but she had listened to plenty of Myles's stories over the past few months and she had grown to feel sorry for the child Dylan had once been, even if she couldn't shake her hatred over what the man had done. She didn't know how she felt about his eventual sentencing, death for death wouldn't bring Kim back, but it was out of her hands.

"Don't forget we need to take pictures to send to your mom." Ethan tugged on Eloise's hand until she got close enough he could snap a selfie of both of them with the bar in the background. Deborah had been completely charmed by Ethan during her brief visit. He'd turned his honeyed southern accent all the way up and called her *ma'am* until she'd blushed and actually smiled at him. Not much of one, but a smile, nonetheless.

The two of them had been a seamless team of support for Eloise ever since. Ethan had been by her side nearly every moment in the early days, comforting her through her nightmares and holding her hand when she had to speak to the police about what had happened that night in the bar. Deborah had been a whirlwind. Charming, scheming, and promising favors until eventually she'd managed to convince the state's lawyers to let the rest of them trade their testimony against Dylan for leniency.

Eloise and Deborah had been on the same side for once and it had helped to smooth out some of the cracks in their relationship. It was like they were truly seeing each other as people for the first time.

"You think she'll like it?" Ethan turned the phone around so Eloise could see the picture, his face alight with pride.

"No, but I think she'll *pretend* to and that's almost as good."

"Hey, you said you like this design," Ethan reminded her. "And you like the colors we picked out when we did the interior."

"I do," she agreed. "But I still can't believe I let you talk me into quitting my job to work here and I think that's the part she probably isn't actually thrilled about."

"Hey," Myles bumped her shoulder with his. "You came up with a great menu for the kitchen."

She couldn't deny that she was happier than she'd ever been, even if this wasn't the future she'd always envisioned for herself, but she was always going to be the type of person who was nervous about new adventures.

"If nothing else, it will give you something to do while you explore your options," Ethan said. He'd been thrilled when she'd quit the job, but she knew he worried about her feeling pressured to work at the bar now that they lived together full-time.

"Maybe I'll become a pumpkin farmer," she teased.

"If that's what you want to do, then I'll support you." He managed to keep a straight face, though only just barely. "I do have one question, though. Can you farm pumpkins in Louisiana?"

"I don't think so." She dissolved into laughter as Myles rolled his eyes. "I guess that's not the right job for me then."

"You're gonna have to do better than that if you want to get out of working here." Ethan kissed her and she clung to him, grateful he was still there and not locked in a prison somewhere. All those favors had gotten him and Myles probation. Ethan had gotten three years for pleading guilty to various crimes Dylan had confessed to them committing, Myles had gotten an additional two years for a conspiracy plea for his limited involvement in the embezzlement.

"I'm not going anywhere," she promised.

"I know." He smiled and leaned his forehead against hers. They stayed that way for a long moment, still awed that they had each other after coming so close to losing their lives and their freedom.

"Are Sarah and Chloe coming to the big reopening tonight?" Myles asked.

"They said they'd be here." Eloise squeezed Ethan's hand as a newly developed nervousness hit her hard. It had been rough for them since everything had come out into the open. She'd done her best to make sure they didn't suffer the same fate as Dylan, but their betrayal had cut her deeper than she'd originally realized. She couldn't find it in her heart to hate them after what they'd been through, but she couldn't trust them either. "Jackson and David, too."

"Those two wouldn't miss it for all the money in the world." Ethan laughed at her skeptical expression. "They'd crawl over hot coals to make you happy."

"Just me?" Eloise pinned him with a hard look. "I don't know if you've noticed but you're their favorite friend since you moved in and started going over there to talk about man stuff."

"Man stuff? The last time I was there, they gave me wine and cheese and made me watch a chick flick."

"They told me you cried, so I want you to know that your secrets are *not* safe with them."

She heard him mutter under his breath, something about traitors, and laughed as he pulled her inside to finish the prep work. They were expecting a packed bar for the opening night. Not just their friends but the people from the community coming out to show support for the business.

Paula had been pressing fliers into the hands of every customer that came through the door of her restaurant and the response had been favorable. They wanted more legitimate businesses in the neighborhood to support the revitalization effort. Property in nearby areas had been bought up by big investors and they didn't want that to happen in their own backyards.

Now Ethan and Myles would get to be part of that, and

they'd already arranged to have monthly donations made available to the local youth center. It was important to both of them that they do what they could to make sure other kids had better opportunities than the ones they were given.

Eloise had been worried that keeping the building would be difficult for all of them after what happened, but the inside had been gutted and completely renovated. The scuffed old floors and warped bar top were gone, along with all the tasteless naked women decorating the walls. They'd put in new pool tables and created a space for a dance floor beside an old-fashioned jukebox. There was a stage for the weekend bands or brave Wednesday night karaoke singers.

Ethan had insisted they splurge on all new glassware and an upgrade to all the bar's service systems, while Eloise and Myles had gone for décor and new kitchen appliances. Top of the line stainless steel made the old kitchen space shine and before long the bar had begun to feel more like home than a place where terrible things had happened to her.

Of course, she suspected that maybe some of the money Ethan was pumping into the business hadn't actually come from selling his house, but if he and Myles had a secret bank account stashed away somewhere with the money they'd gotten working with Dylan, she didn't want to know about it.

It had bought her a lovely new stove and that was all that mattered at this point. Well, mostly. It had also bought her a fryer and a walk-in freezer.

All of which she had put to good use when she'd designed the new menu for the now functioning 'grill' part of the business. Despite what she'd said to Ethan outside, she was perfectly happy in the kitchen. Coming up with new recipes was a thrilling way to exercise her creative mind and she enjoyed the monotony of the prep work almost as much as she enjoyed knowing people were going to be eating the food she'd made.

The idea of the kitchen being swamped with orders was a little unsettling since she hadn't worked a rush shift since she'd finished college, but this time there would be no angry man in an apron shouting orders and trying to grope her ass. She was in charge here and that made all the difference.

Sarah and Chloe showed up just before opening and found her standing in the walk-in, doing a final check to make sure everything was in place before the first customers started arriving.

"You came." Eloise stepped out of the freezer and closed the door behind her. She hadn't seen them since they'd finished their six-month stint of house arrest and she wasn't sure what to do with herself. A handshake seemed too formal and a hug too awkward.

"You know we wouldn't miss it." Sarah smiled and handed over a cup of iced coffee. A small peace offering or a gesture of goodwill. "It's a little late in the day for coffee but I thought you might need this."

"Yes." Eloise took a long sip. "It's perfect. Thank you."

"Ethan's out there prowling around like a caged tiger." Chloe made an exaggerated face. "I think someone's a little nervous."

"Myles is trying to calm him down, but I don't think he's having much luck." Sarah's eyes got misty and she pressed a hand to her face. "Is he doing okay, then? Myles?"

Eloise's smile faltered for a moment, but she nodded. "I think so. He still goes out to her grave sometimes, but I think he's doing better now."

"We were worried about him." Chloe reached for Sarah's hand, a comforting and absentminded gesture as she spoke, and Eloise wondered if there was something more between them these days. It would explain Chloe's attitude toward her all those years, her jealous need to be closer to Sarah than anyone else. Maybe they just hadn't been ready to face it. If there was something there, they'd tell her when they were ready, but she was hopeful that they had found happiness.

"I've been worried about all of you," Eloise admitted.

"Don't worry about me," Chloe said. "House arrest and probation aren't so bad when the other options are death and prison." They'd each gotten eight years of probation after their house arrest terms were up but after what had happened, Eloise was sure it must have seemed like a blessing. They'd also lost their jobs and had to give back all the money they'd stolen but they weren't complaining about that, either.

"Look, I know we talked about all this but ... You two went through a lot. I know you're doing okay now but I still can't help but worry at least a little bit."

They had spent a lot of time in the days following Dylan's arrest talking about what had happened and helping Eloise piece together the events that had led to Kim's death and the near miss they had all experienced at the bar.

It had been hard for her to understand some things—like how Dylan had convinced them to get involved in this scheme of his to begin with—while others were simply surprising. Realizing Sarah had been the one to trash Kim's office, for example. Chloe had slept with one of the security guards and convinced him to turn the cameras off in that part of the building. Eloise had been coming *out* of Kim's office as Sarah had been going *in*. They had all been keeping secrets but they all kept the details of that particular day from the cops.

They had both cried when they'd told her about finding out what Dylan had done. The way he'd threatened Myles and abused Sarah. They'd been living in fear. Even worse than Eloise because they'd had no one to protect them and she'd had Ethan.

"Well, try not to worry today." Sarah batted her eyes and flipped her hair before saying dramatically, "It's your big night."

She hugged them both awkwardly and then shooed them toward the door. "Go ask the very stressed looking blond guy with a beard to make you a drink. Maybe then he'll stop pacing."

"I doubt it, but we'll try."

Eloise had only just gotten them out of the kitchen when Jackson and David came in with their own congratulations and a huge bouquet of red lilies. She let them stay for a few minutes and look over her workstations until Jackson tried eating the ingredients and then she sent them out to wait with the others.

Once the doors were opened, she had no more time to think. Orders came in fast, and her mind narrowed its focus until the food in front of her was all that existed. It was hot and demanding work, but she'd designed her menu and her kitchen well. Her process was efficient and even with the excitement around reopening, she was able to keep up with the demand with only a little help from Myles as he pitched in wherever he was needed.

Before she knew it, hours had passed, and Ethan was leaning against the door frame with a glass of white wine. "That was the last order for the night. Myles just announced the kitchen was closed and we've only got another thirty minutes until the rest of the place closes down, too."

"How did it go out there?" She took a quick drink of the wine to wet her dry throat but set it aside to reach for her bottle of water. There would be time for wine after she'd rehydrated and eaten her own dinner. "Any problems?"

"Not a single one." He looked happier than she'd ever seen him. "Paula came by and had everyone out on the dance floor. Jackson was hustling everyone at the pool tables. Myles was running everywhere but mostly here and the bar and I think maybe even flirting with one of the customers. It was an incredible success."

"You made this happen. This dream is for you and Myles. You've earned it."

"I would never have made it this far without you." He picked her up and spun her around until they were both dizzy, then kissed her senseless. "You were the one that gave me a reason to hope for something better."

"I love you." She beamed down at him, feeling bubbly and free, until he set her down again and kissed her.

"Not bad for an obnoxious neighbor, huh?"

"Hey, you absolutely *were* obnoxious. *But,*" she continued, when he started to argue, "I'd rather have you in my bed than as a neighbor any day."

"Just in your bed?"

His smile was suddenly devilish, and a shiver ran over her. "Where else did you have in mind?"

"Let's get everyone out of here and then I'll show you."

It took more than an hour to clear out all the customers, run through their new end-of-night routine, and pry Myles down off his adrenaline high enough to get him out the door, but Ethan spent all of it tormenting her.

He touched her at every opportunity, never missing a chance to let his fingers dance over the inside of her wrist or the curve of her hip. By the time they locked the door behind Myles and turned to each other, she was eager to get her hands on him in return.

She squealed in surprise when he tossed her over his shoulder and carted her from the doorway to one of the old pool tables he'd stored in the back.

"Did you put it back here just for this?"

"Hey, it's a health code violation to fuck you in the bar's kitchen and I don't want to listen to Myles complain about us messing up the new ones."

"You could take me home, you know?"

He grinned at her from the space between her legs and she

knew she wasn't fooling him. Her thighs were already trembling with anticipation and her voice was husky with want. There were no more secrets between them, and he knew exactly how much she enjoyed this.

"I could." He bit into one thigh and then the other and laughed as she squirmed beneath his teeth. "But what's the fun in that?"

Coming Soon

The Widow's Point Duology

Acknowledgments

Somehow I thought writing my acknowledgments would be easier on my second book but unfortunately it seems the task of trying to thank everyone properly remains a challenge! This book was particularly difficult for me (second book slump is no joke!) and I'm blessed enough to have a wonderful group of supporters that helped me through. If I miss naming anyone specifically, please know that I am intensely grateful to all of you from the bottom of my heart!

I have to begin by thanking my team at Creative James Media. Jean Lowd has believed in me and my books since the beginning and she has been a fearless and generous leader through this entire process. I have learned so much from her and I hope I can put all of it to good use as I continue to grow in this business. I also have to thank my editors, Staci Petroski and Rachel Burchett and my cover designer, Diana from Triumph Covers, for the wonderful work they have done to help make this book a reality. I wouldn't have been able to do this without my wonderful team and I am so grateful to each of you!

Death Sentence was hard for me to write because it was so different from my first book. There were many times that I wasn't sure I had more than one book in me. I wanted to give up. I tried to quit. Thankfully I have many passionate friends and critique partners that cheered me on and refused to let me toss the manuscript in the trash. I have to thank Maria for being my rock from the beginning. I absolutely could not have done this without her. She was there at my lowest moments and I treasure our friendship more than she will ever know. Tristen has been the beta every writer needs! Honest and kind, she always makes me think and work harder. I have to thank her for all the brainstorming sessions and unending encouragement! To all my other betas and every single member of my various Discord servers, you all are the best! I appreciate each and every one of you.

Finally, I have to thank my family because there's simply nothing and no one else in my life as important to me as they are. I have to single out my parents, obviously, and thank them so much for all of their relentless enthusiasm and being proud of my every accomplishment, no matter how small. Evergreen thank you to the sister of my heart, Sassy, for putting up with me for longer than any other friend in my life and still loving me after all these years. My most heartfelt thanks to my husband, love of my life and other half of my soul, I owe him so much of my success! He has always been willing to let me chase my dreams. And finally, all my gratitude to my kids, who are now teenagers and still the biggest blessings I have ever received. May they never read these books but know I love them anyway.

About the Author

Ashley Hawthorne is a contemporary romance author, avid reader of many genres, and shameless nerd. She's a lifetime fan of The Lord of the Rings and Star Wars and has spent nearly as long reading through every book in the romance section of the library. Now, she writes stories that examine what love means to us, how far we'll go to get it, and what we're willing to give up to keep it. She lives in Texas with her husband, kids, and a house full of rescue pets.